From the Files of
Filomena Devlin
Reporter and Nazi Hunter

Agata Stanford
Author of the Dorothy Parker Mystery Series

the three
tomatoes
The Three Tomatoes Book Publishing

Published April 2024
ISBN: 979-8-9891962-9-6
Library of Congress Control Number: 2024905712

For information address:
The Three Tomatoes Book Publishing
6 Soundview Rd.
Glen Cove, NY 11542

Cover and interior design: Susan Herbst

Books by Agata Stanford

The Dorothy Parker Mystery Series

The Broadway Murders

Chasing the Devil

Mystic Mah Jong

Death Rides the Midnight Owl

A Moveable Feast of Murder

The Murder Club

Other novels

Murder Story

A Tall, Imperious Bloom

Everything Will Be All Right!

Dedication

For my Puccio siblings, Rosaria, Benedetto
and Maria Rosa

"Hell is empty and all the devils are here."
Shakespeare's The Tempest

Prologue

The low tide reeked of the decay beneath the calm waters of the canal and rose with the thickening fog. It hit me: I was walking into danger. Danger I was ill-prepared to deal with. But it struck me, too, as a metaphor for the wave of putridity rolling across Europe, smothering and annihilating, and now extending its foul reach to our shores.

I was scared.

What was I going to achieve, alone, unarmed, following these criminals into an unknown place other than to probably get myself killed? For surely, if caught, these men would not hesitate to kill me. They'd already left a trail of dead bodies, so what was one more murder? But I'd come this far to give up now; I had to go on. I was compelled to go on. Too much was at stake.

I stiffened my spine, and with false courage, forced myself to walk quietly over the little Venetian-style bridge. But as I passed over it in my pursuit of the men, the fog dissipated. I was vulnerable now, no trees, no vegetation--nothing to shield me If they turned their heads. I stopped, paralyzed, as they turned left onto a side street.

Off the bridge, now, I cut diagonally across a plot of sandy soil that bordered the canal and ran parallel to the road, scrub oak my only cover. I lost sight of the two men, but I scrambled along, spirals of ghostly mist rising from off the black water, a visual fence from plunging in to guide me.

The foghorn sounded repeatedly like the forlorn moans of a wounded animal, boat rigging creaked along the canal, and a buoy bell clanged somewhere at the mouth of the Great South Bay. The night was closing in on me, its cold swirling breath filling my lungs, chilling my resolve.

Suddenly, light punctured the darkness, and I could see it came from within a structure across the road. I braced myself and headed toward it, stumbling over knotted grasses, and catching my coat sleeve on thorny bushes in my progress. A small creature skirted past and the image in my mind, if not in reality, was of something rat-like scurrying by, its gurgling squeak of surprise in response to my muted gasp.

"Pull yourself together, Filomena!"

The man from Shorty's Garage broke the small rectangle of light from a small bungalow. I scooted across the road, and flattened myself against the wall of the building, invisible from view of the window. Gingerly, I crouched down and moved toward the window ledge, took a breath for courage, and peeked in. Three men were in the room, one, seated at a table before a boxy black appliance with knobs—a radio transmitter!—the man from Shorty's Garage tapped a lever sitting on a small desk. I knew enough to identify code being transmitted. Where was Joe?

I sensed him before I ever saw him. The hair at the back of my neck rose, electrified, and I turned to see the dark shadowy hulk coming from around the rear of the house. It was too late to hide, even had there been a place to hide. The house sat on sand, nothing but low brush across the road near the dark water.

I turned the corner toward the front of the house, in a dash away from his line of vision—or so I thought. The sharp retort of gunfire gripped my heart, took my breath, before adrenaline kicked in and I beelined toward the canal where the fog was thicker. There, a lone leaning weeping willow, dipped its bare fingers over the water, its trunk providing a moment's cover. But he was following my path. I willed the fog to shield me from view, but it did not obey.

This is the test of the Coward verses the Brave Warrior, I thought. I could bluster and posture with feigned heroism, but the truth was I was scared shitless, a pathetic, whimpering coward in the field of battle.

My latent Catholicism kicked in and I prayed to Mary, full of Grace and Our Father Who Art in Heaven when another gunshot sounded, and then another. Frantically searching for a place to hide, I prepared myself for a leap in the canal, shrugging off the Mark Cross satchel to crawl in the darkness toward the timbers at the canal.

New York City,
February 19, 1939 5:46 p.m.

How could I have known—while dashing through the sudden snow squall that swept the city, a powdered sugar slicking the sidewalks, hugging the tree limbs and roofs and fenders of parked cars lining the curb—how could I have known, as I toted my valise, as I rounded the corner from Central Park West, and then climbed the front stoop of Papa's house at 5 West Seventy-Sixth Street, that the course of my life was about to change? A tide of shit was heading my way and I didn't see it coming.

The brownstone, just off Central Park, was the house I grew up in, where Mama died from cancer when I was sixteen, and where Papa, Archibald Devlin, would return from the hospital tomorrow morning to recuperate after suffering a bleeding ulcer. This is the reward he gets after a twenty-year reign as managing editor of *The Morning Sun*. Well, he's just one of a long list of newspapermen who gamble away their health in chasing the next big story. Yep, the newspaper business is riddled with bodies of fallen men. What do you expect when you're always chasing crises, catching naps in lieu of eight hours, drinking, smoking, and choking down greasy spoon fare seven days a week?

I digress . . .

Back to the point, I hadn't lived in this graceful old house since graduating from Columbia University with a degree in journalism, when, in a show of independence I moved into an apartment in Greenwich Village, much to Papa's mortification. *Girls don't leave their family home until they are married!* he had exclaimed, as if it *was written.* Written in the United States Constitution, or somewhere. *There's a bible passage somewhere,* he had argued.

Oh yeah, I had said, *let me know when you find it.*

Don't get me wrong. I love my father. He is a great man and a good, if exacting, father. But it was time, back then, to go out on my own. To leave the comfort of the elegant home for a two-room, cold-water, crumbly walled, roach-infested, tub-in-kitchen, tenement-dump, fifth-floor walk-up in Greenwich Village.

The aroma of pot roast wafted through the crisp air from a neighboring brownstone. The hum of traffic along Central Park West, the gush of the delivery truck's tires plowing through the accumulating road slush was over-ridden by the grating of metal on metal close by. I paused, looked down over my shoulder and caught the dance of shadow and light in the darkness in the well beneath the stoop, where the trash cans were kept in a niche and where a gated door led to the street level rooms of the house, the kitchen and dining room.

The women of the city had been on high alert for the past few months as a murderer had been on the prowl in the residential neighborhoods of the Upper East Side of Manhattan, dubbed the East Side Strangler by the press. It was only a short walk across Central Park to the West Side of town, so it was smart to be on your guard.

A black cat scurred out to dash over the stone wall, crossing my path. I was relieved to know I was safe from the strangler, if not from future catastrophes. I hurried up the stoop and slipped the key into the lock of the front door. My feet trampled over mail dropped through the mail shoot. I scooped up the letters and entered through the etched glass doors to the foyer, dropped everything on the mirrored bench seat, and felt for the light switch. A familiar growl sounded from the hall closet, its door slightly ajar. Out sprang Rascal, Papa's terrier, ten pounds of unbound energy, attacking my ankles in a not very affectionate way.

"Get off me, demon!" I yelled, and he leaped up to grab the hem of my skirt. "I paid seventy-five cents for this hose and I won't have you—"

I lifted him to the crook of my arm and his wet tongue sucked at my face.

"I know you love me," I cooed, the words eliciting his frantic wriggling and the attempt to climb onto my shoulder. "What were you doing hiding in the closet?" But I knew that was where he liked to nest, lying in wait for a passing mouse, or in my case, unsuspecting human. I put him down and called into the parlor.

"Eva?" The house was dark, so of course Papa's house-keeper hadn't yet returned from his bedside at the hospital.

So, now I was back to what I liked to refer to as "my ancestral home." Tomorrow morning, I would bring Papa home from Roosevelt Hospital and get him settled in. I'd stay a couple of days to help where needed, listen to his vocal astonishment that I hadn't changed my mind, after five years on my own, about moving back in to said "ancestral home." Papa was all the family I had left, my very own adorable curmudgeon. He had given us all a scare and I feared losing him. But Eva was in residence, so I really wasn't needed to look after him. I'd be returning to my Greenwich Village sunny, spacious apartment with a wood-burning fireplace, hot water, built-in bookcases, and a tub in the bathroom where it belonged. Sometimes, someone has to die for one to find a decent place to live in Manhattan, and that's how I found this gem. Since Papa started me out writing obituaries and death notices at the paper, I got the first crack at vacancies *before* publication.

The meager light from the chandelier swept over the walnut-paneled foyer, leading to its grand balustraded staircase. This house, five stories tall, the kitchen on the garden floor, servants' quarters on the top, had been built in the past century for elegant, if conservative, living. To the right of the foyer and through the paneled pocket doors lay the drawing room with its high ceiling and intricate plaster flourishes, a trio of floor-to-ceiling bay windows overlooking the street, and at center on the far wall a carved marble fireplace. Beyond, toward the rear of the house, was the library bedecked with built-in glass-fronted cabinetry containing thousands of volumes collected over the years by my parents. A graceful house, I always thought, the space enhanced by my mother's good taste, with style and respect for the occupants of its past.

Memories of childhood awakened and the years slipped away, when I was enclosed within these walls: the smell of lemon wax, of Mama standing in the sunny parlor among the gleaming mahogany tables and walnut paneling that ran throughout the public rooms; the aroma of tomato sauce simmering on the stove and roast beef baking in the oven wafting up from the kitchen for Sunday dinner after church; the music from the radio lilting through the house from the one Papa bought for me when I was accepted to Columbia.

Papa's Giants baseball cap peeked out from under the hall bench and I picked it up and punched the crown. Papa was more than a newspaperman: he was a Giants fan, and I had been dragged into the excitement of his frenzy by the time I took my first steps. I brushed off the old hat and returned it to its rightful place on the hook beside Papa's brown fedora, and to the emotional connection to the house. Truth be told, I loved this graceful, stalwart house the more, probably because I had lived away from it for so long. Although my apartment in Greenwich Village was no model of pristine gentility, it was next door to a coffeehouse, two doors down from a popular little family-run Italian restaurant, and across the street from an "antiquarian" bookstore—more moldy old books than antiquarian anything, really—and the neighborhood apartments were inhabited by old Italian immigrants and poor artists with nothing much worth stealing, and it was my own little sanctuary that proclaimed my independence.

I peeled the soggy rubber shoes from my high heels and flicked the droplets of melting snow off my coat and red tam. Catching my reflection in the hall mirror, my eyes shifted from my features to the reflection of my mother's portrait hanging over the parlor fireplace. Papa was right. I was looking more and more like Mama with every passing year. At thirty-one, I was the spitting image of her, if not at all resembling her in personality. That aspect of my nature I'd inherited from my father. Mama gave my dark hair and green eyes, Mediterranean temperament, my biting sense of humor, and the Italian passion for all the sensual thrills of living; for balance, Papa provided a healthy dose of Irish pessimism, intellectual skepticism, and a gift for blarney that had not always served me well. So, I, Filomena Devlin, relished good food and wine with the joy of the Sicilian, along with the Irish assuredness that famine was only one meal away; I talked with my hands and also had the inherent talent to sell an unsuspecting soul the Brooklyn Bridge, had I the mind to.

I emerged from this reverie and entered the parlor, flicking the light switch, which sparked a moment of illumination before dashing out. Plunged in near total darkness, I cursed a blue streak, a practice inherited from my old man.

"Crap! Damn!"

In the few moments it took for my eyes to adjust, I

began feeling my way along the hall to the stairs leading down to the garden floor, any light from the street fading as I progressed toward the back of the house. Down a flight, I inched toward the kitchen, slamming a knee on a chair, and I cursed some more. A tactile discovery yielded matches on the shelf next to the stove. I found candles in the breakfront.

Moving down a flight of stairs to the basement, I located the fuse box, atop of which were a box of 30-amp fuses. In the flickering candlelight, I tried to discern which fuses were the culprits. None appeared burnt out, their little metal clips intact.

I heard footsteps on the floor above.

Someone was in the house.

But who could it be? Eva? Not likely. She was going to have dinner at her sister's; I now remembered her telling me. And then I recalled I hadn't locked the front door.

Heavy footsteps on the stairs sent a rush of adrenaline through my blood. I was more frightened to be in the dark than to not see who was coming. Looking for a place to hide, I opened the door that formed a cubby beneath the staircase, a little closet where old tennis rackets and fishing poles moldered among toothless garden rakes and rusty shovels. From the hidey-hole I listened and could hear baritone mumblings and then the obscene ranting of an unidentified male.

The door to the hidey-hole suddenly opened and a floodlight accosted my eyes. I clutched a broken umbrella in one hand, the candle in the other, as a tall dark shape shifted. A disembodied voice thundered out, "Identify yourself, thief!"

Light skittered along the sleek blade of a sword pointing at my chest, and before I could raise a hand in defense, I was roughly grabbed and pulled out through the door, my weapon tossed away, the candle snuffed out.

I threw a left hook. The squawk at contact told me I had hit my mark.

"What the—!"

"Unhand me, you brute!" I yelled, even though he had done so at the strike to his nose. The flashlight skittered across the floor, and I blindly bolted away toward escape up the staircase.

"Not so fast!" hissed the man grabbing my skirt.

I fell to the cement floor and then was pulled up to my feet.

"Think you can just sneak into my—"

Light from the felled flashlight brought faint recognition of my attacker, and the voice confirmed my suspicions as he thundered on with theatrical fervor.

"Not only do you rip at my clothes and cut snippets of my hair, invade my hotel rooms, but now you're coming out from behind the woodwork! Are you one of a band hiding in the rafters out to wreak havoc on Hollywood's greatest profile?" he said, clutching at his face.

Through the bouncing light beams, I watched as he peeled off the end of his bulbous nose. "What the hell happened to your face? God! I didn't do that!"

"Why are you *skulking* in the basement, lying in wait for me?" He retrieved the flashlight.

"Get that damned light out of my face, you idiot!"

"What are you doing here, or need I ask?" he demanded as he lowered the light.

"I could ask you the same question, mister!"

But I needn't have asked, because it wasn't just the sword that he flourished that gave him away or my recognition of his features in the spare light: the pencil moustache, the curly dark hair, a lock of which fell over his brow. It was the voice! In spite of one oversize gray eyebrow that was hanging over his left eye, I'd recognized *the voice*, one belonging to a particular man, if displaced from his usual setting.

"Oh, for God's sake, Montgomery Chase!"

He picked up the sword and leaned on its handle, as if it was a walking stick.

"Must you repeat the cry of a thousand cuckolded husbands? But who—You are not one of my imbecilic fans, are you? You know, you look vaguely familiar—"

"Yeah, yeah, I hear it all the time; I look like my mother."

"I don't know your mother—I don't think . . . unless you purport to be the love child from my brief dalliance with Yvonne de Carlo. Same coloring, Latin eyes, *delightful* figure, if I may say so."

"No, you may not say so!"

"No, you are far too *old* to be my daughter."

"I'll have you know—" I objected, about to profess my youth.

"So, tell me, who hired you to hound me?"

He looked ridiculous, half made up in disguise, theatrical putty hanging from his cheek and chin, like peeling skin. "Ah! You're from the press!"

"No."

"Have you been sent by Little Lenny to murder me in my bed?"

"Little Lenny—? Why? Are you expecting a violent death?"

"It's inevitable, my being me, you know."

"You mean, live by the sword, die by the sword? I don't know why anyone would want to kill you. Wait, I take that back."

"Don't you read the columns, girl?"

"The gossips? No. I'm just used to seeing you thirty feet tall on the big screen, wielding your sword, *not* molesting young women in cellars."

My eyes traveled from foot to head of his six-foot-plus frame. "You are much smaller than I thought."

"Men over urinals have died for saying that!"

There was nothing for it but to laugh at the absurdity of his bravado. Was this joker serious?

"You cackle like a hyena; very unattractive."

"Oh stuff it!"

"You don't think you can get away with striking me in the nose, do you?"

"I'm sure the million-dollar profile is insured, is it not?"

It was time to end the game, and I was about to push past him to make for the stairs when the lights flickered on, chasing the brief romance of shadowed intimacy off into the recesses of the cellar.

"Not the fuses, then; a power blackout," he surmised aloud, clutching a handkerchief to his nose. When he looked at it and saw blood he yelped.

"It was only a tap. It doesn't look broken," I said grabbing his nose.

"Oww!"

"Stop the dramatics."

"It still doesn't explain why you were holed up in there, woman. The candlelight from under the door gave you away. I suppose you thought you could sneak into my rooms when I'd gone to bed so you could paw through my drawers to claim a souvenir."

"Rest assured I'm keeping out of your drawers," I said.

"Well, then, why the subterfuge?"

I decided to play the game for a little bit longer.

"What I want to know is why is a movie star, made up to look like Mr. Hyde, wandering around in my house? Did you follow me here? Are you here for retribution? Didn't like the review of your last movie I wrote for the paper? It really was a stinker, and you do have heavy calves, you really do, you know. Tights are not your friend."

"So, you *are* from the press! I'll have you know my calves are all muscle, whatever you say, whoever you are."

"I don't suppose you really are very dangerous for all your sword-swashing and swashbuckling," I laughed. "I'm Filomena Devlin. Which brings us back full circle, now that we know who we are."

"You! But you are—you're Archie's little girl, Filomena—all grown up? You were that ugly little midget, a four-foot butterball, with unruly hair, am I right?"

I flailed out and hit him in the stomach. "I beg your pardon, you big oaf!"

"Archie didn't tell me that you'd be here to greet me, and I didn't expect this kind of rough fare," he said, peeling off the drooping eyebrow and sticking it in his pocket.

My God, he is handsome, I thought.

"But now that I've moved in I—"

"Whaddaya mean, 'moved in?'"

"I live here!"

"Since when?"

"Since about an hour ago when I arrived on the Twentieth Century. I was just unpacking my things when the lights went out. And then—well, you know the rest. I worry now if you can be trusted, especially after those public remarks about my legs."

"Your *calves.* Your thighs are really quite spectacular, actually."

"Well, I suppose you expect me to thank you for that, though you failed to mention them in your review. My question is, are you to be trusted? Archie promised I would be safe here."

"Safe from what?"

"Whom, you mean, from *whom,*" he corrected, following me up the stairs to the kitchen.

"All right, I'll bite. From *whom* will you be safe, Mr.

Chase?"

"Various . . . people who wish to do me harm."

I couldn't help but snigger. "Why would anyone bother? You're just an actor."

"Don't bother to hide your contempt."

"Other than your defiling of Shakespeare where only the Bard might want to strangle you, you're safe; all he can do is roll over in his grave."

"In my line of work, one makes enemies."

"Gable after your hide?"

"Clark and I worked everything out, I'll have you know. Where is my godfather?"

"Archie's in the hospital, Mr. Chase."

"Hospital! I wondered where he'd got to. I wrote to him last week before boarding the train. What happened?"

"Ulcer—or possibly just gas."

"Which was it?"

"The doctors say ulcer, but Papa insists it was something he ate."

"Well, that would account for it. Is he—?"

"He'll be fine, but he can't return to the paper for a couple of weeks. Even then, he has to take it easy. I'm bringing him home from the hospital in the morning. He needs rest and quiet."

"I'll see that he gets that, never fear."

"That's what I'm afraid of," I replied, fetching my valise, Chase following. "Don't you concern yourself, Mr. Chase. I'm here to see that he follows doctor's instructions."

"Must you keep calling me 'Mr. Chase?' That rather

officious tone makes me wonder if you dislike me."

"I only know what I see of you on the screen."

"And you disapprove of my calves."

"I don't concern myself with your physical shortcomings."

"Well, you concerned yourself in that review you wrote! That's a backhanded slap if ever I felt one."

"I'm sure it's not the first time you've been slapped, Mr. Chase."

"You'd think I was your banker, or the taxman or something with the 'Mr. Chase.' I've never heard my name spoken with such contempt!"

"Not even from those cuckolded husbands?"

"They don't call me Mr. Chase, they call me that son of a—well, never mind what they call me! And since Archie is my godfather, that makes us almost like sister and brother, you know. And my sister always called me Monty."

"You don't have a sister," I said, arriving at my bedroom door. "Good night, Mr. Chase."

Monday, February 20, 1939
9:26 a.m.

He really is enjoying all *the fuss, despite his objections,* I thought, as I settled Papa into his chair by the fire and wrapped a blanket over his legs.

"I'm not an invalid!"

Rascal leaped onto his master's lap and began his usual circling dance before settling into a ball. Caught by surprise, Papa dropped all pretense of annoyance to smile and pet his best friend, before reassuming his feigned disgruntlement at the humans in the room.

"So? What are you waiting for?" he said, gruffly addressing the circle of men gathered around him. "Whaddawegot, whaddawegot!"

This was not Papa's usual morning routine as managing editor of *The Morning Sun,* the daily morning newspaper that had been serving New York City for over forty-five years. Archibald Devlin had been overseeing the paper's operation, setting its tone and direction for the past twenty years. This meeting was a daily event of editors cramming into his office at the newsroom. But now that Papa was home, he insisted on holding the meeting at the house. Today, the city editor was AWOL—his wife had given birth during the night.

Skip "Skippy" Hollowid, assigned editor in chief six months ago, leaped in with a rundown of the top stories for tomorrow morning's edition. "It's been quiet these past few days, now that Franco's in charge. Judd Templeton wired his story about the Spanish government's flight to France. . . and the aftermath of the French and British governments recognizing Franco's regime. . ."

"Old news," barked Archie. "What else?"

Skip smiled. He'd known where the Franco story would land—below the front-page fold—before Papa had anything to say about it. After all, it was Skip's job to determine which articles landed where. Today, as a courtesy, Skip was deferring to his boss, who'd been out of the loop for the past two weeks and was worried the paper was going to the dogs.

Skip had been assigned to Archie two years ago, soon after graduating from Columbia University Journalism School—my alma mater. Skip's father was, after all, the paper's owner and publisher. Tall, blond, and patrician, I thought he looked out of place among the grizzled reporters in the newsroom. "He looks like Horatio Nelson without the tricorn, standing on the bridge of the *HMS Victory*," I'd said after first laying eyes on him. That I had a little crush on him was not the point, and not so unusual. Most women he threw a glance at were quickly smitten.

But Skip knew his stuff; he was a born newspaper-man, had learned the ins-and-outs and dos-and-don'ts of the business, and proved himself a fast and masterful re-write man from the beginning. If he kept off the booze and the cigarettes, the common recreational drugs of the business, he might keep his good looks.

"Well, sir, there was the earthquake in Concepción, Chile."

"What about that? I thought we covered that—last month, wasn't it?"

"Well, yes, but thirty-thousand people died and since we have a man down there, I figured we should go with his report on the conditions—"

"Did those poor dead souls miraculously come back to life?"

"Well, no, sir—"

"If they are still dead, nothing has changed and it not news."

"I'm putting it on Page 3, Foreign News," said Skip.

I caught Papa's eye, and he made a face. "Expand the story with pics for the Sunday edition. Oh Christ Almighty!" he mumbled at my silent disapproval. "We're a newspaper! *New* being the key word. Don't we have any murders to report? Hasn't a financier shot his mistress this morning? No mob hits in Little Italy? Is everybody out there getting along just fine, all hearts and flowers? What's the world coming to? Do I have to go out there and murder someone myself?"

Papa's tirade came from *The Morning Sun*'s drop in

circulation during the past three months, and the way to get the attention of readers at the newsstands was to get them with the headline. *If it bleeds, it leads.* An eye-grabbing "wood" decrying the murder of a beautiful call girl was a sure bet to pick up circulation, where the plight of the displaced and suffering victims of a natural disaster offered no salacious interest to the reading public. Give 'em graft among the big politicians, the car bomb in Little Italy and the numbers shoot right up.

"City desk has the run-of-the-mill robberies and muggings so far: a window washer fell off his scaffold ten stories up at Thirty-Second and Madison, the mayor's new task force is in action, and a lion from Ringling Brothers escaped its cage and made it down a mile-long stretch of Tenth Avenue before being caught at a meatpacker's warehouse."

Papa groaned. "What about the East Side Strangler? Has he hit again?"

"Nothing reported," chimed in the city assistant editor.

"What's he waiting for?" mumbled Papa. "No statements from the police commissioner?"

"Let's see what the day brings," said Skip.

Papa turned his glare on Little Dick Trumble, son of Big Dick Trumble the intrepid newshound who passed away back in '25. Little Dick was following in his father's well-worn shoe leather as a crime reporter.

"Couple of winos found dead down the Bowery last night."

"Knife fight?"

Little Dick shook his head. "Died of exposure."

A sneer, a grumble. "Throw it on the Doom Page."

That was Page 7 of the broadsheet.

"What's Hitler up to now?" Archie asked Skippy. "Invade anyplace this week?"

The newspaper's bureau in Berlin had been shut down last September and its sole correspondent, Ken Hartley, was expelled from Germany on the eve of the Munich Agreement because he was just too critical in his dispatches of the Führer's policies. He called the takeover The Munich Betrayal, because France, England, and Italy handed Czechoslovakia's Sudetenland over to Germany on a platter, in an attempt at appeasement, while the Czechs had nothing to say in the matter. That the military alliance between Czechoslovakia, France, and Britain had been ignored, if not discarded, not a shot was fired against Hitler's attempt to seize the region. Was there any doubt that the dictator would feel emboldened to pursue his vision of a Jew-free world under Germanic rule? A month later, the horrors bestowed on the Jews of Germany by the coordinated attacks on more than a thousand synagogues, and thousands of businesses, hospitals, and schools throughout Germany, known as Kristallnacht, sent a roundup of thirty thousand people off to concentration camps. Archie Devlin's editorial the next day read:

"Our paper's correspondent, expelled last fall from Berlin for propagandist activities, could not have shamed the name of Adolf Hitler and his country any more than the heinous events that were perpetrated against the innocent citizens of Germany last night."

Skip said, "Last month Hitler proclaimed to the German parliament he wanted to exterminate all European Jews, threatening, 'If Jewish financiers start a war against Germany, the result will be the annihilation of the Jewish race in Europe.' Nothing new since. I suppose he's holed up in his lair drawing up plans."

"Son of a bitch," said Rudy Rothberg, son of German-Jewish immigrants and our paper's famous sports columnist. His big hangdog features were as rumpled as his suit coat. Rudy's countenance was in stark contrast with his genial nature and natural enthusiasm for the game—any game: baseball, hockey, basketball, horse racing, and the Friday night prizefights. At forty-five, his youthful verve creased the deep folds of his jowls and brows giving the impression of a happy clown. He was a fervent Giants fan, and therefore dear to Archie's heart.

Papa turned to him. "What's your column?"

"Talked with Ed Barrow about succeeding Ruppert as Yankees president, about his plans for the team."

"Good. Now, *we need front-page wood*, for cryin' out loud!" yelled Papa, referring to the front-page headline. "Indictments? Hollywood weddings? Anything?" He turned to glare at each of the men, and landed back on Little Dick, who had been riffling through the *Post*, the *Herald-Tribune* and the *Daily News* for stories missed by *The Morning Sun*.

Feeling the heat of his editor's gaze on him, he slapped the page of *The Hour* with the back of his hand and announced, "This might be something. If not tomorrow morning, then soon. I'll run it by Skip later."

"Human interest?" said Archie. "It's on Page 11—of what? —that ass wiper from upstate?"

"The Bronx isn't upstate, Papa."

The crime reporter chuckled his delight inside the brown paper bag that was his suit, several sizes too big for the delicately built frame, giving meaning to the expression "a bag of bones." His hats, fedoras with wide brims, only served to accentuate his diminutive stature. In spite of how he appeared, Little Dick was a dynamo reporter hanging on to his quarry with the determination of a pit bull.

"Listen to this: 'Last night mourners at the Kemple Funeral Home on the Grand Concourse arrived to pay their last respects to Lillian Hanover, aged eighty-three, who passed away on Friday, February 17. What they didn't expect was the sign in the entrance announcing, "It's a two-for-one Hanover special!"'

"'That's right, two Hanovers were on display in the red-carpeted room with the piped-in organ rendition of *Clair de Lune*, because only a couple of hours earlier, the deceased's husband, eighty-nine-year-old Herbert Vincent Hanover, died on his way to his wife's wake.

"'While traveling from home with his son and daughter-in-law, Henry and Margaret Hanover, Herbert slumped over in the back seat. His last words, according to his son, were, "'When's the flight leave for Rio?'

"'Arrived at the funeral home, the rescue squad was called in and assessed Mr. Hanover's condition and found he was not breathing. Mr. Hanover suffered from a congested heart, and grief over his wife's death had put a strain on his failing heart.

"Pronounced dead, Mr. Hanover was wheeled into the funeral home and his body put into a casket, which was then placed next to that of his wife's.'

"Now, get this, Archie, if you want to hear 'cute.' 'It was so simple and peaceful,' said the couple's daughter-in-law after the service. 'It was fitting; he was a very thrifty man. The only thing he didn't do was to fall into the coffin.'"

"Amusing, in a macabre way," said Archie, "but, damn, Dick, not *wood* by any means!"

I caught Little Dick's eye and smiled in mutual understanding.

"But it might be tomorrow's, if Dick gets on to the story. Don't you see, Papa? The son and his wife murdered the old man."

"What? How'd you come to that conclusion?" asked Archie.

"Who wouldn't come to that conclusion? I'd look into the money angle, right, Dick?"

"All right, Trumble," said Skip, taking back his reins, "look into it."

Papa turned to Skip. "What about Il Duce? What's that crazy fuck up to? I'm sure the maniac couldn't resist saying something stupid since his last public appearance. Find out what it is. Who's he screwing these days? Any rumors? In the meantime, what about Roosevelt? What's he got to say about the Depression, American jobs, and the economy?"

Papa scowled and turned to Ben "Benny the Boo-

Boo" Bogosian, all six-feet-one of him, who came rushing in through the front door, grabbed from him a file he'd started to hand over to Skip, and started to rifle through it.

Benny was Archie's young protégé, an awkward seventeen-year-old. When not attending freshmen classes at CCNY he hung around the office as a sometimes errand boy, sometimes file clerk. Archie saw "something about that kid" that struck him as a potential newshound, since that day back in '31 when he wrote a letter to the editor to say that he'd witnessed a man throwing a big bundle off the Brooklyn Bridge. Because Benny was only ten years old and was known to possess a very fertile imagination—thanks to the fantastic storylines of the comic books he devoured and regularly stole from the candy store in his Brooklyn Park Slope neighborhood—nobody wanted to believe the kid's story. Archie did, however, and after an investigation sprang from the details that Benny provided, the infamous Brooklyn Heights Hatchet Killer was captured.

Having had enough, and attempting to take charge, Skip retrieved a composited file of reports from off the ottoman in front of Archie's chair and handed them to Benny. "Get these to Harry for rewrite."

"Yes, sir," said Benny, leaving the room on the fly.

The men stood up and gathered their things, making for the door, their attention on their varied tasks, now, lighting cigarettes, donning fedoras, checking wristwatches, and exchanging small talk. They didn't hear the boss's appeal.

"What's going to Harry for rewrite?"

I hissed at my father, "Papa, stop, for Pete's sake. Let

Skip do his job. He knows what you want him to do."

Skip Hollowid heard my chiding and sent me a little smile of gratitude. I could almost hear his sigh of relief.

"That's all right, Filly. Archie's right. We need to move forward in a new direction to boost circulation. If it's not good news about the economy, then we've got to grab the readers with the less salubrious fare. We'll go with the Hollywood divorce, Joan Crawford and Franchot Tone—big photo of the couple above the fold, alongside the columns reporting the opening of the San Francisco Exhibition and the rising cost of the World's Fair opening here in New York in April. Then, our British news bureau's coverage of Prime Minister Neville Chamberlain's misadventure, and the reaction of those dozen British Parliamentary Ministers to his conceding the Sudetenland to Germany—preparing to declare war on Germany if Hitler invades France. If anything big happens tonight before press time, I'll flip the divorce story to Page 3. I'll decide the headline later, accordingly."

Papa acquiesced. I knew all his *Sturm und Drang* sprang from his fear of losing control at the paper. I shooed the others out of the room.

When the room had cleared, Papa, waving papers from the file, said, "You! You're a woman—"

"That's what they say."

"Smarty-pants! And what's with those pants you're wearing, Filomena?"

We'd argued last month about my wearing trousers. It had become quite acceptable attire outside the home, and I liked the freedom they afforded me. When last month, a judge in California forbade a kindergarten teacher from testifying as a witness in a criminal court case because she had appeared before the judge in trousers, the reaction to the story from women all over the country was impressive. But the judge found the teacher, Helen Hulick, in contempt and jailed her when she returned the next day wearing slacks. 'You tell the judge I will stand on my rights. If he orders me to change into a dress I won't do it. I like slacks. They're comfortable.' An appellate overturned her five-day jail sentence.

"I want a piece on that girl, the one who is the first girl page in the House of Representatives."

"Gene Cox. Papa, no! It got a column mention last week. That enough."

"Who's in charge here?"

"Well, I'm the Women's Page editor."

"And there's that other one—first woman dean of The New School for Social Research—the Jewess left Germany?"

"Frieda Wunderlich, the economist. I'm doing a story on her."

"I want you to start a conversation about women and their place in society."

"Oh yeah? And where do you think a woman's place should be?"

"I'm not stupid, Filomena! I'm not going to get into a fight with you about it. I'm not against women in the workplace. You're an example of my open mind."

"You want me to start a fight with the public, is that it? Set husband against wife?"

Papa raised an eyebrow, and I watched his lips stiffen as he tried to stifle a smile.

It really wasn't a bad idea, come to think of it. Wunderlich's was an influential voice these days. In her file was a quote from one of her lectures on Nazi Germany:

"It still holds true that in Germany the fundamental principle is that woman is meant for marriage, while in the United States a woman's life is regarded as an end in itself which may find completion without marriage."

I had sniggered at the quote, wondering to which United States Frieda Wunderlich was referring? Was she that naïve about the circumstances in which we American women found ourselves? The battles we fought to have our voices heard and to manifest our dreams of becoming other than only wives and mothers? There might be something to be said for doing an interview with her. But Papa sparked something with his insistence on my setting an agenda. Perhaps I'd do a series of articles; a look at women who were actually making strides—okay, inching along—in American business and industry.

"I like to think of it as expressing the paper's *liberal* approach," said Papa, baiting me.

"Then express your approval in an editorial."

"I want a serial."

"You think it'll boost circulation. Well, you're right, it will start the conversation. But then, I would prefer to make the Wunderlich story the first in a series."

"Nothing wrong with that and it will look like we're progressive when it comes to the weaker sex. Now go out and interview those girls."

Weaker sex. . . Girls. . .

Ordinarily, I would have scoffed at Papa's outdated attitude toward women. But it wasn't worth voicing displeasure. He was aggravated enough.

"You just want me out of your way, I know you do," I said with a laugh, planting a kiss on his head. "Sending me off to do busywork so you can do God-knows-what when my back is turned. Bed rest! That's what the doctor ordered! And I'm here to see that you get it!"

Archie grumbled, and little Rascal squeaked out a challenging objection.

"What? You my boss now? I'll determine what goes on the front page. Just do the stories about those broads, a story on women in power."

"A House page is a woman in power?"

"You know what I mean."

There was no point in arguing and absolutely no hope once he'd made up his mind.

"All right, I'll do what you've asked, and yes, I'll work it into a series, but I have another story I'm working on—and depending on what happens tonight, it might be front-page news for tomorrow's edition."

Well, I decided, I'll do both the women's feature and the political coverage of the German-American Bund and its operations that I'd been quietly delving into over the past few weeks. Tonight was the organization's big rally in Madison Square Garden, and nothing was going to keep me from covering it.

I was leaving the parlor as Montgomery Chase came down the stairs. He was looping his ascot when we nearly collided. He threw a haughty look at me before craning his neck for a peek into the parlor.

"Are they all gone?"

"Who?" I asked.

"The *press*, of course!"

He didn't wait for my retort—for surely there was one forming—when he spotted my father.

"There's the man I've come to see!" he said.

The two men shook hands, and Archie's face lit up with pleasure. A wave of jealousy flooded over me at the look of affection exchanged between them. Monty perched down on the arm of a chair and gave Papa the once-over.

"You don't look so bad, though I've seen you better, Pops. You've got to lay off that fried chicken. Does Eva still make that fried chicken? I dream about it sometimes."

"That's about all Eva knows. Fried chops, fried fish, fried potatoes, fried chicken. I swear if she could figure out a way to make them, I'd be eating fried chicken pot pies."

"Did I hear my name being spoken in vain," said Eva Bellaroma, Papa's housekeeper.

"Never in vain, dearest woman! In awe, perhaps, but never in vain!" replied Monty.

Eva was carrying a tray piled with the silver coffee service, plates, utensils, and a covered dish. Monty leaped to his feet to relieve her of the tray. With a slaphappy grin, Eva pointed to the coffee table, and then began to pour the steaming beverage into a cup, which she handed to Archie.

"What happened to your eye?" she said while handing a cup to Monty.

"Critic. Slammed by a critic," he said, throwing a hostile look in my direction.

"I thought they only ruin you in the press?" said Archie with a chuckle.

"What's this?" asked Monty, as Eva uncovered the dish.

"Your breakfast, my dear." She brought one of the nesting tables to Monty's chair, and he squeezed her around the waist, eliciting a yelp followed by a girlish giggle, charming his way into Eva's good graces. When she placed a linen napkin on his lap, Eva announced, "Fried eggs, crisp bacon, and French toast. Wait! Don't forget the maple syrup," she added, pouring a thick stream from the pitcher.

"You are a dream, woman!"

"Get out!"

"Where's my breakfast?" said Archie.

Eva handed him a plate of dry toast.

"This is it? A pat of butter, at least!"

"Doctor's orders. You have to drop twenty pounds."

"In one day?"

"Don't be ridiculous, Archibald."

"And what is that urine-like stream you're pouring into my cup?"

"Chicory."

"You can't be serious!"

"Best you get used to it. All your meals will be boiled from now on."

"Oh, that sounds appetizing. . ."

"Not very, but as I said, you'll get used to it."

"Now, Eva," Archie grumbled.

Rascal leaped off Papa's lap and nestled in the space between Monty and the chair's arm. "What's this?" said the movie star as the dog nudged his elbow and eyed his plate.

"It's not a show of affection, Monty. That little beggar's abandoned me, and I can see why!" said Archie, eyeing the food he was denied.

"Dear one," said Monty reaching for Eva's hand, "no one is to know that I am staying here, you understand?"

"I don't even want to ask why," I replied.

"Best not to know."

"So, tell me, boy," said Archie, making a face as he bit into his dry toast, "who's after you now?"

Montgomery Chase looked wearily at the women waiting expectantly for his reply.

"The less anyone knows the better."

Archie got the point and nodded conspiratorially; it was not a topic for female ears. Eva stood her ground. I poured myself a cup of coffee. "Oh, for God's sake!" I hissed.

"Tell me, boy, how'd you get here undetected?"

"It took some planning, I must admit. Rocco—you remember my writing to you about Rocco?"

"Your man?"

"Yes, my valet—"

Valet! Was he serious? Lackey was more like it! Pretentious poseur!

"Rocco and I planned a diversion."

"Yes?"

"Well, it was like this: Rocco and I boarded the train in Los Angeles as ourselves—Monty and Man—as brazen as day. Upon arriving at Chicago, Rocco got off and dealt with the barrage of reporters, telling them that I had debarked and had been secreted away in order to avoid the press. Rocco, knowing he would be followed, collected the decoy luggage, got into a cab, and made sure the reporters did not lose his tail until he had checked us into a hotel under the name Sebastian Hunter and his manservant, Mr. Jeeves. While he was leading the chase—excuse the pun—I never left the train. I emerged from Montgomery Chase's drawing room as Otto Rust, pickle salesman from Minnesota."

"But, Monty, no one would mistake you for anyone other than the movie star you are!" said Eva.

"My disguise took only three minutes to affect, my dear: wig, eyeglasses, a bit of spirit gum to enlarge the nose, a change of clothes, and assuming the air of my character."

"Soaked in brine," I said.

"You are a wonder!" said Eva.

"I never had to step foot from the train—only from my drawing room—to walk through the cars to arrive at Otto Rust's reserved compartment. Otto Rust will make an appearance for you later, when I go out."

"Ingenious!" said Papa.

"Yes, isn't it?" agreed the movie star.

"Filomena, you need to get to work."

I pulled a face and topped off my coffee, intending to take it with me as I left the room. I'd heard enough of the adventures of the fading movie star, but to tell the truth, I knew there was more to disclose, so I stirred the sugar cube long after it had dissolved. The men looked over at my clinking spoon and caught my eye. It was all too obvious. They wanted a private talk. Huffing annoyance, I grabbed a slice of crisp bacon from Monty's plate and made for my room.

Monday, February 20, 1939
7:43 p.m.

The demonstration outside Madison Square Garden was huge, an undulating mass of humanity spilling out into the street, the length of several blocks.

Thousands! Tens of thousands! Protesters carried signs; Bund supporters shouted slurs about the Jewish cabal that was threatening to take over the world. Mounted policemen attempted to quell the violence that was brewing as picketers clashed with Nazi supporters attempting to enter the arena.

The rally that had been promoted as "a mass demonstration for true Americanism" promised a George Washington's birthday celebration. But anti-Semitism is at the forefront. Posters plastered the city with the image of a stalwart, square-jawed Germanic warrior brandishing a spear, a serpent caught in the spearhead and set against a shield of stars and stripes. Not everyone is deceived by its patriotic pretense. But many are.

The German-American Bund is an organization spreading Reich-directed propaganda. They are zealots of Hitler's ideology that is currently being spread across Europe by his band of thugs. The message is an incessant mantra of hate and promised retribution. And in the United States they are very well funded.

Across America, Hitler's surrogates are using the weariness of so many Americans who cannot even imagine entering another war with Germany. They are targeting people struggling as our economy is still limping along after a devastating Depression. The experience of these past twenty years left us a nation of dispirited citizens and isolationist leanings are understandable. So, when they pitch the idea that rule by a strongman-led government is more efficient than our often erratic, often bureaucratic democracy, it sounds very appealing. Sit back, relax, and let us make the decisions for you, do the grunt work.

The salesmen who use the promise of easy living through easy solutions when this new idea of modern rule is adopted in America are flimflam men grabbing at power and money and we are the victims they've set their designs on. The sales pitch is given by men of stature with loud voices: intellectuals, writers, daredevils like Charles Lindbergh, populists with big platforms like George Sylvester Viereck and John F. Cassidy, leader of The Christian Front-who use that very weariness of spirit to undermine democracy by sowing distrust of our political system. With mighty big bullhorns to spread their venomous propaganda, they can be very convincing. Father Charles Coughlin's Sunday broadcasts hold sway over thirty million American listeners weekly, claiming the very survival of Christianity is in jeopardy from the Jewish-Communist plot to take over the world and must be stopped by any means, violent means if necessary. These zealots know that every successful revolutionary movement requires a scapegoat at whose feet to lay the troubles *you* have suffered. That scapegoat is richer than *you*, and believes he's smarter and more successful than *you*, but he's cheated *you*, and his soul is black, his features deformed, rendering him *inferior* to you.

And we won't let him take from you what little you have left.

Hitler chooses words that help further inflame his citizens to rise up against that common enemy. Too many weary people are being suckered into relinquishing their individual power to one man on a promise doomed to fail them, because while stripping the inalienable rights of that spooky bogeyman they also forfeit their own. So, when a subsect of a nation's citizenry is labeled "vermin," eradication becomes justified. By abandoning one's morality to the rule of the Fascist exterminator, one loses personal accountability.

And then we are lost.

This is an event I want to report on: the dangerous rise of autocratic rule. It needs to be stopped. The truth beneath the lies must be revealed, and I was not about to be sidelined into human interest stories when there is so much at stake for our nation's survival.

Truth be told, I have no power to do more than report, with objectivity, the events of the evening. Sometimes, though, just presenting the facts are enough for readers to unpack the truth.

With my press badge clipped onto my coat, I circumvented the main entrance for the press door. Passing through a long hallway, the echo of the cheers of the crowd within the hall bled through the steel doors. A guard looked me over and passed me through, into the arena.

Taking in the scene within the great expansive space, through haze created from the powerful lights mingled with tobacco smoke and the breath of humanity, I figured twenty thousand people had assembled.

Could it be? I wondered, amazed that in America there were that many devotees to the Nazi philosophy?

I pushed through the crush of men for a better sight line to the stage, on which stood a dozen drummers beating out a steady rhythm to accompany the orchestra's march. Storm troopers, the *Ordnungdienst*, dressed in gray tunics, black trousers, and forage caps, and carrying Nazi and American flags, stomped righteously in procession down the long sloping aisles at center, right, and left of the hall. The tide of Bund "soldiers" kept on coming, and louder and more frenetic was the roar of the spectators. Deafening cheers rose up suddenly when the orchestra ended its tune and thousands saluted their allegiance in wave after wave proclaiming, "Heil, Hitler! Heil, Amerika!"

What kind of crazy shit was this?!

On the stage, dozens of officers of the German-American Bund stood rigidly—eyes fixed with prideful, *exalted* at-

tention at the spectacle. Chests puffed, like little boys playing soldiers about to take the hill.

Behind them was displayed a thirty-foot-long photograph of George Washington dressed in his Revolutionary
War general's uniform. Patriotic bunting draped the rafters
and yards of cascading stripes of the red, white, and blue
fell from ceiling to the floor beside his image. There, too,
flanking the stage was the incongruous display of American, National Socialist Party, and the German-American
Bund flags, along with the ubiquitous swastikas. At center,
the raised podium promised more exciting entertainment of
racist propaganda to come.

Remove the swastikas and the Nazi paraphernalia
and the stage would be dressed for the Republican National
Convention, I thought.

The incongruity of Fascist imagery against the iconic
image of democratic freedom was inescapable, and I almost
laughed aloud for the absurdity until the feverish mania of
the moment suddenly struck me as sinister. A shiver ran up
my spine at the horror of it. This was serious madness, and
the effect was daunting.

This rally was even bigger than the one held last year.
It was certainly more rambunctious, more *determined*, I realized, as I caught sight of a handful of dissenters heckling the
goose-stepping army and their supporters. Strong-armed
in a scuffle, the protesters were pummeled repeatedly and
dragged out of the arena to the scathing hoots and fist-shak-
ing of the Bund membership. Police officers intervened,
but more punches were thrown as the Nazi marching song,

"Horst Wessel Lied" segued into a crowd-rousing rendition of "Deutschland Über Alles"—Germany Over All.

Excitement charged the air like a bolt of electricity. The acrid odor of masculine sweat, spent tobacco, and lingering shaving soap rose up through the cavernous space, and as I watched, disbelieving the unreality of it all, my gaze landed on a sprawling banner affixed to the balcony wall: Americans—Stop Jewish Domination of Christian America! Disgusted and turning away, another caught my eye: Smash Jewish Communism! I tamped down a wave of nausea.

"Well, this is a surprise," said a familiar voice.

"Skip!" I said and was about to ask what he was doing there, but bit back the question. He was obviously covering the rally for the paper.

"I never thought of you as a Nazi, Filly, so I suppose Archie wanted you to cover this?"

"You know very well he didn't. I suppose you—?"

"Well, it is a big event. How often do you get thousands of Nazis together in the same beer hall this side of the Atlantic? A bit frightening, if you ask me."

"Bat shit crazy, all right! Wait! Don't you think I can handle this story?"

"I didn't mean that. Of course you can and should."

"Listen, Skip, I'm sorry I didn't ask you if I could cover this. I wanted to do the write up, but—"

But I was silenced by the voice booming out through the loudspeakers calling all to attention. The "Star-Spangled Banner" was thumped out by the band and then followed speaker after speaker, until the headliner of the evening was announced with the preface, "We love him for the enemies he has made!"

Fritz Kuhn, the *Bundesfuehrer*, stepped proudly up to the podium and to the cheers of his followers.

"Floor show's over; here comes the main act," said Skip.

"Ladies and gentlemen, fellow Americans, and American patriots," he began, "we are here to honor the memory of the immortal Washington."

"Oh brother!" I said.

"You all have heard of me through the Jewish-American press. I am a devil with horns and tail. . . "

"Oy vey. Here comes the good stuff!"

"The Bund is fighting shoulder to shoulder with patriotic Americans to protect America from a race that is not the American race, that is not even a white race."

The hairs on my neck prickled at the blatant anti-Semitism and racism.

When he referred to America's president as Frank D. Rosenfeld, there was much sniggering, and when he called the New Deal the Jew Deal, the response was much foot-stomping and cheers. "The Jews are enemies of the United States!" he announced to much applause and a scattering of dissent, which was swiftly silenced by the well-placed thugs in the audience.

"German-American bunk!" yelled a woman's voice out of my line of vision. It only took a few moments to identify that the source of the outburst was journalist Dorothy Thompson, who had just been named by *Time* as the country's second most influential woman next to Eleanor Roosevelt. She was roughly shuttled out of the arena, and not for the first time. She'd been evicted from Berlin after her published interview of Adolf Hitler in which she described him as "a little man."

"Well," said Skip, "There's our headline."

Kuhn ranted on, spewing his hate, and defending his right of free speech guaranteed by the United States Constitution, while accusing that the "Jew-press" would have him silenced. "We must stop the Jewish-Communist influence in our schools, in the movies, on the radio, and in the press!" he declared.

Finally, after demanding German-American representation in Congress and denouncing the Bolshevik Jewish-American leadership and the "Moscow-directed labor unions" his speech ended with a plea for a return to "a Gentile white society."

"Heil, Hitler! Heil, Amerika!" he yelled to the crowd who echoed his appeal.

"I'm gonna toss that chicken parmesan I ate for dinner," I stated, "I need a hot shower to scrub off this stink."

"After you've cleaned up, you've a story to write, Miss Devlin," announced Skip. "Unless Hitler annexes another territory, or some dame at a Park Avenue address gets knocked-off tonight, your coverage will be tomorrow's front-page lede."

"You are sounding more and more like a hard-boiled newsman, Skip. It doesn't suit your patrician—Wait! You mean, you're letting *me* have it?"

"Sure. Why not?"

"Byline?"

He nodded.

"You're a mensch, Skip!"

"Is that a good thing or a—"

"A mensch? A very good thing. And a *Yiddish* expression."

I beamed gratitude at the handsome man while more hoopla and war-dancing followed.

About to make my escape for the newsroom to type out the story for the morning edition, I spotted a figure towering over the crowd. I pushed through to better confirm my suspicions. He was sporting the very disguise he had been wearing before he left the house several hours earlier. It just didn't seem likely, but then again, what business could Montgomery Chase have here at a Nazi rally?

A little closer still, and I might be able to hear the conversation he was having with a pudgy, bespectacled man. But then the crowd enthusiastically voiced their appreciation of the Bund's agenda all over again, drowning out the quiet conference.

Nearly at his back now, Montgomery Chase and the pudgy man parted in opposite directions and disappeared into the crowd. That's when the pudgy middle-aged fellow walking in my direction caught my eye.

Curiosity reigned, and I made a split-second decision to find out the identity of the man. Skip was an arm's length away, alongside Jerry Hiller, a photographer from the paper. There is an almost telepathic communication among newspapermen, and with a gesture and silent appeal, Jerry followed after me. A moment later I caught up with the pudgy man and positioned him for the camera.

"Hello! I'm a reporter with *The Morning Sun*, sir, and I see you are a supporter of the German-American Bund."

The man stared with goldfish eyes. When I touched his arm, he recoiled and looked down at my hand with alarm.

"You are wearing an armband and the Bund's insignia, sir, so I assume you are a supporter of the cause?"

He appeared to relax at my smile. The tense expression melted, and his doughy features deflated like poked rising bread dough.

"As a follower, can you tell me of your reaction to the festivities tonight?"

"I am an American citizen—since 1928!"

A citizen, hmm? I wanted to reply, "That's even more appalling," but kept my opinion to myself.

The camera flash lit up his spectacles, and he scowled with a look of horror, a hand leaping to his face. He motioned toward Jerry, as if to stop him.

"Thank you, sir. And what is your name?"

Eyes and mouth narrowing with suspicion, he turned away from the camera, attempting to retreat into the crowd.

His back to me now, I touched his shoulder to stop his progress. He shrugged me off.

"I will quote you in the newspaper. Front page tomorrow morning," I said appealing to his ego. That always got them, the idea of seeing their names in print.

"That is not necessary," he said, curtly.

"Oh, but think how proud it will make your family to say you were quoted in *The Morning Sun*!"

When I looked up from my shorthand pad, he was slicing through the thicket of bodies. Leaving Jerry, I followed him. I wanted to know why he was reticent to express his opinion, but mostly, I wanted to find out why a movie star was cavorting with this little Fascist.

At times, I almost lost him. Being short, time and again the crowd closed in on him, his ubiquitous brown overcoat indistinguishable from hundreds of others. There were a few hurtles to conquer as I pushed through the oncoming tide of rowdy worshipers and a line of storm troopers pressing on toward the stage. I caught sight of his balding head when he cut through a battalion of Hitler Youth in uniforms resembling wayward Boy Scouts. Out through the doors toward the street, I was sure to lose him. Once he donned his hat, I feared he would melt into the sea of bobbing fedoras outside the Garden.

Why was I following him? Was it because of Montgomery Chase's unlikely association with him and with this crazy rally I asked myself?

The timely reappearance of the taller-than-average pickle salesman from Minnesota, Otto Rust, a.k.a. Montgomery Chase at the pudgy man's side confirmed my suspicion that something peculiar was going on.

The bands of protesters proved thick and unwieldy: labor unionists and socialists banding placards, signs, and banners twenty-feet-wide obstructed car and pedestrian traffic. A line of a dozen mounted policemen stood at the ready. Barriers lined the streets. I caught up to the two men when they were forced to wait at the curb while an officer stopped the flow of pedestrians for traffic to pass across the avenue. They continued uptown through the thinning crowds toward the Theater District and turned west toward Ninth Avenue. Halfway up the street, they hailed a cab from a line of taxis awaiting the release of theatergoers who would, at any moment, charge out from under marquees at final curtains. I hopped into the back of a taxi, and when I saw the men's cab pull away from the curb I said, "Let's go."

"Where to, lady?" said the driver, flicking the meter lever.

"I don't know yet. Just follow that cab."

"You've got to be—"

"No, I'm not kidding. Really, follow that cab!"

Up through Central Park West, and a turn onto Ninety-Third Street, before my quarry's taxi pulled to the curb. Chase and the man got out of their cab. I told my driver to pass and pull up farther down the street. Cash ready, I paid my driver and got out in time to see the men climb the stoop of a brownstone.

What to do now? And why was I doing it?

I walked to the brownstone, one of a string of identical residences that lined both sides of the street.

The odd pairing of a famous movie star in disguise cavorting with a Nazi enthusiast had driven my curiosity. What on earth could they have in common? The bigger question in my mind was, why had Montgomery Chase gone to the rally in the first place? And more pressing, why had he attended disguised as the pickle salesman Otto Rust? Obviously, he didn't want to be recognized for the movie star he was. But was there some other, more clandestine purpose to the masquerade? Maybe he wasn't masking his real identity to just duck reporters or a cuckold husband. Maybe he was a Nazi sympathizer!

The building they entered was dark, except for a rectangle of light at the second-floor window. I watched from the sidewalk behind the cover of a tree trunk.

What now? I thought.

A rooming house, I surmised, from the cardboard sign in one of the first-floor windows offering rooms to let. What to do next? Walk up the stoop, enter, and walk up the hall stairs to listen at the door of the second-floor front apartment?

What do I have to lose, I thought, before my mother's voice echoed from my memory about curiosity killing the cat when I was eight years old and had nearly electrocuted myself in my attempt to take apart the toaster while it was still plugged into the socket. "But cats have nine lives," had been my retort.

I was about to sprint up the stoop but first looked up at the window, made opaque by its shade, where silhouetted figures danced furiously on the bright screen. Gunshots rang out, two, in rapid succession. Lights came on throughout the building and in surrounding houses. Screams of "murder" screeched in a high nasal voice from within.

I ducked for cover behind the short wall at the basement-level apartment entrance as window sashes flew open along the residential street; heads popped out cautiously to see what drama might be happening on the street. Shielded from view, I heard the *whoosh* and *thump* of the front door opening and footfalls on the stone steps. Peeking over at the sidewalk I saw the pudgy man clutching a briefcase and hurriedly making for Columbus Avenue. A barely audible clink of metal hitting the pavement alerted me that he had dropped something in his retreat. Something metallic.

About to climb the stoop, I saw movement behind the glass panes of the door. Back I retreated into the stoop well, holding my breath, my heart pounding loudly in my ears, as I peeked up and saw Otto Rust on the sidewalk only inches away. He turned toward Central Park West and then stopped, turning his gaze toward Columbus Avenue. For a moment I feared he'd discovered me, so I slunk down deeper into the shadows. When his big shadow, cast by a streetlamp, moved, I let out a breath. He was walking brisk-ly in the direction the pudgy man had taken.

To follow him or to investigate the source of the gun-shot?

I had to know how and *if* Montgomery Chase was involved. Upon stepping out from my hiding place, I re-trieved the object Pudgy had dropped, slipping it into my coat pocket. There were more pressing things on my mind than sidewalk treasure.

There was a good chance that the front door was un-locked, since the two men had fled in a hurry. The door gave way, and as I entered through the foyer, I was met with the slamming of a door at the rear of the downstairs hallway.

I raced up the stairs to the second floor. The smell of gunpowder filled the hall. The door to the front apartment was swung wide open. Splintered wood marred its panel. About to enter, I stopped short at the sound of movement above me. I looked up and glimpsed the wary face of a young man, his auburn hair a tousle of curls, peering down over the rail of the third-floor landing.

"What's going on?" he said, accusingly.

"Didn't you hear a couple of gunshots?"

He was buttoning his shirt, and in the shadow behind him was a woman, a pretty blonde woman. They each wore a startled expression at my arrival. A kiss on the man's cheek and the woman whispered, "Hurry!" as she helped him on with his coat.

The furtiveness of her plea made me suspicious. And I was even more certain when the man came flying down the stairs toward me that he harbored ill intent. If not for the hat tossed from the rail by the blonde, I might have followed through with a kick to his most precious parts, until I saw that the clandestine affair was simply a clandestine affair of the heart and nothing more sinister: woman leaning over the rail and a handsome disheveled young man making his escape. I caught the fedora on the fly and popped it on the young man's head. He smiled shyly.

People were coming out of their rooms, a door at the foot of the landing creaked open and quickly shut at the appearance of strangers loitering in the hall, tenants on the floors above and below voiced speculations about whether they'd heard a gunshot or a backfire. Someone was ringing the police. A woman's shrill voice was giving the address.

"Oh God! I'll never get out of here before the police arrive. Her brother can't find me here!" said the young man looking up toward the young woman on the floor above.

An officious-looking middle-aged man came up the stairs from the first floor and cast us an accusatory look. Obviously, the landlord. Sirens squealed along the avenue. I wasn't there to help young lovers out of a jam, after all, and I didn't have time to waste before the cops arrived and I'd get dragged into things. I entered the apartment.

A man was lying on the floor, blood pouring out from a wound to his chest.

Kneeling at his side, I tried to assure him help was on its way. He gripped my shoulder, pulling me down closer as he struggled to form words.

The young man peeked in from the hall, a furtive look.

I leaned in closer to the man's lips, at the same time stanching the flow of blood with the dying man's wool scarf.

"Hmm. . ." the man struggled to say, his eyes wild, staring into the distance, beyond the walls, beyond the door, as if into some unfathomable abyss.

An urgent, nearly soundless, murmur, "Hmm!" as he grabbed my wrist with force, as if clinging to me for dear life. And then his hand fell away. He was gone, the expression of terror frozen in his eyes.

The young man leaned warily against the doorframe.

The landlord appeared, mumbled about the damage to the door—a bullet hole!—and generally expressed his distress, swearing and protesting that these things don't happen in his establishment.

"Shut up, will you!" I hissed at his outrage. "Who is this man?"

"I don't know!" he said, and as he regained his composure so did his indignation. "Who are *you*, lady, and what are *you* doing here?"

"We heard a gunshot," I said, taking a visual tour of the room: lumpy, shabby sofa, worn-out upholstery on its companion chair, faded chintz over the window blinds, overturned lamp on a desk strewn with papers, the smell of soiled wool, tobacco smoke, and general neglect mingling with gunpowder.

"Whose room is this?" I pressed on, as I strode over to the desk to peruse the papers, my back to the men.

"Miss Werner lives here."

If this was a woman's apartment, there was no sign of it. There were no personal items, no picture frames, no feminine touches. The bed in the corner looked as inviting as an army cot.

"And where is this, Miss Werner?"

"Away to care for her sick mother in New Jersey."

Convenient, I thought.

"How long has she lived here?"

"Since last October, but she is often away on business."

"What is her business?"

"She sells stockings to the stores and such."

"Do you have a telephone number or address of her ailing mother?"

"But what business is it of yours?"

It is none of my business, I thought, about to change the subject, until I saw that the young fellow, so worried about being found in the building by his girlfriend's brother, was still hanging around.

I glimpsed a familiar gray homburg lying under the knocked-over desk chair, and to divert attention I said to the landlord, "And shut that door, would you, and for God's sake don't touch anything."

Before the young man tentatively covered the dead man with a blanket from off the bed and the landlord closed the door, I took my Rolleiflex camera and flash attachment from my bag. With his and the landlord's backs to me, I retrieved the hat and stuffed it into my bag. Snatching an envelope and a little black book from off the desk, I slid them into my coat pocket. When I turned, I saw the young man looking through the dead man's pockets.

"You shouldn't be doing that," I warned. "That's for the police to deal with. You're corrupting the scene and any possible evidence the killer may have left."

As if I hadn't lifted possible clues. But there was something. . .

His look of effrontery prompted me to say, "I thought you were in a hurry to get out of here."

"You're right," he said, rising up, touching the flap of his coat pocket.

"Did you find his wallet?" I asked.

"Nothing on him."

I doubted that. The dead man was dressed in street

clothes. What man didn't carry a wallet when he left home?

I was surprised the landlord didn't question why I was taking photographs of the dead man, until he asked, "Who are you?"

"Press," I said, matter-of-factly. "I was passing by when I heard the shot."

I studied the dead man, his arm thrown out at a forty-five-degree angle from his side, his other thrown over his chest. He looked like a school crossing guard who'd met up violently with a truck. He wore no wristwatch now, where moments ago he'd had a very expensive Swiss brand on the extended arm where I had checked for a pulse.

So, I thought, this fellow who looked so innocent, who was playing the Romeo and Juliet scenario with the girl upstairs is a petty thief. Papa taught me how to play poker with the boys. This guy's "tell" was the pat to his coat pocket. I'll fix that, I decided, right after I got a few more shots of the room. He turned away when I flashed in his direction.

And why was he still hanging around? A few minutes ago, he was anxious to get away.

"Okay, let's go," I said, pushing past the startled landlord, shuffling the young man through the gaping onlookers.

"You got a name, buddy?"

"Ahh, I'm Joe."

"Just Joe?" I said, easing past a portly bald man wrapped up in a well-worn bathrobe, who reeked of onions.

The hallway and stairwell were crowding with people. Now was my chance. I steered my larcenous companion into a rail-thin spinsterish woman in hairpins and flowered housecoat, who let out a cry of surprise at the collision. Joe's back was to me, wedged between the flowered housecoat and an ambulant beer belly, so I wedged myself between them, and in the perfect position to do the deed, I lifted the watch from Joe's pocket—and a billfold—with ease. The oversize fit of the overcoat made the fishing easy as pie. Thank you, Freddy Four-Fingers, Papa's reformed pick-pocket friend who fed Papa leads on Mafia activity in city. Four fingers, one might ask? Freddy was caught red-hand-ed once and the punishment was just a warning.

As we exited, the police swept in, a veritable posse of reporters in their wake, held back by cops manning the front door. I flashed my press badge, clipped on the under-side of my coat collar, sure it was a guarantee that I'd be kicked out to wait for the details, the story, with the dozen or so other reporters who had followed in the wake of the squad cars from the precinct house a dozen blocks away, where they would sit all day playing card games to kill the time waiting to catch a hot lead for their morning editions.

And there among the newshounds stood Little Dick Trumble, all five feet of him, caught in the oncoming crush of the well-padded shoulders of his confederates, all jock-eying for position. He wore a dogged expression, and in a minute would undoubtedly squeeze through as a front-row spectator to land the story. I was pretty sure he hadn't seen me. How could I explain my presence there? Once the po-lice took over, the reporters would not be allowed in the room to ask questions and take photos of the crime scene until fingerprints and the forensic team had gone over the place. I had a slew of shots and felt guilty about not letting Dick know I'd gotten the scoop.

But even though I had the story first, I wouldn't be writing it, or probably even telling Little Dick or anyone at all that I had been in the apartment. Because Monty, my father's godson, had been there as witness, or worse, the perpetrator of murder, I had a lot to think about, a lot to find out. As I passed the darkened brownstones along the street on my way toward Columbus, I tried to make sense of what I'd seen. What was the connection between the dead man, the fellow I now called Pudgy, and the so-called pickle salesman from Minnesota? Montgomery Chase in disguise at a Bund rally strained credulity. And why had they conspired in the room of a Miss Werner? What did this woman have to do with anything? I was the only person who knew who was in the apartment, even if I didn't know the details of what had transpired before violence ended this stranger's life. There were questions needing answers.

I dared not tell Papa, or talk of my suspicions about Chase, at least, not until I knew more. First, I had to speak with Chase, confront him.

A movie star, a Nazi supporter, and a dead man.

Right now, I wasn't ready to offer the police much more than wild speculations, and if I revealed my presence at a murder scene, I might implicate myself. The only people I spoke with at the apartment were the young lovers involved in a tryst behind her brother's back and the owner of the rooming house. The lovers—albeit the man was a thief—would not tell the police about my appearance for fear of the discovery of their affair; the owner thought I was one of a score of reporters. But the presence of Montgomery Chase and his sudden departure from the brownstone apartment after the unexpected gunshot nagged at me.

Down the sidewalk and away from the commotion, I was not surprised that Joe was no longer at my side, nowhere to be seen at all. Sneaky fellow. I headed west, toward Columbus Avenue, at a brisk pace, my head cleared with the cold night air. Icy windswept snowflakes bit my face. I needed time to think. But first I had to do the write-up of the Bund fiasco at the Garden before the morning edition was put to bed. This was my first big story, thanks to Skip, and I couldn't blow it. It was my chance to break out of the women's section of *The Morning Sun*. I walked toward Broadway for the IRT subway station.

Police car sirens and ambulance bells rang in the night, the vehicles converging at the intersection of Ninety-Third Street and Amsterdam Avenue, before turning west toward Broadway.

Odors of frying oil and spilled liquor wafted from a bar on the corner as I hurried toward the strobing lights. It was a busy and violent night in the city, I thought, while heading to see what the racket was all about. A bar fight? But even before I got to the corner, I sensed that what was happening, beyond the wall of backs that had closed in on the scene, disrupting traffic on the divided boulevard, had a connection to the murder in the rooming house.

Pushing through gawking onlookers, I glimpsed the

prone and broken body of the man I'd come to call Pudgy. I felt a sharp sense of remorse. Gathering from the snippets of conversations from eyewitnesses, the man had simply lurched into the road, unaware of the taxicab driving up the divided street. An elderly gentleman had been the first to attend him, I heard said, and had yelled for someone to pull the police alarm.

I asked a woman, who appeared quite stricken at witnessing the tragedy, if the Good Samaritan was still around, but when she didn't spot him, I pressed for a description. Through her tears she said, "Just a man."

Grabbing my camera and flash from my bag, my hand brushed the hat I had secreted away.

"Was he wearing a hat?" I asked her. "The man who helped, was he wearing a hat?"

After a moment of reflection the woman shook her head, "I don't—!" she whimpered, before submitting to another round of weeping. The tears abruptly stopped, and with a faraway look in her eyes, as if flitting through memories, the woman gave a description that confirmed my fears.

I searched the assembled crowd for the elderly gentleman, described as very tall, distinguished-looking, and wearing a dark overcoat. No other man in the crowd was hatless on this cold winter's night.

As I snapped picture after picture of the scene, I continued to search the crowd for that suspected "elderly gentleman," straining to catch a glimpse of his figure lurking in a darkened doorway of a shop along the avenue.

A policeman was taking statements from witnesses. I

pried through the thickening crowd to eavesdrop on the interviews. Flashing my press card, the cop refused to tell me the name of the victim until family was notified. But vanity prevailed, and combined with a flirtatious smile, a gazing, starry-eyed expression, along with a promise that his picture would be in the morning edition, the officer relented.

"No I.D.," he said.

It was almost midnight when I filed my stories of the Bund rally and a column about the traffic death. Had the victim been a celebrity or one side of a salacious triangle love-nest murder, or hit by mobsters instead of a wayward taxi, it would have warranted full-page coverage and an obit. But death by crossing a Manhattan street was a common occurrence and not considered newsworthy. I was glad, for once, that I didn't get a byline for the news column; there was a chance, albeit small, that Montgomery Chase might put me at the scene of Pudgy's death.

Little Dick was pounding out his story of murder at a rooming house on West Ninety-Third Street, and I longed to see what other facts he may have uncovered about the crime. Like who was this mysterious Miss Werner in whose room a man had been murdered? I dared not interrupt his progress, he was on a roll, and I would have to wait until Dick's story appeared in the morning.

I quickly looked through the scores of photos I'd snapped at the rooming house, the negatives developed, printed, and delivered to my desk as I worked, before I threw the lot in a manila envelope, covered my typewriter, grabbed the file on Frieda Wunderlich, the Jewish economist who'd left Germany and was now presiding as the first woman dean of The New School for Social Research, and stole out of the newsroom.

Satisfied with the ease with which I had churned out the coverage of the rally, complete with Jerry's photos of the event's highlights, I was about to leave the building and hop into a taxi, exhilarated, if exhausted, to return to Papa's house. But uneasiness nagged at me. Because of Montgomery Chase, the night's gruesome events had hit too close to home. Too close to Papa. I needed a stiff drink to calm my nerves, a warm bed, and a good night's sleep, and then in the morning I would attempt to figure out what to do next.

But instead of pressing the lobby button on the elevator, I pressed the button for the sixth floor, for the newspaper's morgue. I had some research to do. I needed to find out everything I could about Montgomery Chase—who he really was, had been, and was now—before I could decide what to do. An hour later, armed with a bit more knowledge of the man—albeit much of what I'd read was from the Hollywood publicity machine—I entered Papa's house and headed for the stairs and that much needed bath.

But first, I wanted to look in on Papa. I was worried about him. It was against his nature to be sedentary. His life had been one of constant motion, conflict, and I'm proud to say, his dogged dedication toward exposing truth beneath lies. The recent drop in the paper's circulation was probably only a temporary dip, and although it had happened in the past, Archibald Devlin, managing editor of *The Morning Sun*, could not take the slight lightly. It was personal!

His mission was at stake: the paper was the vehicle through which one informed and engaged the public and affected democratic change and justice through fair and unbiased reporting. *This* is what drove Papa, and it was so intrinsically a part of *who* he was, the purpose of his life. Ironically, his physical health was dependent on his slowing down and managing his condition. His spiritual and emotional well-being was dependent on his return to his life's work.

Tuesday, February 21, 1939
1:14 a.m.

The house was dark as I entered but for light spilling in from beyond the parlor, the library. *Could Papa still be awake?* I wondered, worried that he was not tucked in bed, but had stayed up so late. Eva would never have gone to bed without being sure Papa was in his bed when she turned in. And Rascal wasn't lying in wait when I opened the coat closet. . .

I walked quietly across the parlor toward the library, expecting to see Papa fallen asleep on the cushy sofa. He was sitting in a wing chair, its back to me, so he didn't see me, his hand reaching for the glass of bourbon on the side table. Horrified, I came around to confront him for sneaking booze, which was lethal in his condition, when I stopped short.

"You're burning the midnight oil," said Montgomery Chase, looking up at me as I rounded the chair. "Why do you look so. . .upset?"

I caught my breath.

"I thought you were Papa."

"Ahh," he said, considering his glass, holding it up, tilting it before the light from the lamp on the refectory table across the room. "No, this would be very bad. No, he shouldn't have this."

"I want to look in on Papa."

"I just did, actually. He's sound asleep. All is well," he slurred, the precision of his speech washed away with drink.

"Okay. Thanks. Well, good night."

"Why don't you join me?" he said, a quiet appeal, but an appeal still. And then he reached over and touched my arm.

I wanted a drink, I really did, but I didn't want to face the man, not tonight. Not with what I'd learned about him. He was involved in a murder, if not himself a murderer, and he was sleeping in the room next to mine. What terrible secret had he brought into this house? I almost confronted him in that moment, but when he rose slowly from the chair and went over to the liquor cabinet, atop of which was a bottle of caramel-colored liquor, something stopped me. Fear? I was alone with him, Papa and Eva upstairs, asleep, and might put myself in jeopardy if I spoke frankly. Not that he was going to kill me or anything. But he'd been drinking for a while, I could tell from his languid movements and the timbre of his voice, and somehow, he frightened me.

"It's Rémy Martin. Good stuff," he said, pouring several fingers' worth into a crystal tumbler and handing it to me, his hand lingering on the glass.

God, he was gorgeous, I couldn't help but think; standing there tall and substantial, his dark waves glinting in the low ambient lamplight; his eyes, a mystery in shadow gazing down on me from his towering height. He had cast off his Otto Rust disguise and was wearing a navy blue silk robe over matching pajamas. Why was I feeling. . .drawn, at the same time, shrinking away? He looked at me for a long moment, which didn't seem fair, since I was facing the light, and his features were a secret.

"You're not wearing your sheep's clothing," I said, idiotically, defensively.

"So, Filomena Devlin," he said, returning to his chair, "You are quite a surprise to me. I never knew you before. Well, not since you were very little. Even so, I knew *of* you, Archie's little girl. But I don't remember much."

"Yes, so you've told me, with a most unflattering image, I recall. But I remember you. You were here with your parents. I was seven years old. A party. You were a teenager."

I didn't tell him how well I remembered, because seven-year-old Filomena was struck, mesmerized by the handsome boy who my father and mother and everybody at the party had turned their attention toward. Not only struck but annoyed, as well.

"Oh?"

"After playing a Beethoven sonata on the piano, you got up on a chair and began reciting from Shakespeare."

"Oh. . .from *Julius Caesar*. . .'Friends, Romans, Countrymen!'"

"Made yourself the center of attention," I said, and then wished my tone had sounded less resentful.

"It was *Rhapsody in Blue*."

"What?"

"I performed Gershwin's *Rhapsody in Blue*, not Beethoven."

"Yes, and to much applause, if I remember. At *my* birthday party."

He let rip a laugh. "Did I ruin your party? Is that it?"

"What?" I was taken aback. "That's absurd."

"Is it?" he laughed, a silly giggle. "Did you really detest me? Do you still?"

"I have no opinion of you."

"Of course you do."

"I don't consider you at all."

"That's worse. And a lie."

"Why would you say such a thing?"

"The way you sound, the way you look at me. Like you're ready to tell me off, but then decide you are above the dirty task. Such contempt! I wonder why?"

I downed the liquor in one long drag. The heat of the cognac lit a fire in my chest. "I really think that you. . .misunderstand me. My review of your film was nothing personal—"

"I don't give a damn about your review. Nobody cares about *your* review; it's of no consequence. I'm Montgomery Chase. People come to see my films because they care about me. I star in them. Do you have any idea. . .? Oh never mind.

It doesn't matter what you think."

"Who's contemptuous now? What's behind all this, Mr. Chase?" I said, treading dangerous ground. "Are you feeling guilty about something, so you've decided to take it out on me?"

Sharply, he turned to look at me, and it was unsettling to see the narrowing of his eyes burning into me. Was he trying to determine how much I knew about tonight?

"You're shivering," he said. I thought I heard a tone of contrition.

"It's cold outside—in here—I'm tired."

"Let me pour you another drink."

His hand reached for my glass and his fingers covered mine, lingering. I felt small and insubstantial in his presence. I didn't like it. I hesitated, held fast, until I realized I needed to let go of the tumbler.

"No." I turned away from him and walked away. "I've had enough. I'm going to bed."

He didn't reply. I left, confused and conflicted about our brief encounter, wondering why I had spoken when I'd not meant to. But something about him brought out the nasty in me, the part that clicked in whenever I felt on the defensive. Exhausted, yet wound-up at the same time, I dumped my things on my bed and began to review the events of the night.

Tuesday, February 21, 1939
8:21 a.m.

I was rudely awakened by Eva rapping on my bedroom door. Papa's housekeeper didn't wait for a response, she just barged in, threw open the blinds, and told me to get out of bed with the very good imitation of an army drill sergeant. I considered the consequences of hiding beneath the covers and decided not to prove difficult; Eva would undoubtedly win the contest of wills. Since Mama died, she'd been successful in running the business of the house, and because I planned to remain in residence for only a couple of more days, I acquiesced.

"Breakfast in fifteen minutes," she announced.

I was about to say, "I just want black coffee," but that wouldn't wash where this short order cook was concerned. I'd have to swallow down a stack of pancakes, a couple of eggs, and bacon.

"You sleep in your clothes?" she said, accusingly, as I sat up on the edge of the bed.

"It was a late night."

"Gallivanting about town, were you?"

"Not the way you think, Eva. Newspaper. . ."

"Dick Trumble wants you to call him."

"Isn't he downstairs with the boys?" I asked.

"Been and gone."

"What about Monty?"

"In the shower."

"Hope he leaves me some hot water," I said weakly. I never got that bath last night.

"You should be nice to him."

"I'm nice enough."

"Why'dya roll your eyes?"

"Let's not get carried away, now," I mumbled at Eva's back as the door closed behind her, her mission accomplished.

Killing time while waiting for the boiler to heat up my bathwater, I took out the file on the illustrious female dean of The New School and flipped through it. I wanted to get rid of the feature as quickly as possible; it wasn't hard news, and there were more pressing topics to investigate and to hold my interest. But journalism often entailed grunt work. I left the file out on my desk—a relic from days at school—and pulled out the hat stashed in my bag, crushed under the Rolleiflex and flash attachment, notebook, pencils, and Juicy Fruit gum wrappers. The hat was in a sorry state, resembling the indistinguishable gray remains of some poor dead wood critter. After punching out its crown and smoothing its wavy brim, I wondered what to do with it? He might be a conceited blowhard Hollywood actor, but for some reason—perhaps his loyalty to Archie—I didn't think Monty was a murderer.

Toss the hat in a garbage can put out on the street on collection day? I wasn't sure what to do. It was evidence, stolen evidence from a crime scene. Why had I taken it? I reasoned that there were thousands of hats just like this one worn by men all over town. There was no reason it might be connected to Monty. But then, as my thumbs smoothed the inside hatband into its correct position, I saw the movie studio label sewn in, stating "property of."

Why, in heaven's name had a movie star, disguised as an elderly pickle salesman, attended a Nazi rally? Why would he fraternize with a person such as Pudgy—a peculiar individual, to say the least—and then go with him to a shabby rooming house uptown? What was their connection? Was it true that Monty really was a Nazi sympathizer? If he was an innocent witness to the shooting, why did he bolt?

But then, I reasoned, had he remained at the scene, he might have feared the police uncovering his true identity under his disguise.

Could it be that the dead man was his blackmailer? Or a hatchet man employed by some outraged husband? Had Pudgy been hired to kill the fellow I'd found shot to death in the woman's apartment? Perhaps Monty's story about leaving Hollywood was true. Someone was after him—or he, cagily, was the pursuer, stalking his prey!

I had no answers, just wild speculations.

Although exhausted last night, I had taken time to peruse the packet of photos I'd taken at the rooming house and at the Broadway accident. Now, sitting down in the rickety chair at my old school desk, I spread them out to study them more closely.

The stark black-and-white images were quite crisp in detail, and as I shuffled through the photos of Pudgy lying dead on the street, and of the onlookers loitering along the police line, I searched for answers. Something was wrong, and I couldn't quite figure out what it was. With a magnifying glass, I studied the faces of the people surrounding the corner crossing. If there was a clue there, as I suspected, I wasn't yet seeing it.

I looked over the photos taken inside the rooming house. Seeing the one I'd snapped of the desk strewn with papers, I remembered the envelope and the black book I'd slid into the pocket of my coat. I tossed loose change and subway tokens, a couple of chewing gum wrappers, a tube of lipstick, and the brass buckle loop onto my bed. In my other pocket I discovered the loot I'd not meant to walk away with, but for the distraction of the arrival of the cops at the scene: the dead man's watch and billfold! Holy Jesus! I'd stolen from a corpse! Or "lover boy Joe" had—initially, anyway. Still, I was in possession of stolen evidence.

The wallet held over two hundred dollars in crisp new twenties, a driver's license proclaiming he was forty-four years old and lived in Bronxville, and a Hanover Aeronautics I.D. card identifying the dead man in the rooming house as Henry Hanover, senior vice president of the company.

What was he doing in Miss Werner's apartment?

First things first.

Flipping through the small address book I found noth-ing unusual at first, just an ordinary little book with names, addresses, and telephone numbers, the kind one would find in any woman's possession. I wondered why, if the woman went away to take care of a sick parent, she would leave be-hind her address book? I put it aside for a later, more thor-ough, inspection.

The envelope was unopened, addressed to Miss Hedy Werner, the return address, a dentist's office in the East Eighties. A dentist's bill?

I was about to slit open the envelope, not so much concerned about committing the federal offence of mail tampering—after all, I'd already sullied the scene of the crime by walking off with a dead man's watch and wallet—when footsteps padded along the hall to a whistled refrain of "Stairway to Paradise." Monty from his bath.

I tossed everything into the top desk drawer, a trea-sure trove of my adolescence, where spent erasers, paper clips, broken fountain pens, elastic bands, tin school badges, and crumpled graph paper was like a time capsule buried back to 1925. I resisted the pull of nostalgia but was caught by the sight of my science fair ribbon squashed flat under the metal three-hole punch. The Kewpie doll temporarily tore at my heart, the memory of a steamy summer night at Coney Island, the doll won for me by Teddy Lambert, a third-year Yale man, who had died, tragically, later that summer in an automobile crash. I sighed and said goodbye again to Ted and to 1927 by shutting the drawer.

I slogged to the bathroom, ran the bath, soaked for a lovely five minutes, brushed my teeth, combed my hair, and went back to my room to dress. A turtleneck and trousers, argyle socks, and oxfords, and I didn't care if the Kate Hepburn look was a bone of contention with Papa.

Noises of jovial appreciation and feminine encouragement wafted up from the parlor floor. About to hit the stairs, I stopped suddenly and retraced my steps. Monty's room was next to mine, and it was my chance to take a look around before he returned to it. If my calculations were correct, Monty would be stuffing his handsome face with the delicious breakfast fare provided by Eva, his most enthusiastic admirer.

The door was locked.

A skeleton key was handy, kept in a hiding place flat atop the inside bedroom doorframe of my bedroom, right where I had hidden it when a teenager, as a way of locking my room from the outside. I had behaved no differently from most teenagers trying to put one over on their parents, and those naughty nighttime escapades during my high school years, although innocent enough (except for that time in my senior year when a bunch of kids taxied up to the Harlem jazz clubs and got tight), was a rather tame attempt at rebellion during those couple of years after Mama died. Most of the times when I snuck out, we'd take the streetcar up to Grant's Tomb and set to guzzling the most disgusting bathtub gin Eddie Hirschfield purloined from his father's basement still. Me, Teddy, Eddie, and Harriet, my best girlfriend. I'd never really gone off the charts, even if Papa and the venerable Miss Eva thought I'd gone too far when I'd moved out of the brownstone and into the Greenwich Village apartment, the summer of college graduation, fearing I'd gone over to the dark side, and would live a life of bohemian decadence. Girls just didn't move out of the house until they were properly married.

I pulled over a chair, stepped up, and found the dust-covered key, my passport to forbidden places. So, I thought, there was a place that Eva could not reach to dust, that polishing maniac!

I stepped through the hall, hearing the party going on downstairs, and made fast work of entering Monty's room.

His trunks had arrived; the room was littered with clothes draped haphazardly across an opened steamer, and three valises had their contents spilled across the bed. But, as the trunks had arrived, so must have Rocco, arrived from Chicago, after his decoy demonstration for the pressmen. Rocco must be installed on the third floor, no doubt, if not in the parlor enjoying breakfast. I had no time to waste.

I didn't really know what I was looking for, as I rifled through the linens in the steamer trunk, fine silk and cotton shirts, an array of neckties, the usual and a few unusual items of a gentleman's wardrobe. It was a wonderland of extravagance, and I tried to nix the desire to examine the gold shaving apparatuses—solid gold razor? I thought, uncharitably, *I sure hope he contributes to the grocery bill while he's here.*

I flipped open an elaborate enameled box holding a

variety of diamond and sapphire studs, cuff links, and tie-pins. The beautifully tailored dress and evening suits lying prone on the bed bespoke a masculine elegance. Stocking garters hung from the rod of one of the opened steamers. I had wandered into the male sanctum, the mingling of shaving cream, cut tobacco, and intoxicating scents—a whiff of sandalwood—all decidedly masculine in nature, and at the same time evoking thoughts of mysterious Arabian nights. The bass notes of Guerlain's Mouchoir de Monsieur spoke of exotic places and sent an unexpected thrill through me, not unlike an intimate touch, a feeling I quickly tamped down. The effect on me was only the result of a stuffy room, the steam heat rising from the radiators, I rationalized. I had yet to have my morning coffee, which accounted for the weakness in my limbs and the flutter in my stomach. I was not immune to the attraction of a man as handsome as Montgomery Chase, even if I didn't particularly like him. But I had to get down to business, searching for evidence of Otto Rust's activities.

There, in an old case tossed in the closet, I found the tools of the actor's craft: wigs, moustaches, and a box filled with makeup, spirit gum, and fleshy appliances with which to pull off a number of disguises. A wardrobe of slightly worn and unfashionable suits and trousers, vests, and shoes had taken up residence in the closet. And deeper within was a briefcase, the accordion style with flap and belt buckle closures, its brown leather, ordinary, if old and battered, one of the straps missing its hardware.

A light dawned! The thing that was missing from the

photos I'd taken at the traffic accident was the briefcase! Pudgy had been clutching a briefcase as he ran out of the brownstone. I'd remembered the metal clink of the small buckle as it hit the sidewalk, the brass loop I'd picked up. The briefcase wasn't lying beside Pudgy's body because Otto Rust had retrieved it, taken it away with him, and the proof of that was in this closet!

The briefcase was weighty. I unbuckled the one fastened strap and stared at what stared up at me: a black gun. The smell of gunpowder proved that it had recently been fired. Fired by Pudgy? If he had been in possession of it, probably so. . .unless the gun belonged to Monty, and he'd hidden it there. . .

Underneath the gun was a sheaf of papers, but when I pulled it out I saw that it was one large sheet folded many times over. Blueprints! A mechanical plan for some sort of devise. The Hanover Range Finder, it stated beneath the Hanover Aeronautics company legend atop the page.

On impulse, I charged out of the room and fetched my Rolle and returned to Monty's room, where I unfolded the blueprint, laid it out on the floor in the light from the window, and snapped several photos. Eva's voice sounded, calling out my name.

Panicked, I refolded the blueprint, shoved it and the gun back into the briefcase, closed the flap, and returned it to the closet. Quickly, I left the room and locked the door.

"I'll be right down," I called out, and went to my room to check my coat pocket for the bit of metal I'd found on the sidewalk. It was the brass loop fallen from the buckle closure, fallen from the briefcase.

I sprinted down the stairs to join the fun in the parlor.

Papa, ensconced in his favorite armchair, was holding court over the movie star and attended to by the watchful Eva. The parlor was scattered with half a dozen morning editions of competing New York papers. Rascal made for my ankles, but they were covered.

"Foiled, you little bugger!" I said, picking him up and patting his head.

A tall stranger turned in greeting. He smiled disarmingly. I couldn't help but notice how comfortably this young man fit in his skin as he leaned forward with an easy air of elegance. Was this the ingenious valet who'd tricked the press in Chicago? Taken aback, expecting Rocco to be a brawny brute from the way Monty had described his body-guard-slash-valet, the Hollywood stereotype of the punch-drunk-but-cheerful speakeasy bouncer, I felt both under-dressed and totally disarmed, chiding myself for failing to check my lipstick and mascara.

Lounging on the arm of the sofa, Monty—his high-blown and animated tale of the behavior of an ornery camel during the desert filming of an Arabian adventure, in which he played the role of a tribal sheikh—frowned at my appearance in the room, obviously annoyed at the interruption, and tossed off, "Rocco, meet Miss Devlin. Now, what was I saying? Oh yes, the microphone. That critter was determined to eat the damned thing!"

"How do you do, Miss Devlin?" said Rocco. That easy air of elegance as he moved in his suit extended to his speech; the dulcet tone and precise diction confirmed an English public school education.

This man should be in the movies, or installed in an English country manor, I thought, as he took my hand, and with the most natural and inconspicuous manner, bowed over it ever so slightly, his eyes never leaving mine. Anyone else his age—he couldn't be more than thirty—would have looked preposterous, and other than an elderly bewhiskered baron in a costume drama, could not have pulled off such a Victorian appeal. Warm blue eyes twinkled with good humor; butter-blond hair, untamed by tonic, a whirl of waves breaking shore. I liked him immediately.

"Please call me Filomena—or Filly, if you like."

"I'd be pleased if you'd call me Rory," he replied in mellow tones.

My raised eyebrow prompted him to add, "Mr. Chase addresses me as Rocco, I know, it's an affectation, but you see, my surname is Rockford, hence, Rocco."

"How are you this morning, Papa," I said, planting a kiss on Papa's cheek. He actually looked rosy-cheeked—or was that the effect of high blood pressure? He did seem content in Monty's company. I placed Rascal on his lap.

"I see you were busy last night," said Archie, indicating the morning edition of *The Morning Sun*, the long-shot photo of Bund soldiers in the foreground saluting Kuhn addressing the crowd.

Although I was desperate to see my reporting in print, on the front page above the fold with my byline atop, I was not about to display my excitement in front of Papa and

Monty. I slapped the page, the photo that Monty was holding up, and nonchalantly said, "I love a parade and men in uniform—"

"Why do women have this thing about men in uniform?" asked Monty.

"Skip told me he'd assigned the story to you," said Papa.

I wanted to kiss that beautiful man! *Thank you, Skip!*

Papa raised a skeptical brow, but to my utter surprise, said, "Not bad."

I wanted to ask, "Does that mean it was good?" but refused to drag it out of him; it might sound like begging for approval, and I wasn't about to do that, not with Monty in the room.

"I thought it was spot-on," said Monty, surprising me, "the way you described the disparity between the philosophy of our nation's forefathers and that of the Third Reich's exclusionary tactics. How the Bill of Rights gives license to the expression of the Bund, no matter how distasteful their cause might be. . ."

Not a Nazi? I thought, or was Monty just saying what was expected of him?

"Thank you, Montgomery," I replied, tight-lipped.

". . . I especially enjoyed the comparison of the goose-stepping army, likening them to automatons—and then, let me read it! Here it is: 'brought to mind images of a herd, urged on by their manic sheepdog, Kuhn, in a misadventure over the cliffs of history.'"

"Yeah, well it was as far as I could go without saying those people are bat shit crazy. I suppose my story this morning transported you to the Garden last night," I was taking a chance when I turned and looked him straight in the eyes and blurted out, "as if you'd actually been there."

No reaction, just, "Sounds like you had a roaring good time!"

"How did you spend the evening?" I asked, amazed at how refreshed he appeared, not betrayed at all after his encounter with the Rémy bottle in the wee hours of the morning.

"I never kiss and tell."

I grabbed a wedge of buttered toast from the rack and took the coffee cup offered by Rocco. "I've got work to do," I announced as I started from the room, grabbing one from the stack of *The Morning Sun* on the hall table. "Glad to have met you, Rory," I said, as I made for the stairs, Monty climbing up behind me and then lingering at his bedroom door. I could feel his eyes on me as I entered my room and closed the door behind me.

Alone in my room, I would be able to look at the paper without the scrutiny of others witnessing my delight. I flattened the fold crease of the newspaper and sat by the window overlooking the street, relishing the sight of my reporting and my name in print atop. My first reporting byline on the front page! I'd been doing the feature stories, the human interest stuff, as the Women's Page editor, but this might help to convince my father I was ready for investigative reporting.

The photo was perfect in showing the manic fervor of

the Bund event, Kuhn, buffoon-like, shouting from the dais. After rereading my story, as if I hadn't read it a dozen times before filing it the night before, I turned my attention toward finding Little Dick Trumble's columns on the brownstone murder. I had to telephone Dick as soon as I could be assured a private moment at the hall telephone, or call him from the luncheonette pay phone around the corner. Too many inquiring ears in this house, I thought, turning the pages, until I spotted the story on Page 6. I was so shocked that I needed to find out if there had been a mistake. But it would have to wait, I decided, as I glanced out the window an hour later. It had to wait.

An hour later, I watched the pickle salesman, carrying a large suit box, walk down Archie Devlin's brownstone stoop. I grabbed my hat and bag and flew down the stairs, threw on my coat, and bolted out of the house in pursuit. He was half a block away, heading down toward Amsterdam Avenue, but I knew I had to keep my distance. I followed as Otto Rust walked briskly up the avenue. At Eighty-Sixth Street, he crossed west at the traffic light, and was almost lost to me when a taxicab cut me off just as the light turned red, splashing melted slush over my pant legs. Momentarily dumbstruck, and then cursing as I backed to the curb, I caught sight of Herr Rust as he crossed to the north side of the street.

The traffic signal changed and slogging across in my wet shoes and dripping pants, I tried to keep him in my sights. With a wall of car and pedestrian traffic preventing my crossing again, I kept him in sight as he casually walked

on. Free at last to catch up, I was challenged by a black road-
ster, determined to have the right-of-way in spite of the signal, and when the driver braked within inches from my hip,
I thumped angrily on the hood while emitting several more
obscenities, which elicited a shouted response from the man
behind the wheel. The incident served only to distract, and
for a moment, I lost Monty, until—there he was!—walking
into a storefront business. The elegantly painted sign above
the door read Martin Randolph Bespoke Tailor.

Pleated drapery obscured the interior view of the
shop from the sidewalk. Should I enter? Or should I wait for
Monty to exit the store? A thought struck as I gazed down at
my wet legs, and my decision was made.

A bell above the door announced my entrance, and
with a quick glance I saw that Monty wasn't in the showroom. A small, dapperly dressed man came from a curtained
back room to greet me with a smile.

"I wonder if you might help me," I said, using a dam-
sel-in-distress edge to my voice, "but you see, a cab splashed
me awfully bad—"

The man looked down at my pant legs and clucked
and nodded.

"I have a job interview just up the block this morning,
so I don't have time to go home and—"

"Well, my dear, let's see what we can do for you," said
the shopkeeper in a soothing tone, as he ushered me into
a fitting room. "We can dry them quickly," he said. "Hand
them through to me, and your hose, too. Your shoes need a
wipe. . ." he added as he left through a door at the rear of

the dressing room.

I tied the robe he had handed me, and then sat down, wondering, where had Monty disappeared to? He hadn't come out of the shop's front door, or I would have seen him. If he left now, while I was half-naked—but I would hear the door's bell jangle. Could he possibly be in another fitting room? Doing what exactly? Getting a new disguise sewn up?

Gingerly, I cracked open the door to the back room and peeked through. Cutting tables, sewing machines, block forms, bolts of fabric stacked on shelves filled a large workroom. Racks of silk ties, and linens filled a corner. A tailor was suggesting a choice of fabrics from a stack of swatches to a customer. From an alcove beyond the workroom sounded the hiss of a steam press and the clean scent of laundry starch filled the room. A woman wearing a smock carrying my clothes and shoes was fast approaching my fitting room. I closed the door, sat down, and after she rapped, bid her enter. Quickly, I dressed—my socks dry and still warm, pants pressed, and my shoes wiped clean.

From the showroom I heard Monty's distinctive voice. He was close by, just the other side of my door. I could hear every word distinctly, between him and another man—the gentleman who greeted me upon entering the shop, whose speech was decidedly foreign.

"That long?" said Monty.

"I don't see how it can be ready any sooner."

"Yes, but the ship sails at midnight, tomorrow."

"I saw in the papers about—"

"It's been taken care of. All cleaned up. Hanover was—well, it's not a problem now."

"Is there any way—"

"I wouldn't worry about that. There's no connection to you. Our people are looking for him. The case is closed as far as the police are concerned."

No more talk, just the jangle of the bell over the front door.

The small man smiled at me as I exited the fitting room, and when I opened my change purse he said, "No charge, my dear. Good luck getting the job."

Once out the shop door, there was Monty across the street, heading south and then disappearing down the steps of the subway. His arms were free of the suit box he had carried into the tailor's shop. Even if I tried, I knew I'd not catch up with him. I headed back toward home. I stopped at the Columbus Avenue luncheonette and dialed Dick Trumble.

Tuesday, February 21, 1939
11:50 a.m.

A fter finally tracking him down, we arranged to meet right at the luncheonette in half an hour. I knew what I wanted to ask Little Dick, but wondered why he'd want to talk with me? Had he seen me at the murder scene?

I ordered a cheeseburger and a chocolate malted while I waited for him to arrive. What I had to ask Little Dick would have to be carefully phrased. Any mention of Monty's presence at the murder scene, or his presence in Manhattan, for that matter, had to be kept to myself for now. My own presence at the murder scene also had to be kept to myself. I trusted Little Dick, just so far as anyone could trust any newshound, but talking about my appearance at the murder scene would bring up too many questions, ultimately subjecting me and Monty to police scrutiny. Until I knew more, I had to remain mum.

Marty, owner-waiter-chief-cook-and-bottle-washer brought over my order.

"Long time no see, kiddo. Where you been?"

"I live down in the Village, Marty. I'm staying with Papa a few days."

"How is Archie?"

I filled him in with the news of Papa's bleeding ulcer, and Marty, who'd known the family for twenty years since he opened the restaurant just after the war, said to send his regards to Archie.

There was nothing as good as Cherry's Luncheonette's grilled burger, I told him. The restaurant was named after his wife, who had passed away soon after my mother died. But Marty carried on, through the worst of the Depression, lowering his prices and feeding many a hungry man who happened by without a dime. I took my first bite into the juicy burger just as Dick walked in.

"I'll have what she's having," he called out to Marty, sliding into the booth, "but double the order." He picked a French fry from off my plate and popped it into his mouth.

"You didn't want to talk on the phone, so what's it about?" I asked, after a sip through the straw of my malted milk. "About your story—"

"Aha!" he spurted out, "you noticed it!"

I wasn't sure how he could know about my confusion about the cause of death, knife verses gun, but I was really worried that he knew I'd been in the rooming house and I feared he was going to confront me about why I'd been there. "What do you know about it?" I asked, careful not to offer information.

"The dead guy."

"Yeah, you wrote that he died. . .of a stab wound."

"Yeah, but that's not what I wanted to talk with you about."

"It isn't?" I replied, my half-eaten burger suspended in my hand as I waited for him to reveal that he saw me at the scene.

"The stiff was Hanover, Henry Hanover."

I was still trying to process that the cause of death was not from a bullet but from a stab wound. I must have appeared wide-eyed, waiting for Dick to spit it out, all the while wondering how the dead man had been identified, since his identification was in his billfold, which I had stashed away in my old desk. I dragged a fry through a puddle of ketchup. "Oh yeah," I managed to whisper inanely.

"You don't seem surprised."

"Well. . ."

A couple walked in and took the booth behind me.

"You're a smart cookie, Cookie! You are Archie's daughter, after all."

"I try to stay on my toes," I replied, circling the fact that I didn't know what the hell he was talking about.

"When they let us in the rooming house and I saw the guy lying there, I had a hunch it was the same man from the funeral up in the Bronx from that article I read yesterday morning at your pop's—in *The Hour*."

Funeral, Bronx, article Dick read at my father's. . . ?

I saw the light and it all came together. "Right!" I pointed a French fry at him for emphasis. "The dead old couple 'two-for-one special' funeral? That's what I wanted to ask you about. How'd you know for sure it was the same guy?"

"Henry Hanover was the dead old codger's son!" said Little Dick, pulling out a tattered sheet of newsprint from the inside breast pocket of his equally tattered trench coat, which he smoothed down with the palm of his hand, scattering cigarette ash like a benediction on the page as he pointed at its photo.

The bereaved son and his wife—whose features were obscured by black veiling—outside the funeral home bore a striking resemblance to the man who lay dying in the rooming house. There it was in print: . . . *Henry Hanover and his wife, Margaret. . .*

"That's what I meant. The son was shot?"

"Stabbed."

"There ya go, Dick! You identified the body?"

"I never forget a face, you know."

"I thought the name, Henry Hanover, was familiar—the old coot's son—when I saw the dead guy's name mentioned in the paper this morning, 'cause I remembered the story." I was talking too much, a sure tell I was not quite telling the truth. "You certainly have a nose for sniffing out crime. And you told the cops you suspected the man are one and the same? Just by the picture of him in *The Hour*?"

"Yeah, but actually, his name was on the tailor's label sewn inside his suit coat. Just confirmed he was who I thought he was, looking at his face. But that's not the crazy thing, you know?" he said, before pausing as Marty placed two plates loaded with two cheeseburgers with a double order of fries and the malted milk in front of him.

How could Dick eat so much and remain so scrawny? I wondered with envy.

"I told the detective in charge of the case who I thought the dead man was. I told them about the two-for-one funeral, that seemed suspicious to me—to us—and this morning when I stopped in at the precinct and saw the detective on the case to ask if they had a suspect in the killing, so I could follow it up—the detective—he was weird—he said the case was closed and brushed me off."

He squirted a stream of ketchup on the hamburgers and fries and tucked into the first.

"You wrote that the man—this Henry Hanover—was stabbed to death. I read somewhere in another rag that he was put down by a bullet."

"That's another crazy thing," nodded Dick as he continued speaking, ketchup dripping down his chin. I pulled a napkin from the napkin holder and handed it to him. "The whole rooming house and the neighbors heard a gunshot. There's a hole in the apartment door from a bullet, too. But it was a knife wound killed him."

"It's a strange coincidence that this Hanover fellow gets killed just a couple of days after both his parents kick off."

"If you believe in coincidence."

"Absolutely not!"

"I think this is what went down—"

"Oh? Enlighten me, Dick."

"It's like this, see," prefaced Little Dick, tossing the

straw from out the glass, and then taking a long drag of his malted milk. I pulled another napkin from the holder and sent it his way. He wiped the milk moustache from his upper lip and said, "This guy Henry and his wife kill the old man on the way to the funeral home, see?"

"Why?"

"Maybe for the insurance money; maybe the old fart was a pain in the ass, who knows?! There was insurance money by the way; I looked into that angle yesterday, after the meeting at your Pop's. A hundred grand! Plus, what his recently dead wife was worth both alive and in life insurance paid out to the old man then goes to the son, Henry. *And*—a house in Bronxville and a mansion in Sands Point, right on the Sound. The old man was swimming in cash, too, since the war. Aeronautics. The Crash didn't hurt him at all. I'm figuring the son, who's now dead, stood to inherit close to a million. All goes to his wife now."

"That ain't hay!"

"So, I figure maybe the old man's son, this Henry, is followed to the rooming house of this woman, see, this woman Hedy Werner—and she's this guy's mistress, see?"

"How you figure that?"

"It's the dame's room, after all, and why else would Henry be there, in that dump, unless it was to meet his mistress?"

"You sound pretty sure. Maybe she's a relative or an old family friend he went to tell of the news of his parents' deaths. Damn! Maybe this woman was his dead father's mistress, not his, for all you know! Or maybe Henry was just an innocent victim, lured to the apartment by a gang who wanted to steal his wallet—his wallet was missing, after all—and he put up a fight, maybe."

"How'd you know his wallet was missing?"

I had to shut up and let Dick talk. But I had an answer, "You said his name was on his suit label."

"Right." Dick flicked his lighter, the cigarette halfway to the flame, when he stopped, frowned, and stared at me. "What you getting all worked up about, Fill?

I had to get him off track, at least for a day or so, until I finished my own investigation, so I said, "I think you're jumping to conclusions. Have you found out anything about this Hedy Werner?"

I already knew that Hedy Werner was often out of town, a saleswoman, according to the rooming house landlord, but I could not offer the information to Dick.

"I'm looking into it. I'm gonna talk to the landlord this afternoon; see what I can find out. But listen, I heard him tell the police there was another woman in the apartment when he found the body."

I hoped Dick couldn't hear my heart throbbing or see the blood rushing to my cheeks.

"A real looker, too, who said she was from the press, but the landlord didn't buy it because she looked tough and mean as hell."

"What? What the—" I was about to say a bad word for which Mama would have washed out my mouth with soap but caught myself—"landlord say? The beautiful woman looked tough?"

Dick nodded. "I'll bet it was Henry Hanover's wife, Margaret, that the landlord was talking about, the woman he found leaning over the body."

"Is that what he said?"

"He said she was dark, but the wife, Margaret here"— he picked up the newspaper and slapped the photo, smudging ketchup on the page, which he swiped away with the back of his hand—"is blonde. See her hair beneath the veil? Maybe she was wearing a wig, who knows! She stabbed the cheating double-crosser."

Decision time. I wrestled with myself, trying to calculate what to give away and what to keep to myself. As things stood now, I had been personally described as a vengeful and murderous woman, at least by the landlord's overembellished testimony. I needed Little Dick's help. *How* he was going to be of help, I had no idea yet. But if I could have him on my side instead of trying to figure things out on my own. . .Little Dick Trumble was the notorious "pit bull" of reporters who could wheedle the evidence from the most unsuspecting sources. Should I just level with him?

No, I decided, not until I could find out exactly how Monty was involved.

Little Dick was looking at me with an odd glint in his eyes, and I wondered, had he, after all, seen me leaving the rooming house and was he just stringing me along?

"I think you got a good story there, Dick, but until you find out for sure that this Henry Hanover had indeed been stabbed by his wife—I mean, does the wife have an alibi?— you might want to look elsewhere."

"You think I don't know that?"

"Of course, you do, I'm sorry. What's your next move?"

"Look, the reason I asked your Pop to have you call me was because you were the only one, out of that whole bunch of harebrains, to suspect the old man's kids had done him in. Oh, by the way, the old man was buried without so much as an autopsy."

"Of course, there wouldn't be a call for one; they probably thought, since everybody knew his wife of fifty years had just died a day or two before, it was a broken heart done him in, since that happens sometimes when a spouse dies and the remaining one is in distress."

"Yeah, I know a case or two. Broken heart."

"But *you* saw the dark side."

"What do you mean? Oh, that it might not be as cut-and-dried as an old man croaking from a simple heart attack."

"Right. And I can't get very far with this...investigating...because the police have closed the case and I'm a man."

"Huh?"

"I think you can help me get to the bottom of this double—no triple murder."

I shifted in the booth, toyed with the last French fry on my plate.

"Triple?"

"The three Hanovers—Mom, Pop, son."

"You suspect the old lady—"

"Listen, kiddo, you've been begging Archie to let you do some real reporting. Your first shot was front-page wood this morning on the Bund rally, but you need to follow up with an investigative piece to move up and out of the Women's Page. This is your chance. I'll share the byline if you help."

"All right, but I want to keep this only between us. I don't want Papa or anybody at the paper to know what we're investigating, even though he told you to look into the two-for-one funeral story."

"I'm sure he's forgotten all about it. But sure. I'll zip my lips. We don't want anybody getting a jump on us, that's for sure."

"What do you want me to do?"

"Get to this woman, Margaret Hanover, Henry's wife—rich wife now, and find out all you can about her."

"Find out if she killed her husband? How do you know she's going to talk with me?"

"I'd talk to you before I'd talk to me," said Dick, as I waved yet another napkin and pointed at his hopelessly soiled necktie.

He had a point. As well-fed as he was, as sharp-minded, there was a sad seediness about his countenance, with his rumpled clothes and hangdog features. I'd known Little Dick and his father, Big Dick Trumble, the intrepid Pulitzer Prize-winning reporter, all of my life, so I always looked past his unkempt appearance. Dick was fully aware of his own limitations in dealing with women. He was an unattractive little fellow, and those who did not know and admire him, as I did, might find him a little creepy, and not the kind of sympathetic fellow you'd want to open up to.

"All right. The question is how I get in?"

"I suspect there'll be a funeral for her husband, Henry."

Tuesday, February 21, 1939
1:28 p.m.

For the second time today, I planted myself in my room, near the window, so I could watch for the moment when Rocco left the house. Earlier, when I'd returned to the house, Rocco said it was his day off and he wanted to see a Broadway musical matinee and I suggested Kurt Weill's *Knickerbocker Holiday* starring Walter Huston. I telephoned my friend at the paper, drama critic Jim Weisman, and secured Rocco's seat as well as my opportunity to search Monty's room again.

Earlier, while waiting for Little Dick to arrive at Cherry's, I wrote in my shorthand notebook the conversation I'd overheard from behind the fitting room door. Thanks to my ability of recall, I was able to note down verbatim what was said between the shop owner and Monty. Now I attempted to dissect from the conversation its various possible meanings:

I don't see how it can be ready any sooner.

What was it that would take so long to be made ready? Made ready for what?

Yes, but the ship sails at midnight tomorrow.

Obviously, something had to be ready before a ship sailed tomorrow midnight. Because the conversation was held at the tailor's, could it be a suit or dinner coat Monty had ordered cut? Was there a suit in the box he'd carried to the shop? Was he sailing somewhere tomorrow night? That was a possibility. What I wanted to believe. Perhaps something was going to be sent overseas? Cargo? I made a note to check the shipping news to find out which ships were departing tomorrow night. Dozens, most likely.

Why the shift in the conversation to the rooming house murder victim, Henry Hanover?

It's been taken care of. All cleaned up. Hanover was—well, it's not a problem now.

Monty confirmed that the tailor knew about the murder and needed assurances from Monty.

Who took care of cleaning up what?

There's no connection to you.

This had to be in reply to the man's concern of being implicated in the crime. Obviously, he was involved, but how? Why would this kindly little tailor have anything to do with murder in a rooming house?

Our people are looking for him, Monty had assured him.

Who was "our people," and for whom were they searching? Pudgy was dead, Monty was the only other man, surviving man, present in the apartment. . .and—

I went down to the next line in the conversation.

The case is closed as far as the police are concerned.

This is what Little Dick told me, too! Now, why would the police close a case file before solving the crime? How could it be all wrapped up without first catching the perpetrator? Suspicious. Something to look into.

Unless the police played a part in the crime. Sure, there was corruption in the force. There'd always been bad cops.

One thing was certain: things didn't smell right.

I heard the familiar thud of the front door closing, looked out the window, and watched as Rocco walked down the sidewalk for his matinee. The coast was clear.

Eva was busy downstairs in the kitchen. Papa was napping on the library sofa, with Rascal curled up at his feet. I entered Monty's bedroom with my skeleton key, and thought it suspicious that Monty would lock the door in the first place. This wasn't a hotel; it was a family home. There were no strangers mucking about the house, so why the locked door? Eva wouldn't snoop; no one would snoop— well, all right, but I had reason. What was he trying to hide, as if I didn't know? Well, I didn't know but was determined to find out.

First things first. Straight to the closet searching for the briefcase. It wasn't there, just as I'd figured. It had to have been contained in the suit box Otto Rust had delivered to the tailor shop, for sure. But why? Why all the subterfuge? Where was the gun?

I riffled through the dresser, but it was too obvious a place to hide anything. Eva might come across it there, if she returned folded laundry. Just spare blankets. I checked under the mattress, as well as in and behind the armoire. Nothing.

The steamer trunks appeared organized. I opened their drawers and found only apparel and grooming items; the suits and shirts that had been tossed across the bed this morning had been hung in the closet. No doubt by Rocco since his arrival. Could Rocco have knowledge of what went down last night and be involved in all this? A little box hidden under a stack of silk undershirts revealed Nazi paraphernalia—a swastika tiepin and cuff links, and a business card. I read the name of a dentist whose office was on the Upper East Side. The dentist! The same dentist whose bill I'd pilfered from Hedy Werner's desk!

But no gun.

I looked over the room to make sure I was leaving it exactly as I'd found it and went to the door. I noticed the matchstick on the floor and tried to remember if I'd seen it or simply walked over it when I entered. The floor by the door was a gleaming, light stained wood, and I couldn't have missed seeing the match when I'd first stepped in. There was a pack of matches on the bedside table, next to an ashtray, and I went over to take a closer look. The match was from the same pack. Monty used a gold lighter—I'd seen it earlier that morning among his things. The match cover advertised a beer garden on East Eighty-Sixth Street.

It dawned on me. All the subterfuge, the disguises: the matchstick had fallen from between the door and the jamb, set there to inform Monty of the presence of intruders while he was away! I replaced the stick, above eye level to any possible intruder and locked the door.

Back in my room, I opened the "bill" envelope addressed to Hedy Werner.

So, Monty knew this dentist, Robert Armbruster, D.D.S. . . . and it was probable that he also knew the woman, Hedy Werner, Armbruster's patient, I figured as I carefully lifted the envelope's flap.

It was just a bill, an ordinary bill for work done, a gold crown molar, nine dollars.

That was cheap for a gold crown! Dental work like that would cost triple that.

I stuffed the bill back into the envelope and stuck it in my desk drawer.

But the thought came into my head: if Monty was taking precautions, like locking his room and setting alerts with matchsticks, my room might not be the best hiding place for my loot, which included Henry Hanover's wristwatch and billfold, the crime scene photos, and the dentist's bill. I looked around my bedroom for a more secure hiding space and found the room was too spare, my only remaining possessions from my youth were my bed, a chair, the desk, a bureau, and a couple of photos on the wall. I stuffed my "loot" into a Bergdorf's shopping bag I found on the closet shelf and topped it with a sweater taken from my valise, leaving the bag next to the valise, out in the open, not hidden but in plain sight. As soon as I could, I would bring it to my apartment and away from prying eyes.

What did I really know about Monty? Just that his father had been my father's close friend. It was time I found out more about him. It was time I talked with Papa.

I found him awake when I went into the library, sipping a cup of tea.

"If you want to call this tea," he scowled, when I poured myself a cup.

"Chamomile."

"Dishwater." He nibbled on a zwieback biscuit, and then returned it to the plate. "What am I, a baby? I have all my teeth. You've got to get me some real food, Filomena."

"Eva only means well, Papa."

"She'll kill me with kindness by starving me to death."

"Tell you what. I'll call Dr. Harriman right now and ask what you can't eat and I'll make sure you get everything you can. Since Eva runs the show and does the cooking, I'll bring her in on it."

I called the doctor's office, and his nurse gave me the rundown: no fried foods, hold the butter and cream. That left plenty of vegetables, fruit, lean meats, and oatmeal. I gave Eva the list and she balked at first, saying that's not what her sister ate when she returned from the hospital.

"Gall bladder surgery is different from a bleeding ulcer. And Papa can have Indian tea, eggs, and jam or honey on fresh bread. No onions or garlic, keep the peanuts and walnuts away, and no more fava bean soup. Empty the liquor cabinet. No more bacon or ham or corned beef. Broil, bake, or boil."

After several "harrumphs," I gave her a hug, a kiss on the cheek, and told her how we could never do without her. And it was true; she kept everything going, and I was grateful for this little widow in her fifties, with her curly tendrils always escaping her bun, her sparkling black eyes, and winning smile that surprised you by transforming a rather plain countenance into one of beauty. Today she wore one of her Sunday dresses, I could tell, because of the lace collar, in place of the usual cardigan over floral sackcloth. Well, Monty was in the house, and having a movie star around raised the fashion bar. That she was sworn to secrecy about his presence here must have been hard to bear, especially since she could not brag to her church ladies and sewing circle friends, I was sure.

"Eva, are there any cookies around? I'm starving and dinner isn't for a couple of hours—"

"You're hungry, huh? Vanilla wafers."

I took a stack from the box she handed me, and went to leave the kitchen.

"He shouldn't have too many," she said, seeing through my deceit.

"I set up an appointment to meet with Frieda Wunderlich, Papa," I prefaced, handing him the cookies. "I've started the profile on her, chosen photos for the spread and compiled my questions. I'll schedule the feature for this coming Sunday."

He nodded, placated with my compliance and a bite of the wafer. I went on with a list of other stories that would appear in the Sunday section; including the latest fashion rage—bold plaids with calfskin accents—and a feature of the fashion designer, Mainbocher's, his new salon opening on Fifty-Ninth Street, next door to Tiffany's.

"All right."

I was surprised, a little, that he appeared so resigned. Or was he just savoring the taste of the cookie?

"Papa?"

He must have read my thoughts, because he came back with, "I don't know how I'm going to last two weeks here, just lying around. Doing nothing is more aggravating than the newsroom."

"You have to slow down, Papa. You have to recover. And then you've got to stay well."

"The paper is what I do, Filomena. I'm not ready to be put out to pasture."

"Nobody is saying you should retire or anything like that. But in future you can't ignore your health. You've groomed Skip in the business, and you don't need to worry about him. It's still your paper, Papa. You still point the way; you still have the last word. But like you always said, the smart man delegates."

"I don't want to talk about it anymore."

I sipped the tepid tea, and searched for something innocuous to say as a lead-in to my questions, when Papa stated, "Monty's having dinner with us tonight. You will be here?"

More a directive than a request.

"Yes, if you like."

"I would like."

"Okay."

"It's good to have him here. He doesn't come home to New York very often. But now I suppose that will change and we'll see him more."

"Oh? You mean he'll be visiting more often?"

"No. He's staying."

"Here?!"

"Until his penthouse is ready."

"What? When will that be?"

"A couple of months."

"I don't understand, Papa. What about his film contract? How many films does he have to make a year that he can hop back and forth from coast to coast?"

Papa looked at me with that tight-lipped, narrow-eyed expression, the way he did when I was a kid and he suspected I was either hiding something or was up to something. His silence prompted me to explain.

"What I mean is, I'm glad that you're happy to see him and have him stay here—"

"But?"

"Isn't it an imposition—more work for Eva?"

"She's delighted."

"I suppose she is. But she's supposed to be taking care of you, not him."

"You'll be going back to your apartment—when? Tomorrow? Why should it concern you if he's living here?"

"It doesn't. Not at all. Why should I care? I don't care what he does."

Why couldn't I *just. Shut. Up!* I protest too much, and Papa was looking at me with that *look*.

The silence was palpable. Papa continued his steady and uncomfortable scrutiny of me, absent-mindedly breaking off pieces of cookie and feeding them to that little beggar, Rascal, who took full advantage of his master's distraction. Of course, it was not in my nature to keep quiet for long. I just couldn't help myself.

"What happened? Didn't the studio renew his contract?"

I must have guessed right, because Papa's eyes shifted away and his amused expression morphed into a frown, and instead of answering my question he said, "Monty's going to do a new play on Broadway next fall."

"I see. . ." I floundered, trying to understand why Montgomery Chase would leave Hollywood when he was at the top of his career as one of the movie industry's most sought-after leading men? I couldn't believe the studio would not renew his contract. Unless it was Monty who opted out. Papa answered my silent question.

"He doesn't care about the money. He's an artist, and he wants to get back to his roots—the theatre."

"I see," I said. "Bully for him."

Damn, there I go again! I just couldn't keep the sarcasm out of my voice! Not only did I keep putting my foot in my mouth, I kept swallowing it, too.

I was rescued by the ringing of the telephone. Papa leaned over and picked up the receiver. It was my chance to escape. My questions about Monty would have to wait. I kissed Papa on the forehead and dashed out of the room. I had work to do at the paper and only a couple of hours to get it done before dinner was served.

Tuesday, February 21, 1939
2:35 p.m.

Fortunately, as women's editor, I had underlings, and heeding the advice I had just given to Papa, I delegated to the two women, Grace Miller and Terry Hayes—graduates from Smith and Vassar, respectively, to do my bidding. First, I had to make the lie I had told Papa the truth: the research on Frieda Wunderlich for my article had to be done and a bio sketched out. I assigned Terry to that task. Grace, fashion savvy—her interest grounded to the runway—I sent to compile fashion photographs using plaid fabric with calfskin accents. Grace immediately chimed in about Clare Potter, whose Fall '39 collection showed last week. Grace rattled off that the designer won this year's Neiman Marcus Fashion Award, only a year after winning Lord & Taylor's Sportswear Award. I didn't give a crap about the accolades as long as Potter designed clothes with plaid and calfskin accents.

The deadline for Sunday's advertising pages was

Thursday noon, and the usual retailers had their spaces mocked out already—B. Altman, Bergdorf Goodman, Lord & Taylor, Macy's, Gimbels, Lerner, Peck & Peck. But Bonwit Teller wanted an additional ad fitted next to Tiffany's, and thereby decreasing column space. It would all get done. It always did. I'd bought myself some time, time to investigate how murders and Montgomery Chase were connected.

Now I needed to attend a funeral. I checked with the reporter filing the obits, but the Henry Hanover entry didn't mention a funeral home or the calling hours. I got the telephone number for the Hanover house in Bronxville from the operator and she connected me. After three rings, a woman picked up, told me she was the housekeeper, and that Mrs. Hanover was not at home. With a few further questions I found out that, no, Mrs. Hanover was not at the Sands Point estate and that there would be no calling hours and no service. Mr. Hanover's body was to be cremated the following morning.

"But I'd like to speak with Mrs. Hanover—Margaret—to offer my condolences. We are old friends and— "

"I can't say when she'll return, Miss—?"

"I'll call her again. Tomorrow, perhaps?"

No reply, just the click of disconnect.

So, I thought, she doesn't want to talk to anyone, even old friends. I wasn't surprised, really. Her husband and in-laws were dead. I thought about it. She must be in a state. Distraught at the loss. There was nothing that pointed to her being responsible for any of the deaths, really. She may have just been an unknowing victim of bad luck. Bad luck. Even though she just inherited a fortune it didn't mean she had instigated events leading to the windfall.

Could she have had anything to do with murder?

Tuesday, February 21, 1939
7:10 p.m.

66. . .then your father, Monty, he sees the man kick the
dog off the pier, hears the dog yelp in pain—or surprise—
landing in the river. He jumps in after the poor mutt, into
the river, cause he's gonna rescue it," Papa was saying when
I arrived home and took my place at the dining room table.
He flashed me a look that read, *You're late, Filomena.*

"Sorry, got held up at the paper."

Monty, Rocco, and Eva were spooning up their soup.
I was about to sit opposite from Papa, who was at the head
of the table, when he indicated I come around to sit next to
Rocco, which put me directly across from Montgomery.

I raised a hand for Eva to remain seated and helped
myself to the soup from the tureen. I caught Monty's eye,
as I ladled out my portion, before he turned back to Papa.

"All right, so my father jumps into the East River. . . ?"

"How old were you two?" asked Eva.

"Well, Fred was a year my senior. So. . .twelve? No,

thirteen."

"Go on. Archie, what happened then?" prodded Monty.

"Well, your father wasn't much of a swimmer, and then waves from a passing barge started knocking him around. I watched him struggle for a minute, and I got scared he'd go under, so I started yelling for help and threw off my shoes and trousers and jumped in after him. But that dog, that mongrel he was trying to save, he didn't need to be rescued, wasn't in any trouble of drowning. He was happy as pie, just paddling along, enjoying the cool bath."

Papa made like a swimming dog, paddling his hands like paws through water, lifting his head, as if clearing the water line. Musing in his childhood's past.

"So!" exclaimed Papa, returned from his reverie, "When that dog heard Fred's cries for help—he was spitting water now—wouldn't you know, that mutt spun around and made for him, swimming a beeline toward Fred, and before I could swim anywhere near him, that dog, that crazy dog, grabbed your father by the collar of his shirt and dragged him to shore! By golly, you should've seen that!"

"Father never told me about that."

"You should have seen it! There were half a dozen kids jumping around cheering them on, and then the crowd got bigger—longshoremen came running, truck drivers, and the cabbies!"

"That must have been something!" said Eva, laughing.

"Now I know why he made me learn how to swim," said Monty, "why he took us to Manhattan Beach on Sundays. Made me tread water for God knows how long, taught me lifesaving, too!"

"It was one hot summer, back in '93," Papa chuckled. "And that dog was happy to cool off."

"Father must have been—"

"He was mad as hell at that dog. Everybody was laughing and patting the dog—feeding him frankfurters from the vendor, ice cream from the cart, like he was the hero, you see. And Fred was humiliated because the crowd thought he'd just fallen in off the pier. They never saw the man beat and throw the dog in the river, you see. Fred caught his breath and pushed the grown-ups away. Boy, was he mad! Where was his frankfurter, his ice cream cone? He started to run off—half-naked, still—the mongrel ran after him—and I followed, and the kids followed, too."

"Like a parade," nodded Rocco.

"Like a parade, all right!" said Papa.

"To further humiliate him, I'm sure," said Monty.

"But, Archie," chimed in Rocco, "I still don't see how Monty's father got his nickname?"

"Was he a very skinny boy?" asked Eva.

"Fred? Nah. We were all on the scrawny side, but that's not it—hold your horses, kids, I'm not finished!" Papa laughed. "You see, as he was trying to run away from the dog—"

"Was the dog attacking him?"

"No, Monty, the dog only wanted to play! Big black dog, lapping tongue—and I'm dashing after them both with a trail of others—and I hear your father yelling at the dog,

"Get away from me!" Papa broke off to laugh and pound a fist on the table, trembling my soup dish and rattling the glasses before he continued, trying to form his words through his laughter.

"'I'm not a—stick!'" spat out Papa. "'I'm not a *stick!* Get away from me, you!'"

"Oooohhh!" bellowed Monty, and everyone chimed in, including me. "Now I know why they called him *the Stick!* I thought it was his love of stickball."

"If you want that version, sure. Fred was the best batter on our street. But it wasn't the street game that got him his name."

"So much I didn't know about my old man, Archie."

"And there's a lot I'll never tell you, if you know what I mean? All the kids had nicknames."

"What was yours, Papa?"

"Mine wasn't so flattering."

"Oh really? What did you do to deserve it?" asked Eva.

"I was born, that's all. Born Irish. I was *the Mick.*"

"You're right, not so flattering," said Rocco.

"Yeah, but we were kids. We addressed each with good fellowship. There was Little Irish, Belfast, and Sean the Leprechaun. There was even a little chink we labeled Ricky Rickshaw; his parents ran a laundry. Your father grew up just on the German side of the German-Irish boundary on the East Side, Ninety-Third Street, Monty."

"You're German," I said, as if I hadn't just done my homework at the paper's morgue.

"You know how we became friends?" said Papa.

Monty gave my father his full attention.

"I was nine years old and my ma made me take my little brother, Danny, home from the house on Eighty-Seventh Street, where she worked for a family, cleaning house. Germantown. I don't remember why she brought us there that day, but to get home Danny and I had to cross the German-Irish boundary. A gang of kids started messing with us, and it was your papa came to our rescue, and made the others let us pass. Walked with us the rest of the way to our building. By the time we got to the front stoop, we'd become fast friends. We played marbles on the sidewalk and a couple of other Irish kids joined us. It's easy when you're kids. Easy to make friends."

"Sounds like your father was quite a guy, Monty," said Rocco.

"Yes, sounds like it. Rescuing little children and mongrel dogs."

"I didn't know you were German, Monty," I said again.

"Yes," he replied, matter-of-factly. "On my father's side."

"Do you speak German?" I asked.

"I do."

"Fluently?"

"Yes."

"Interesting. . . What is your real name?" I pressed on.

"Trumbauer."

"Why'd you change it?"

"Well, it wasn't my call, actually," he said, turning toward Eva and Papa to explain. "The studio didn't like the sound of Trumbauer. Too harsh. Too German. All things German were not appreciated, if you remember, back in '21, when I first came on the scene. 'Sounds like a villainous Hun,' the studio chief said. I suggested Chase, from my mother's surname, Chashnik."

"I see," I said. "But Montgomery? Wasn't your real name Rudolf?"

He turned wearily to face me. "Well, at the time there was already a very popular 'Rudolph.' Rudolph Valentino. The studio publicity people thought that one was enough."

"I suppose there's a nice flow to the name," I said. "Very. . .British."

"Very harmonious," said Rocco.

"Innocuous," I said.

"Glad you approve, Filomena," said Monty.

I held his fiery gaze until Eva rose and asked me to help bring in the roast. But then the telephone rang.

"Saved by the bell," said Monty.

"Do you need saving?" I asked as I went to answer it.

It was Little Dick Trumble calling to tell me that the body of Henry Hanover had been released to his family—to his wife.

"Now get this: since I didn't get squat from the detective assigned the case—"

"Yes, you told me he said the case was closed." I told him about my phone conversation with the Hanover family housekeeper.

"Gotta track down Henry's wife." He switched over. "But why would they close a murder investigation? Only if they had the perpetrator locked up, right?"

"So who done it?"

"That's just it. This beat cop I know at the precinct—I stood him for a couple of rounds at Dirty Pete's and a fin— he tells me they don't have one—not even a suspect. Seems there was a phone call, see? Drop the investigation. From someone high up in the department."

"So, what do you make of it?"

"I can't make anything of it. Henry Hanover wasn't an undercover cop, and they probably know who whacked him, but they're keeping mum. He wasn't related to any- one in the NYPD or in the mayor's office, so it doesn't look like a cover-up. This guy, Henry, didn't even have a parking ticket, let alone a criminal record or ties to the mob. So I asked, was there a big fish out there swimming around the city who they want to nail for more than a murder rap of a law-abiding citizen who might have just been at the wrong place at the wrong time?"

"What did your friend think was going on?"

"That the back-off order came from outside the de- partment."

"So, what do you think we should do?"

"Here's the thing: if we investigate things might get sticky."

I recognized a hesitancy in his voice, the kind I was familiar with, when I wanted to break a date with a guy—a nice, if boring, guy. You don't lead them on, and you let them down gently.

"Are you thinking we have to back off, too?"

"Hell no, not me! But you maybe."

"What? I thought we were in this thing—"

"It's too dangerous, kiddo. Archie would have my hide if anything happened to you."

"Well, I appreciate your concern over covering your ass from the wrath of Archibald Devlin, but—"

"Come on, it's not safe for you."

I didn't take his warning lightly. Dick had a sixth sense about things, he listened to his gut, intuition—whatever it was that led him to uncovering facts, solving crime puzzles. And I could not share with him all that I knew about the case. At least, not yet. I wouldn't cover up Monty's involvement in the murder, but for goodness's sake, it looked like he would remain living, according to Papa, in this house for months to come.

"Okay, okay, Dick. This is more than just a crime of passion, a crime for money, like we first thought." I didn't give him a chance to weasel out of my helping.

"But forget about Hanover for now, Fill, until I find out more about what we're up against. Just step back, until I call you in again."

If he called me in again.

"Okay, boss, I'll sit tight."

"Aren't you going to argue with me? Put up a fight?"

I must have really blown his mind by agreeing to play by his rules.

"Hell no, Dick. I'll let you call the shots on this."

Back at the dinner table the mood had turned from gregarious to somber. When I returned, everybody was chowing down on the main course. Eva's roast was memorable, as were all the side dishes that went with the feast, so the lack of conversation was understandable. I should visit for dinner more often; I made a mental note to myself. I'd forgotten that when Papa wasn't dictating the menu of deep-fried everything Eva could put out one hell of a spread. Satiated, Rocco gave us his review of the matinee he attended, and Eva asked Monty about the various Hollywood stars she admired, besides Monty, of course. She was startled to learn that Carole Lombard "cursed like a drunken sailor," Gable had false teeth and bad breath, and Charles Boyer, who wore a toupee—"Say it isn't so!" declared Eva— was one of the nastiest characters you'd ever want to meet. I served dessert, ice cream, and soon afterward, Papa settled in the library with a book and a cup of Indian tea, satiated from his first meal of "real" food in weeks. Monty announced he was going out, Rocco said he was going to bed with a good book, and Eva refused my help washing up, for which I was grateful. I wanted to be ready to leave the house when Otto Rust descended the stairs.

Tuesday, February 21, 1939
10:23 p.m.

How was I going to unobtrusively walk into a German beer hall? Because that's where Otto Rust's cab dropped him off on East Eighty-Sixth Street, the part of town better known as Germantown.

Following him across town was challenging enough, because although I was lucky to hop in a taxi, the driver didn't like that I wouldn't give him a destination. It was past his shift, I was the last fare, and he complained he "didn't want to end up in some hellhole neighborhood in the Bronx without the chance of a return fare."

"There's a big tip," I said, to shut him up. "If you would just follow that damn Checker cab three car-lengths ahead."

Some people have no sense of adventure.

I tossed the fare with an extra quarter when I got out of the cab, but he didn't seem pleased. "I'm a working girl, mister. Count your blessings you landed this side of the

Grand Concourse."

I would just have to use my imagination, and some fast thinking, and possibly fast-talking to get into the restaurant undetected by my quarry. Yes! I said to myself, I was a hunter, and although it was not the stalking of the wild rhino in a heady African adventure, it was a stalking nonetheless, my prey, a Nazi. I was a Nazi hunter! The idea emboldened me into action. I simply walked in through the front door, along with a party of four, and before the host noticed me, I circled around the edges of the noisy and crowded room, past busy waiters serving bratwurst and pitchers of beer to diners packing the tables. Tobacco smoke snaked in a cloud over the heads of diners and diffused into a blue haze at the high-vaulted ceiling, the smell mingled with the pungent odors of cabbage and sour beer.

Where was Otto?

Momentarily distracted by a waiter—I was intercepted when he lifted a particularly mouthwatering slice of apple streusel from his tray to pass at nose level—I finally spotted my prey. He was seated at a table near the bandstand, its musicians pumping out a brassy oompah-pah polka, and across from him sat a distinguished-looking man, sleek black hair combed back from a middle part, thin moustache, and dapper threads. With all the racket of the band and gregarious socializing, I realized that even if I got close enough—like at the table next to theirs, where I'd surely be discovered, the noise would drown out their conversation.

So, from behind a pillar that blocked being seen, I could at least watch their exchange. A waiter deposited steins of beer at their table and soon departed. Then, with slow and deliberate movements Monty placed an envelope on the table, which his companion deposited inside his coat. I watched them for a while, as they appeared to make small talk, and then the next thing I knew, Monty had risen to his feet, and was walking in my direction. I slinked backward, hugging the pillar to avoid being seen, circling around with no thought of what was behind my back, until I collided into a waiter serving a table of five.

The impact was followed by the clamorous crash of silverware and porcelain, the scrape of chairs, the shrieks of startled and splashed customers, and the smell of spilled beer. What I saw when I turned to see the damage made me close my eyes for a moment: the poor waiter sprawled across a table in a pose that brought to mind da Vinci's *Vitruvian Man*—only face down—the table pitched at a precarious angle, ruined suits and dresses, strings of sauerkraut dangling from a fashionable chapeau.

It was not a pretty picture.

And then the big thud, when the tabletop hit the floor, the waiter sliding face first under the legs of a woman diner. An additional round of shouts ensued.

It was not exactly catastrophic—a plate of Wiener schnitzel lay unscathed, its parsley garnish undisturbed, having hydroplaned to a gentle stop. And although the waiter may not have agreed, the vocal reaction was more from surprise than injury. Fearing retaliation for the trampled spaetzle under my shoe, I had to get out of there, before the finger-pointing began along with cries for restitution, but when I turned to flee the fiasco of my own making, I spotted Monty hesitating in his advance to the door as he cast a glance in my direction, the epicenter of the commotion. I ducked to the floor.

Suddenly, a gentleman, believing I had fallen, came to my aid, blocking Monty's line of vision. I thanked him, after he lifted me to my feet. When I looked up into his face, my heart skipped a beat.

"Are you sure you are all right, miss?" said Monty's drinking buddy, his accent decidedly Germanic. "You are not injured?"

I smoothed down my beer-splashed coat, feeling in my pocket for a handkerchief to wipe it off, and of course, I couldn't find one. When I bent down to peek around the man's waist, to see if Monty still lingered, I felt the dreaded tickle running down along my shin. "Another fifty cents' worth of injured pride," I replied at the sight of my right stocking.

I must have appeared off-balance, or at least, shifty-eyed, as I again threw glances around the room behind him, like a boxer avoiding a punch to the head, because he asked if I had, in fact, hit my head. "No," I replied, once more scanning the room. Monty was nowhere in sight. "I have to go," I said, removing his hand from my elbow.

"Let me help you."

"That's not necessary, thanks."

"I insist. Where's your party?" he asked, handing me his folded handkerchief and pointing to my face. I wiped some gelatinous liquid off my cheek. He handed me my handbag.

"Umm, they are gone, left. I must go now."

As I started for the door, my heel made contact with something slick. Spaetzle? I was about to make a hard landing on my rump, when suddenly, arms gripped me from behind. I fell back into the pillow of his chest in what might have otherwise appeared an expert dance move. He steadied me to my feet.

"I'll walk you out."

I let him lead me out to the street. I thanked him for his help, distractedly, while looking up and down the street for my movie star.

"You are looking for something? Someone?"

"Umm. . .no," I said, a little defensively. He studied my face, which made me uncomfortable.

"Shall I hail you a taxi?"

"Umm. . ."

"Are you sure you're all right?" he said, as he took hold of me and looked into my eyes. I waved him off with the handkerchief I still gripped in my hand.

"Oh, this is yours. . ."

"You are quite shaken."

"Well, it's been an eventful evening."

"Look, can I buy you a drink? You look like you could use one."

"I should be going."

"There's a nice little bar, just a few doors away—or, my office is right there, across the street. You see the sign?"

"Really, very nice, but. . ."

"I'm Robert Armbruster, the dentist, see?"

The otherwise unobtrusive fellow made splendid in his sealskin overcoat with mink collar, white silk scarf at his neck, placed his homburg on his head and looked me over.

I looked where he pointed, to the shingle outside a brownstone. Robert Armbruster, D.D.S. it read in block letters. My mind flipped back to the rooming house where Henry Hanover had been stabbed to death, the envelope I pilfered from the desk addressed to Hedy Werner, a bill from her dentist, *Robert Armbruster, D.D.S.!*

I had to make a decision. Monty was nowhere in sight. At best he had returned to Papa's. But chances were he would be lost to me amid eight million city souls. I reasoned that his man, Armbruster, might prove important, might provide me with proof in my investigation of Monty Chase. Proof to expose Monty as a Nazi. I'd read all I could about Monty this afternoon, his activities in Hollywood, his German parentage, his fluency in the language, even the fact that he was involved with the Hollywood Anti-Nazi League. Incongruous, but what better way to deflect suspicion from himself, while infiltrating the group? This chance collision with Armbruster was serendipitous!

"I do feel a bit faint. I'll take you up on that drink, Dr. Armbruster."

"Robert, call me Robert."

He took my elbow and guided me across the busy thoroughfare, dodging two-way traffic and streetcars.

We entered the house. Off the hallway was a door with signage leading to the dental office. But the dentist led me up a flight of stairs, where the landing opened into a large living space.

He flicked the light switch and the room illuminated a rather old-fashionedly decorated room: forest green brocade and gold bullion-fringed chairs and sofa of a matching suite flanked the fireplace and dominated the space; an ornately carved credenza and tables held fringe-shaded lamps and stood on Bauhaus carpets; carved dark wood tall-back chairs shouted their palatial origins; oil paintings—on first glance Old Masters—were stacked threefold up the walls, and a large tapestry—medieval from the look of it—took up the narrow wall opposite the room's street-side windows. It was all so. . .heavy-handed, and what might have been a stylish and cozy space was weighed down with a claustrophobic air.

Armbruster, his hand at my back, ushered me into the room, taking my coat and draping it across one of the medieval monstrosities. I kept my satchel. Inside it was a good-size, sharp-as-hell hatpin. Just in case.

"Have a seat, my dear," he said, waving a hand toward the overstuffed suite. I sank deep into the down cushions, wondering if I would ever be able to get up out of it. He walked over to a cabinet that housed an array of liquor, and without asking what I'd have, poured several fingers of brown liquid into a tumbler. I took the glass, sniffed it, and sipped. It was the good stuff. Really good cognac. My nearly soundless sigh of approval prompted him to say, "Courvoisier."

"Very nice," I said, nodding.

These Nazis and their French cognac, I thought, thinking of Monty and his Rémy.

He smiled, and when I took another sip, asked sternly, "Well, I have to say I find it a bit disturbing, unfair."

"Excuse me?"

"Well, now you know who I am," he said, a frown on his face as he stood over me.

I, mired in a quicksand of down feathers, fight versus flight responses kicking around inside me at his suddenly ominous demeanor, sat frozen.

Yes, I know who you are! I might be clumsy, but I'm not stupid. A Nazi! You're a Nazi! But I sat mum.

Armbruster was most definitely a Nazi, I knew, just from his association with Montgomery Chase—the clandestine meeting, the passing of an envelope across a table.

"Yes," I answered, my chin out, a hand scavenging in my satchel for the hatpin. "I know who you are."

"So," he laughed, his stance relaxed as he took the tumbler from my hand and went to refill my glass, "You know my name, that I am a dentist, and that this is my home."

I waited, uncertain, fearing.

"But I don't know your name," he continued, walking back to me, having refilled my glass. "I admit, I am curious. What is your name?"

"Oh," I said, hoping he didn't hear relief in my voice. I must have hesitated, taking a breath to replace the one I'd been living on for what seemed forever, because he laughed, sat down on the sofa across from me, and with a conspiratorial wink said, "I won't tell anyone that it was you who caused the ruckus in the restaurant, if that's what you're afraid of." He ended with peals of almost girlish giggles. "It was quite funny, like Carole Lombard in one of her movies. I like Carole Lombard, you see."

I joined in the laughter, sparingly.

"So, who are you, this other Carole Lombard?"

"It was an accident, of course," I replied, searching my mind to come up with a fictitious name. Of the thousands to pick from, nothing came through.

"Of course! I wouldn't suggest it was otherwise. What do they call you?"

"They call me butterfingers, clumsy, trip-over-her-own-two-feet crazy."

A giggle, but his raised eyebrow and silence told me he was waiting.

"Carol."

"No!"

"Yes!" I smiled, nodding. "My name *is* Carol."

"Just Carol?"

As I scoured my brain for the right name for an answer, my eyes landed on the Master's woodcut print on the wall behind Armbruster. "Durer. Carol Durer."

"A good German name!"

"One of the best."

The doorbell rang. Armbruster frowned and then apologized that he had to answer it. "It might be a patient."

"I should be leaving. But may I use your telephone to call my, ah, brother?"

"Yes, of course. The telephone is right there," he said, pointing to the desk. "I'll see who's at the door."

Now was my chance.

Armbruster had secured the manila envelope Monty had passed to him under his vest. I saw when we had arrived at the apartment that he had slipped it into his desk drawer. I hurried to the desk, and uncoiled the string from the envelope's fastener. Inside was a passport, American, and issued to Laura Miller. I looked hard at the photo. Blonde, green eyes, five-feet-seven inches.

I grabbed my Rolle from my bag, turned on the desk lamp, and snapped a photo of the interior of the passport.

An envelope from the Hamburg America Line for passage on the *SS New York*, sailing at 11:59 p.m. on Thursday, February 23.

Snap!

Another envelope on simple white stationery, unsealed, and addressed to Miss Mae Brown, Pittenweem, Scotland. I unfolded the single sheet of paper within. Not bothering to read the letter, I smoothed it out on the desk.

Snap!

But what seemed completely incongruous to the other items in the envelope was what I discovered when I untied the bow of string from a thin brown paper-wrapped package: a handkerchief with a floral embroidered edge and folded into a fan shape, then nestled into a flat, clear, celluloid-covered box. The sort of thing found in any Woolworth's 5 & 10. With it was a birthday card with an odd message inside:

Happy birthday, My dear Peacock!
Chivalry is not dead!
This gift I sent. Was not the plan.
I would have delivered it.
But I'm in New York!
Best regards from Laura.
I hope this arrives. Before you leave Southampton.
Auntie Belle
Snap!

I heard voices from below, and I quickly rewrapped the gift and retied the string.

Footsteps on the stairs, as I returned handkerchief, the letter to Scotland, the passport, and ticket into the manila envelope, coiled the fastener and shut the desk drawer. I lifted my glass of cognac to my lips as Dr. Armbruster entered from the hall.

"Please forgive me, my dear. My bookkeeper has arrived for some papers," he said, making for the desk, where he retrieved the manila envelope, and tucked it under his arm. "I won't be more than a minute," he said, before charging out the door. As his footfalls faded down the flight of stairs, I prayed that he had not seen my camera, which I held behind my back.

I have to get out of here!

I headed down the stairs to the first floor and past the door of the dental office. I wavered as I opened the front door to the stoop, and decision made, I turned back, knocked on the office door, behind which I could see shadowy movement through its frosted glass. The dentist stuck his head out the door.

"Miss Durer!" he said, equally surprised, "I am so sorry, but I have—"

"Oh yes, I was just—I wanted to say goodbye and to thank you—"

He shook his head, his lips pursed, eyebrows twisted as he took my hand and bowed his head. "Oh no, it was my pleasure to assist you."

"I must run, you see. I telephoned my brother to let him know—"

"I very much enjoyed our conversation and hope that perhaps—"

"Thank you, again," I said with a smile, catching a glimpse of a blue hat atop a blond head through the crack between the door hinges.

Was this the Laura Miller of the passport?

And out through the front door, down the stoop, and to the curb I ran to wave down a taxi.

I told the cabbie to park a few doors down the street, in sight of the dentist's residence. "Yes, of course I expect you to flip the meter. I don't expect a free ride."

Ten minutes passed before the blonde, draped in an extravagant silver fox-trimmed evening cape of violet-blue velvet over a matching violet gown, floated down from the brownstone steps.

Laura Miller of the passport photo!

A few feet down the sidewalk, she was chauffeured into a two-toned Cadillac saloon. I told my cabbie to follow the car when it passed by, and he turned to look at me.

"Really!" I replied to his smirk. "Now let's get going. Don't lose it."

"Who can lose that beauty?"

We were off through Central Park to the West Side, and down to Columbus Circle. The Caddy drove toward Times Square, the Theater District, where, at Forty-Eighth Street, in the triangle that divided Seventh Avenue and Broadway, it pulled to the curb, and the chauffeur opened the door.

Blondie waltzed past the uniformed doorman and into the new Cotton Club, where a lavish revue with a star-studded cast had been captivating Broadway theatergoers for more than a year, since the club moved downtown from Harlem.

I paid my cabbie and followed her into the nightclub along with a round of camera flashes from newspaper photographers, hoping to catch sight and a picture of any famous patrons for their next editions. I scooted through the door and continued to the showroom on the top floor.

The lobby was crowded with parties waiting to be seated, so I was not conspicuous, as I moved in closer to stand within earshot, knowing, though, that it was only a matter of time before the host approached me. Through the draped entrance to the big room came the upbeat jazz music of the world-class Cab Calloway Orchestra, and the stage lights illuminated scores of dancers dressed in skimpy yellow-and-red satin costumes skittering along the stage. The blonde passed the coat check and walked toward the lounge. The plush potted palm and a party of gowned women and black-tied gents gave me cover as the blonde was met by Rocco.

She offered her cheek to kiss, and then let him remove her cape. They walked a few steps to the cloakroom, where the hatcheck girl gave Rocco a ticket. As they turned toward the big room, the nightclub, there was Montgomery Chase, exiting the elevator, now appearing as himself, having shed his Otto Rust disguise for evening clothes.

My coat sleeve button caught on a frond, and the palm shook from the drag, as I tried to reposition myself farther out of their sight line. Panicked, I sank down on my heels.

But what really shook me, was not the palm alone, and not just the sudden appearance of Papa's godson, it was the way the blonde greeted Monty, the way her finger traced along his cheek, the way his hand stroked her bare shoulder that I found most disturbing—disturbing to me, I admit, because the gestures suggested an intimacy more disquieting than a kiss, while confirming my suspicion that I was witnessing a collaboration of spies. And another Monty conquest.

Monty had ditched the Otto Rust disguise, so he obviously was not concerned about being recognized for fear of being caught out by any mistress's angry husband. And why had he gone through all the trouble of meeting with Dr. Armbruster to deliver the envelope, when the woman was on Monty's arm right now?

What game was he playing?

I was angry, but more, I was disappointed, let down, betrayed, and more than a little light-headed. Monty had betrayed Papa's trust and faith in him, his godson! A Nazi in our midst, in our home!

Treason! It was treason!

But it was more than that. Much more, and I was not about to entertain such thoughts.

There was nothing for me to see, I told myself, as the threesome was greeted by the host who led them through to a table, members of the audience twisting in their seats upon sight of the movie star and his glamorous companion, a flutter of murmurs pulling attention from the stage. Monty nodded left and right, waved to several patrons, as Cab Calloway's musical vamp was tootled out by the brass section. When the song and dance man came out onstage to welcoming applause, I turned to leave.

Wednesday, February 22, 1939
12:15 a.m.

Juliet Vicente lived at the red brick house, trimmed with wrought iron scrollwork, at 130 MacDougal Street, where reportedly Louisa May Alcott had written *Little Women.*

Juliet was a world-class photojournalist who covered the activities of the International Brigades during the Spanish Civil War for *Life* magazine, until she was caught in crossfire, suffering injuries that almost cost her her left leg. Leg saved, she returned to New York last autumn to recuperate. Being put on the sidelines made her furious, and she was anxious to get back into the action. If the events brewing in Europe were any indication of imminent war, Juliet was determined to follow the story at the front lines. My best friend and, a couple of years my senior, she was a big sister, mentor, and voice of reason when I needed guidance. She did not answer her doorbell.

But I had a hunch where she'd be: Chumley's.

I walked the couple of blocks around to Barrow Street, down the narrow alley that led to a hidden courtyard entrance to the bar. A popular speakeasy during Prohibition, Chumley's was also rumored to be the hub of Communist activity, where, it was said, was planned to "overthrow the United States government" in the secret meeting room on the second floor, accessed by a dumbwaiter hidden behind shelving in the ladies' room.

I spotted Juliet through the smoke haze, sitting in a booth with three men, none of whom I knew, but I supposed were writers or artists of one variety or another by their sorry states of apparel, stubble growth, wiry hair, and generally wretched demeanors. I always wondered why Juliet gravitated toward the company of men who were inferior to herself. Highly educated and from a wealthy family, the beautiful, statuesque redhead seemed to engage these sad specimens for a short time before tiring of their neuroses and moving on to the next intriguing sorry sack. I told her I thought her heartless, stringing them along, but she just replied that she was not heartless, just easily disillusioned.

She caught my eye as I approached.

"What are you doing here at this hour? I thought you were uptown taking care of Archie." She shoved the fellow hemming her in the booth so that she could get out, and focusing her attention on me, dismissed them without a word of goodbye, as if they'd evaporated into thin air—they all looked up at her with sad cow eyes—took my arm for support, along with her cane, and moved me toward the entrance.

"You look like hell. You're all flushed. Want a shot?" she said as we passed the bar.

"No—yes, but not here. Can we go back to your place?"

"All right."

"And I need to use your darkroom."

She paused and threw me a sideward glance, eyebrow raised.

"I'll explain," I said, helping her on with her coat.

"What have you been up to—wait! I saw your front-page story this morning! Good for you, honey!"

We had settled into the apartment, which was part photo studio, part living space, the two areas undefined. Photographic equipment—half a dozen cameras, tripods, lenses, even a movie camera—took up residence around the otherwise eclectic space. Large prints of war photos were pinned to the walls, juxtaposed alongside portraits and city-scapes. Books were tossed on every surface, artwork by fa-mous and the not-so-famous were hung haphazardly or sat propped against the walls or table legs. Clothes were tossed on chairs and scarves littered the sofa. All in all a charming, wonderful space.

I lifted a sweater from off an old, overstuffed chair she'd rescued from a trash pile on Sixth Avenue. I knew its origin since I'd helped her carry it up three flights. That she so revered its lovely lines, and the comfort of the cushions was a winning quality, I thought, since Juliet could well af-ford to live in a more fashionable part of town, with design-er-chic furnishings. Exhausted, I swished my behind back into the chair, my head into its cushy back pillow and accepted the drink she'd poured me.

"Spill. What's going on?"

"I'm not sure. . .but I think I've landed in a pile."

"Oh dear. . ." She sat across from me in the leather Stickley Mission chair—another secondhand find. "Take your time and tell me all."

I started from the beginning, trying to unravel the events of the past three days, from the unexpected arrival of Montgomery Chase to the discovery of a murdered man in a brownstone rooming house, the traffic accident that killed a man, my discovery of blueprints from an aeronautical company, the tailing of a pickle salesman from Minnesota to clandestine rendezvous around the city, and an encounter with the oily German dentist. I tried to relay the story without prejudice, without emotion, without revealing my anger and disappointment with Monty, at least I thought I had, but when I finished and looked at my friend, she just stared at me for a long time, as if trying to decipher some unspoken truth, lit another cigarette, refilled her glass with bourbon before resuming her seat, taking my hand in hers, and stating, "You have it bad for him."

"What?! What are you talking about?"

"Well, he is quite alarmingly attractive." She smiled wanly.

"Oh stop."

"Not my type, of course."

"You like them fragile, neurotic, I've noticed."

"Don't strike out because you're hearing the truth."

"I'm just worried. . .worried that Papa is harboring a Nazi spy."

"Yes, of course you are, being patriotic and all," she said, studying her cigarette and picking a bit of tobacco off the tip of her tongue. "But what makes you so sure he's a spy?"

"After what I told you? What I've witnessed? He isn't escaping cuckhold husbands, that's for sure, even if he has that sort of reputation. You should have seen him tonight at the club, strutting like a peacock, posing for the press boys."

"I don't know about those things, really; I don't follow the movie rags, even though I would suspect that he's a husband's worst nightmare." Her head thrown back, a throaty gurgle of laughter escaped her lips.

"He may be a member of the Hollywood Anti-Nazi League, but that is only a ruse to cover his Nazi activities."

"They're all Reds, you know," she added, matter-of-factly, blowing out a stream of smoke.

"Who are?"

"Hollywood League members—well, a few of them, anyway. The others are well-intentioned, if misguided."

"Are you saying—"

"Believe me, the Reds are running that show, just like they did in Spain. Won't everyone be surprised when they figure out who's behind it all: the most Fascist of all governments. No altruism there, just deceptive Soviet propaganda."

I was astonished by the revelations, but I trusted that Juliet knew what she was talking about. Her cynicism was not misplaced. She'd seen and heard enough during her assignment in Spain to have learned any underlying truth.

"So, Filly, have you discussed this with your friend? The reporter at the paper?"

"Little Dick?"

"You're joking!" she laughed. Then, with a sloe-eyed glance asked. *"How* do you know?"

I tossed off the inference. "I wanted to be sure, first, about what's going on. Can we develop my film?"

An hour later, we stared at the images of the photos I'd snapped in Monty's room of the blueprint from Hanover Aeronautics. Because the blueprint was printed on such a large sheet of paper, I'd snapped six sections in natural sunlight. Now, we trimmed the overlapping sections and taped them all together to form a facsimile of the original. I knew now what I didn't know at the time I discovered it in the briefcase hidden in Monty's closet: that Hanover Aeronautics had been founded by Henry Hanover's father, Herbert. Had Henry's old man been killed for that blueprint? Had Henry stolen the plans and while handing it over to Nazi spies, something went wrong?

The passport photo page of Laura Miller gave her a home address in Philadelphia.

"That's the woman I followed from Armbruster's, the woman who met Rocco and Monty at the club. But I don't believe that's her real name, if you want to know."

I picked up the photo of the envelope addressed to Miss Mae Brown, Pittenweem, Scotland, and then read from the letter within:

Dear Mae,

The weather has been miserable here in Lisbon. Cold and rainy most days. I am planning to go fly-fishing in Spain next month with George. He knows the best rivers to go to. So don't expect me to return until the end of April.

Your brother, Ryan

"What do you make of this, Jules?"

"Maybe this 'Ryan' is trying to put one over on his sister."

"You mean, he's having the fling of his life, and he wants her to believe he's somewhere he's not?"

"Been done before. . ."

"Look at this," I said picking up the photo of the birthday card and laid it alongside the one of the handkerchief box:

Happy birthday, My dear Peacock!
Chivalry is not dead!
This gift I sent. Was not the plan.
I would have delivered it.
But I'm in New York!
Best regards from Laura.
I hope this arrives. Before you leave Southampton.
Auntie Belle

"Another drink?" asked Juliet, as I gathered up the prints and followed her into the living room.

"Sure, why not?" I said, handing her my glass.

"So, the passport is a fake, obviously, and this spy, this so-called Laura Miller is sailing tomorrow night at midnight."

Juliet lectured me on how *not* to snap a photograph at close range. "Now, if you are going to go around snapping bad quality photos, I just can't have it."

She rummaged through a cabinet and, finding what she was looking for, handed me a miniature camera. "Take this for now, honey. A Kodak Retina. 35mm film—see? You can load the cartridge even in daylight. German-made, so appropriate for your counterspy work. I'll find you a Leica—that's even smaller."

"Wow! It's so tiny."

"Well, yes. When you can't lug the gin jug you carry a flask."

She showed me how to use it, loaded it up with film, and handed me an extra roll.

"Now you're prepared. But the question is, what are you going to do with all this information?"

"Oh, I don't know," I said.

What was I going to do with this stuff? I thought, gathering up the photographs.

"Hey!" said Juliet, turning on me with concern in her eyes. "You're not planning on confronting these people on your own, are you?"

"Well. . ."

"Now listen to me," she said, all seriousness as she planted her hands on my shoulders and looked me in the eyes, "if these people are in fact who you think they are, they are up to no good. If they are who you think they are, they don't play around. They won't hesitate to do whatever it is they have to do to prevent being exposed. Even if they have to kill you. And I don't hold much value to misplaced valor."

This woman's warning, this spirited and fearless creature, who had followed the XV International Brigade on its offensive and was recovering from wounds when caught in the crossfire in the Republican attempt to take territory in Aragon last summer, was not to be dismissed.

"I'm going to the Bureau of Investigation with this," I said.

"Why don't you wait a couple of days, honey? Just to be sure."

"I don't think I can wait. A ship sails at midnight tomorrow. And I don't think that the 'midnight' reference that Monty made in the tailor shop is coincidence, Jules; I think it may have to do with this sailing. I don't know what's planned, but if I don't find out fast, I'll have to call in the big guns—the Bureau."

Wednesday, February 22, 1939
7:00 a.m.

I returned to Papa's house a little after three in the morning, more than a little drunk from the several shots I'd tossed back at Juliet's. I fell into a fitful sleep, but by seven, I was washed, dressed, and down in the kitchen helping Eva prepare breakfast.

"You look like crap," said Eva, nudging me aside so she could flip a pancake. I had burned the first three.

"Thanks," I said. "Big breakfast this morning. Is Monty up?"

"Didn't come home last night, and Rocco, too."

"So, he's not in the house?"

"That's what I just said. What's wrong with you?"

"Nothing's wrong. Stop looking at me like that," I said, looking over the counter at the dish of scrambled eggs, a dozen stacked pancakes, Canadian bacon, and a steaming coffeepot. "I was just wondering why you're making breakfast for twenty."

"They'll be hungry when they get in."

The wooden spoon she held up in her hand descended into the saucepan of the farina she was cooking. She added a pinch of salt, and furiously whipped it all up and turned off the gas.

Testy this morning.

"I suppose everything's running smoothly, now that Papa's home."

"I always try to see to things."

Careful, Filomena, I said to myself.

"I'm staying at my place tonight."

"Suit yourself."

"But only if you think—well, I can stay if you think—"

"I've got things all under control."

"—But I'll stop in tomorrow. And if you need me to do anything—go to the grocer's or do something around the house. . ."

"That's fine."

Something was irritating her, but I didn't know if it was something I'd said or did, or didn't do, and from past experience, you couldn't just blurt out, *What the hell is your problem?* I was fond of this little woman who was dedicated to my father, and I didn't want her to feel unappreciated.

"Listen, Eva, I have an interview this morning, but I'll be back here by noon. Why don't you take some time for yourself? Didn't you say something about getting your hair done? In the style of Myrna Loy? I think it's the perfect cut for you."

She thawed, and when she nodded, I said, "I'll get the

maple syrup."

I slipped a ten-dollar bill into her purse before I left the house.

I was exhausted from the mental calisthenics I'd engaged in over the past day and was still conflicted about what to do about my discoveries. I needed to keep moving, doing, and there was a lot to get done before midnight. In a couple of hours, I had an interview to do. And then came the rest of today's to-do list rolling out before me.

As I left the house I heard the delighted giggle of Eva in response to the coddling, rich tones of a baritone voice. Monty had returned.

Now, waiting in the outer office to meet Frieda Wunderlich at The New School for Social Research, I checked my face in my compact and reapplied my lipstick.

The timing of this interview was serendipitous. Beyond the feature story I was about to write, I needed Dr. Wunderlich's firsthand insights and perspective to gauge the immediacy of the threat of Nazi aggression to America's shores. I needed allies, people above reproach, who might steer me in the right direction, guide me toward a decision of what I should do. Might she allay my fears or confirm that the nature of Nazi activity, including that of the German-American Bund in America, posed a real threat? There were those who opposed the United States's involvement in the struggles of Europe, just as there were voices urging American intervention against Hitler's aggressions. The isolationists urging Washington to stay out of any involvement by turning a blind eye to the ravages of Nazi Imperialism and Hitler's targeting of an entire race of people through fear and blame might call themselves patriots—but were they all patriots or were they supporters of Hitler's despicable philosophy of exclusion?

When I was announced by Dean Wunderlich's secretary and walked through the door into her small office, I was surprised to see, rising from her chair behind the desk and extending her hand in greeting, a petite woman of about fifty-five years with graying hair, a fine aquiline nose, and soft brown eyes. She was dressed in a navy blue knit wool suit trimmed with a lacy ecru crocheted collar and cuffs. She smiled as we shook hands, and her long thin Modigliani face brightened, giving off warmth and charm, and a glimpse back to her youth.

The secretary returned with a tray of coffee, and after we had settled in the alcove off the main office, a small sitting area consisting of a sofa and twin chairs, I took out my pencil and dictation pad and posed my first question.

"Dr. Wunderlich, you were the only woman among the eleven members of, what has been called, 'the university in exile,' here at The New School. And now, you are dean. Actually, the first woman *elected* dean of any secondary educational institution. You emigrated to the United States in 1933—in exile—and I would ask you, what events precipitated your leaving Germany?"

"I had little choice," she replied, with a smile, her accent slight and her voice cultured and mellow.

Such power behind the soft bell-like tone, I thought, proving one did not have to be loud to be commanding.

"I was forcibly 'retired' from my post as professor and other positions I held."

I asked her to elaborate.

"I was *removed*. I was removed from my positions as a member of the German Democratic Party and the Berlin City Council and of my appointment to the German Supreme Court for Social Welfare."

"Because you were Jewish?"

She nodded. "As a Jew I had been marginalized for a long time. No Jew at university has ever been granted tenure, and as a woman this was assured. Women have become even more restricted since Hitler took power. Women may not hold any employment outside the home except for the most menial of positions. But being Jewish and a woman holding important posts was not the primary reason I was forced out."

"Because you spoke out against Hitler?"

"Yes. As editor of *Soziale Praxis*, I—we criticized Hitler. The journal was a forum for discussions of social and economic problems that Germany had been facing since the end of the war. As you probably know, Germany was greatly in debt at war's end, as consequence of starting that war. The penalties were imposed by the Treaty of Versailles, dictating millions in reparations to France and Belgium and huge losses of territory. Germany's failure to make a payment, in 1922, along with the loss of natural resources from the Saar Coalfields—Alsace-Lorraine given to France, and the loss of the Ruhr Valley's industry—created mass unemployment and hyperinflation. As an economist I did not agree with the government's methods at recovery."

"How do you account for the rise to power of a despot like Hitler?"

"The National Socialist German Workers' Party grew from a series of political parties that were anti-big business, anti-capitalist and anti-Communist in the early 1920s. It is now the party of the totalitarian regime since Hitler became chancellor.

"One must understand that postwar conditions had crushed the people of Germany, so much so that the deprivation gave birth to fear, fear for their future existence, and with fear there is further instability, which accounts for the rise of Adolf Hitler and his party, who promised to elevate the nation from the shame of defeat to a world power once again. As with all tyrants who seek control over a people, the way to unite a defeated and humiliated people is not just to promise to improve their lives; it is to restore their national honor in the world."

"The treaty was a harsh punishment, you say?" I asked.

"Yes, because all of Germany's resources were taken, by territory distribution, for restitution. There was no way for the government to pay the fines because there was little source of revenue."

"So, what you are saying is, the German people were desperate for any solution to their predicament?"

She nodded.

"And Hitler took advantage of that?"

"Oh, he may have been patriotic at first, but he became hungry for power. A disease of many politicians."

"But how did he convince a nation to adopt the policies he offered as the solution to their plight?"

"After his release from jail for his failed coup in '24, he and his cronies regrouped. The lesson learned, the way to gain control of the hearts of the people, is to wage a war against a common enemy—foreigners—Jews, Romany, those who are not racially desirable, those who are said to have polluted the Aryan race from within the national community. It is a sad truth that many find great pleasure looking down on those you are told are inferior to you. The existence of an enemy justifies immoral acts against any opposition, pointing to a race of people as the cause of the nation's predicament, the root of all that is plaguing the nation.

"So, National Socialism has become what I see as a substitute for religion, 'a mystic society bound by blood' with the smug belief that the German race is superior to all others. Therefore, it then becomes necessary to eliminate detractors—voices of reason—because it is loudly proclaimed that they pose a threat to national purity. I, and many thousands of others, was among the chorus speaking out against Hitler's rhetoric. I had to go."

"What were the challenges you faced in leaving Germany?"

"Initially, I was to emigrate to England, but at the last minute, the position I had secured was rescinded. And then, five years ago, I was offered a teaching position here at The New School, for which I was very lucky and am very grateful. The challenges of having remained in Germany would have been far greater."

I asked about her work on women's issues, her activism for maternity leave and guaranteed employment for mothers, knowing she had written about women's rights all the way back to 1924. And this led to a question about women in the United States compared to their sisters in Germany. I quoted her words:

"'I have recognized that in the United States, women's lives were not necessarily considered incomplete without marriage, as I observed they were in my native Germany. In the U.S., their lives were an end in themselves.'"

As we were ending the interview, I took the opportunity to ask my own most pressing question. "Do you suppose, Dr. Wunderlich, that America is at risk?"

"How do you mean?"

"That America will engage in a war with Germany again?"

"Well, it is possible, if Hitler tries to invade France and England as he has threatened."

"No, what I mean to ask is—well, I was wondering about your thoughts about whether or not Hitler has designs on American soil?"

"Invade America?"

"It seems farfetched, I know; there is a vast ocean between us, but still. . ."

"America is the prize!"

"You mean that it is—"

"Yes, Hitler most certainly has designs of invading

America. He already has positioned himself in South America. He supports Franco, and there is Mussolini. There are more Americans of German ancestry than any other nationality living here in the United States, and he hopes to appeal to their sense of heritage. Not all citizens are American patriots."

My delayed response was response enough, and she caught my eye when I looked up.

She was scrutinizing my face, then smiled, touched my arm with her delicate birdlike fingers, and said, "I did see the front-page coverage in your newspaper of the German-American Bund rally the other night in Madison Square Garden. The only person missing was Adolf Hitler himself! You yourself wrote that the Bund's membership is estimated at two hundred thousand members, and they have a war chest of over twenty million dollars!"

"So, there is probably a Nazi spy network here in the U.S.?"

"I'd be surprised if there was not. Given the numbers and the fervor of their public rhetoric, I'd say, no doubt.

"German immigration to this country has been greater than from any other nation in the past eighty years. And after Germany's defeat in the Great War, along with the suspicions and social persecutions during the war years against those Americans of Germanic heritage, there has existed much sympathy for what some German-Americans call their *Fatherland*. Many have relatives in Germany. They feel as connected and proud of their heritage as the Irish, the Italians, the Swedes. They want to see their homeland made whole again. It is only natural. But there are those factions in this country who share the tenets of the Nazi Party as the means to restoring Germany's greatness on the world stage. And they will work toward that end. So, yes, I believe my adopted country, that took me in and gave me opportunity I never would have had in Germany, must beware those who wish to undermine the interests of America."

I left the interview with her words echoing in my head.

Beware those who wish to undermine the interests of America.

Wednesday, February 22, 1939
10:50 a.m.

It was time to level with Little Dick Trumble.

When I left The New School, I headed for the newspaper offices. The snow had melted, and the streets were a mess of slush the color of wet cardboard. I took the subway downtown.

The music of the city room was the lullaby of my childhood, a familiar melody that stirred the blood and invigorated those bitten by the reporting bug: the *tick-tick-tick* of the teletype delivering events from around the world; the random *brrrriiiiiiing* of a score of telephone bells demanding immediate attention; the frantic *click-click-click* of typewriter keys pounding out human dramas. This was home, had been since Papa first brought me here when I was a little girl. I'd sit on the radiator cover pretending to read the newspaper, the pictures telling me stories invented from my imagination, watching the chaos in his office, the reporters and editors moving in and out the door in a choreographed flurry, impatient or contrite, with Papa the stage manager calling the show. I'd sport the visor Papa gave me and type out nonsensical reports on his Royal, delighted when the carriage hit the bell. Who needed a jack-in-the-box?

So, I was hooked early and permanently from the age of three, spending my summers from the time I was twelve running around from desk to desk doing the bidding of reporters I'd come to know as "uncles." Big Dick Trumble, Little Dick's father, the fearless crime reporter who used to point to his desk drawer, where, when I opened it, there'd be licorice strings or Jawbreakers or Cracker Jack boxes with prizes inside, just for me.

When he died in '25, I was devastated by the loss. The craggy-faced man with a noontime five o'clock shadow, who smelled of tobacco, hair tonic, and typewriter ribbon ink—the intoxicating smell of the newsroom mingled with the warmth of the male sex—and who always changed his demeanor from a frown of intense concentration to a smile and an easy manner when I'd stop at his desk. He called me "kiddo," like Little Dick does now.

And he taught me the elements of writing a news story—starting with a strong attention-grabbing lead; the five *W*'s and *H*: who, what, when, where, why, and how; significance, proximity, and quotes. And the difference between what was newsworthy and what were human interest stories. *Too many prepositions, kiddo. Vague, this statement is wishy-washy, kiddo. Cut this out. Too many adjectives, and nobody cares about your opinion, so just give 'em the facts. So what if you have a good vocabulary? Save it for your novel, I'm not impressed. What's another word for—* By the time I was at Columbia, I had been well prepped by a master.

No one knew where Little Dick Trumble was. He wasn't in the newsroom, so he might be at Hold the Presses, the saloon owned by a retired typesetter from the *Tribune* and watering hole for the newshounds from all the rags in the district, or he might be at the 18th Precinct hanging around to chase whatever call came in.

I looked for my other "uncle," Rudy Rothberg, sports columnist and Papa's baseball season buddy, who taught me what was happening on the diamond when I was five and brought me around to meet the greats—even if they weren't Giants stars—like the team's manager John Mac-Graw, and players Irish Meusel, Casey Stengel, Dave Bancroft, and Heinie Groh; and then there were the Babe and Bob Shawkey, and Irish's brother, Bob Meusel playing for the Yankees, and of course, players from that other New York rival team, "Dem Bums", the Brooklyn Dodgers. The elation in the Giants's World Series victory over the Yankees in '22 and the misery the following year when the Yanks took the trophy and the ticker-tape parade down through Wall Street. But to Rudy, a great player was a great player, didn't matter what team he played for.

I caught up with Rudy just as he was heading out of the office to take the train south for the Giants's spring training. He might know where Little Dick was, because they were not only colleagues, they were poker game, fight night, football stadium buddies, as well as having shared the same wife.

Rudy's second wife out of three failed marriages, Lydia, became Little Dick's first. Little Dick vowed she would be the last Mrs. Trumble. The common enemy bonded the men, and although Rudy never said, "I told you so," he pointed out that *One should learn from the mistakes of one's superiors.*

You mean, learn from my elders? That what you mean, old fart? tossed back Little Dick. They were always sparring, harmlessly, affectionately.

When I caught up to him at the elevator, the rumpled, rubber-featured face shone with joyful anticipation of sunny weather and witnessing the first pitch from the mound; his hair and suit were pressed, for a change.

"I heard him talking to Skip about a new lead in a story he's doing," he said when I asked after Little Dick.

"Did you hear which story?"

"A murder?" guessed Rudy, just as the elevator door opened and out walked Skip. Rudy entered the elevator, lugging his suitcase and his Underwood portable typewriter case, just like the one I had, too; a graduation gift from my "uncles," who had chipped in to get me exactly the one I'd lusted over, the same model Rudy lugged around to the games—a three-bank portable in a green body.

I followed Skip, telling him what I had to ask was very important—life or death—as he walked toward his office, soon trailing a line of reporters after us, an unseemly conga line snaking through the aisle to his door.

"This must make me look very important," he said, throwing me a side glance, and indicating the others wanting to speak with him. He opened the door for me, ushered me in with a hand to my back, and shut the door in the faces of the five frustrated newsmen.

"I'm wary of leaving the office, because then I have to return, and it's like a traffic jam." He took off his waistcoat and began rolling up his sleeves.

"Papa will be back in a couple of weeks. But someday. . ."

"All this will be mine; I know. And the bleeding ulcers. But after these past weeks, I'm not in any hurry to take the reins."

"Where's Little Dick?" I blurted, impatiently.

"Interviewing someone for that story he's working on—that murder uptown on the West Side."

"Okay, but who and where?"

"I don't know. Wait—the victim's wife. Yonkers—no, Bronxville."

"Crap almighty!"

"I suppose you don't approve?"

"He may be walking into trouble."

"You serious?"

"Maybe."

I yelled at myself for not having pursued the wife of Henry Hanover, as we'd agreed I would, but I hadn't had time, the housekeeper was cagey, and I knew more about the whole story than Little Dick knew. I had decided that talking with the woman was of least importance until now. I chided myself for not having leveled with him, and it appeared I was too late. My only consolation was that because he knew so little about the murder in the rooming house—

well, less than I did—his ignorance might be his saving grace.

"He can take care of himself, Little Dick's a big boy. I don't believe I said that," said Skip, settling at his desk piled with folders, and news copy. "Look, Filly, he's due back in a little while, and then he has to go over to the printing plant for me—don't ask: we're all pitching in until Archie returns. I'll tell him you were looking for him."

"Since he'll be in my neighborhood, ask him to stop by my place in the Village. It's urgent."

"Oh?" He raised an eyebrow and gave me his full attention. Relenting to my reticence to tell him more, he said, "I'm not even going to pursue that. Send in Johnny when you leave." I followed his glance through the open venetian blinds that hung over the office's glass partitions overlooking the newsroom. "He's chomping at the bit."

I did so, and as I was crossing the floor to the elevator, Benny the Boo-Boo Borgosian spotted me from across the room, waved, called out my name loudly, and the gangly teenager, whom I knew had a crush on me, weaved through a dozen desks to join me at the elevator. Five minutes of small talk, his plan to start college in the fall, sweet kid, but I didn't have time to shoot the breeze. The elevator doors opened.

I returned to Papa's house to find a note from Eva saying she had gone to the beauty parlor, after which lunch and shopping with her sister, adding that Monty and Rocco had returned midmorning, went to bed, and shouldn't be disturbed.

Perfect, I thought. I didn't want to face them, so I gingerly climbed the stairs to my room, where I packed my bags, locked my portable Underwood in its case, gathered the Bergdorf's shopping bag filled with my evidence against Monty, and carried them down to the foyer.

Papa was in his chair in the library, and we talked for a few minutes about my interview with Frieda Wunderlich, which brought us to discuss the series I would write about women in power.

"I want you to follow up on the Nazi Bund story," said Papa.

I was surprised by his suggestion. Broadsided, actually. I couldn't have heard right.

"The women of the Bund?"

"No. Not the Women's Page. I want you to look into what these Fascist bastards are really doing in this country, besides dressing up like aged Boy Scouts marching in the July Fourth parade, while pretending to be American patriots."

"You want *me*—"

"Yeah, you should do it."

"Are you telling me you want a feature story?"

"Feature, sure—and news coverage, whenever they do something. I want you to keep an eye on them. Ferret out what else they're really up to. If there's a rally, you cover it; when their *Bundesfuehrer* Kuhn says something inflammatory, write about it. These jokers need to be shown for what they are: Fascists!"

"But Martin is your political reporter."

"Not anymore. I'm sending him to France as our new European bureau chief. Russ Talbert's quit."

"So, you want me to stay women's editor, and at the same time cover—"

"For the time being, Filomena."

I must have looked dazed because Papa laughed and leaned over, grabbed my hand, and said, "It's time, honey. Skip was right giving you the rally assignment. I want you to expose what's going on behind closed doors."

My silence was a lie of omission. Papa didn't know I went to the rally of my own accord. That Skip had planned to cover the story, and he only gave it to me because I must have looked desperate—and he was a nice guy.

"Papa, they're doing it out in the open, these Nazis posing as patriotic Americans."

"You don't have to tell me. We broke the Rumrich scandal."

The Morning Sun broke the story last December about a naturalized American-turned-Nazi spy, Guenther Rumrich. He was sentenced to a short prison term for his cooperation so that the Bureau could round up the others in the ring. The agent in charge, Leon Turrou, told the spies that they'd have to appear to testify before a grand jury, and after the interviews, they were released. The release allowed them all to walk out of the agency's office. Like rats in the dog ring knowing that the pit bull was about to rip them apart, they scattered. Worse, during this time, Turrou leaked information to the press, and was even contracted by a publication to write articles about the investigation.

He was fired, and the FBI, whose role it had been up until now to fight the criminal organizations that had been the source of trouble since the Volstead Act was enacted to police Prohibition, organizations like Murder, Inc., and other mobster activity that plagued the cities was scrambling to find a way to best handle this new threat of international espionage.

"It's time we stop these people. And we do that by showing exactly who they are and what their intentions are."

"All right, Papa."

"Those youth camps—one on Long Island, another upstate, another in Jersey, out west—where they're indoctrinating little kids. Nazi Youth," Papa said with a look of disgust. "Let's let the country know about these monsters!"

I was stunned at this promotion to investigative reporting, because I just hadn't anticipated it happening so soon. And, as much as I should have been thrilled, since it was my dream becoming a reality, I dreaded the implications. Papa wasn't aware of what was going on under his own roof, and I feared his distress when he learned the truth about the godson he loved.

I left Papa for the kitchen, to heat up the chicken soup Eva had made for lunch. I was going to bring a tray up to the library, but while I was heating rolls in the oven Papa came downstairs, and we ate at the old oak kitchen table, talking about the new Giants drafts picks. His mood was improving with his health, and I was elated to see it.

But tonight, Montgomery Chase would be exposed

for the Nazi spy he was, and *Oh, Papa, what might these revelations do to you?*

Wednesday, February 22, 1939
8:15 p.m.

My Greenwich Village apartment was on MacDougal Street, in a walk-up a couple of doors down from
Razzazco's Italian Restaurant, Louis's Luncheon and Swing
Rendezvous (lesbian bars half-a-block away), the Caffe Reg-
gio, where cappuccino was introduced to Americans (Mama
had prepared the foamy hot milk espresso for Papa's breakfast long before it became "the thing"). It was also within
spitting distance of Washington Square Park, a plot of real
estate that had once been a parade ground, later a potter's
field for those executed by hanging from the big elm on
the park's north side, and later still, the burial ground for
the twenty thousand dead from the yellow fever epidem-
ic that swept the lower part of Manhattan during the early
nineteenth century. Eventually, when the town houses were
built on its north side, it became a park, the front-yard play-
ground of the well-to-do and respectable families of New
York. Such is New York: it never stops reinventing itself.

The red brick building that housed my apartment stood huddled amid dozens of bars and cafés that came to life at night in a community that was born from the descendants of Dutch and English settlers of the seventeenth and eighteenth centuries, residing in those modest town houses of Henry James fame, along the northern fringe of the park; Italians, Eastern European Jews, and a smattering of Irish and Ukrainians who migrated a couple of miles west from the congested tenements of the Lower East Side. But the heart of this melting pot that was the Village and the influence that so permeated its culture was the heterogeneous array comprising the bohemian society of freethinkers, proponents of free love, and the intelligentsia that have gathered here and spread the district's fame throughout America. From Edgar Poe to Henry James to Eugene O'Neill, Edna St. Vincent Millay, Isamu Noguchi, and Buckminster Fuller, the square mile is teeming with the spirit of individuality and rampant creativity.

I loved my little corner apartment on the third-floor front, with the eastern and southern exposure that let the light spill in, the high ceilings, and ebony stained wood floors that shone beneath my scattered Orientals, the bookcases an old boyfriend built along the entire length of the wall opposite the fireplace that warmed cold winter nights. Ragtag overstuffed chairs I disguised with slipcovers and throws to cover the imminent threat of popping seams. Hugo—the name I gave to the mahogany framed club chair because I thought it was the sort of chair the famous writer, cognac in hand, might have settled into after a day of writing at his desk—was my favorite and the most comfortable seat in the house. The alcove that led to my bedroom I'd furnished with an old fainting couch found at a secondhand shop on Seventh Avenue. Beside it, an old mahogany cabinet held a brass lamp. The alcove walls were painted red. The cozy space served as my reading nook, a place to curl up in to listen to the radio shows I liked to tune in to, or the records I'd play when I was in a somber mood. My little sanctuary.

If not for the clanging and shaking water pipes in the bathtub and sink that presaged a flood, the miniscule kitchen with its overactive refrigerator that needed defrosting every month, the tenants across the hall who stumbled vociferously up the stairs in the wee hours of the weekend, drunk and violent as a pair of Parisian Apache dancers, threatening one another with death by strangulation or gunshot (the Fighting Frasiers, I dubbed them), Salvatore, the Italian janitor who pretended he didn't understand English—"The light!" I shouted, repeatedly, modulating an octave with each attempt while pointing to the flickering hall light, "Musta fixa da lighta!"—this apartment would be perfect.

As I didn't want to live uptown in the big house with Eva as my jailor and Papa replacing St. Jerome's Sister Mary Joseph with her squinty-eyed scrutiny of my chastity, I learned to screw in lightbulbs, and keep my head down on weekends.

And there was James Kennedy, a mild-mannered man on the second floor, who became a dinner partner and regular chess opponent with whom I had struck up a friendship over the past few years. He was a font of historical knowledge, a retired World History professor from NYU—never boring, never condescending of my youth, and never critical of the occasional young man with whom I might attempt a relationship—and I relished his fatherly concern and affection, returning it in kind.

I lugged my valise, overnight case, portable typewriter, tote, the shopping bag containing evidence I'd collected over the past few days, and a meatball hero from Razzazco's up three flights of stairs to my door.

Breathless, I dropped everything on the tile floor and searched through my tote for my key. Finally found, as I brought the key to the lock, I saw that the door was open.

Could I have. . .? I was in a hurry when I left my apartment for Papa's, but—No, not possible. I had locked my door!

Had Salvatore entered the apartment on some pretext—a burst water pipe? Radiator? Gas leak?

I picked up my typewriter case, lifted it over my head, and pushed the door open slowly with my foot. It creaked, and I cursed to myself for not having oiled the hinges.

The apartment was dark, the curtains drawn, as I'd left them, only light from the streetlamps filtering in. After a moment, my eyes adjusted to the gloom. I listened for sounds of life within. Silence, except for street traffic. No light came from my bedroom or the bathroom.

I lowered the case, flicked on the lights, and looked over the room. Someone had been in the apartment, I was sure. On first glance, nothing appeared to have been disturbed except that a chair's seat cushion had been replaced the wrong way—back to front. I circled the living room, noticing a section of books had been disturbed and hastily reshelved, their bindings not flush with the edge. A bookmark had fallen to the floor. The surface of my desk, which was always a study of chaos, did not look any different from how I'd left it. That's when I noticed that the paintings on the wall had been touched, since one of them was hanging askew.

I grabbed an umbrella from the entry closet, and armed, peeked into the bedroom, flicked on the light switch. The bedspread was slightly awry, and the rug beside the bed was off-kilter. The closet door was slightly ajar. I flung it open, ready to stab the intruder hiding within, but no one sprang out at me. My hatboxes and storage boxes had been moved; they were not returned to their original positions. The contents of my dresser appeared undisturbed, but they were always a jumble, try as I might to achieve some order to them. I could see that the dresser had been pulled away from the wall; there was a scar on the wood floor from where its front leg had scraped and unearthed dust balls floated alongside it.

The bathroom was as I left it. But, on turning away, I noticed the wall hamper open.

It wasn't a burglary, I was certain. My jewelry boxes were untouched, and with great relief, my sable coat, once worn by Mama, was on its hanger. Nothing of value was missing. Someone had searched for something in particular.

The trespasser had made an effort to make it appear that no one had entered the apartment, only he or she had neglected the details. But, perhaps, whomever it was only wanted to frighten me by leaving signs of his intrusion. To show the vulnerability of my sanctuary.

I discounted Salvatore fishing through my things. He had keys to all the apartments. I'd lived here with him as janitor for five years, and, lazy as he might be, he just wasn't the snooping sort. And upon revisiting the front door, and inspecting the lock, I could see scratches across the brass, new and untarnished by time. It was not a key that had turned the lock.

I spent the next hour looking for some indication of who might have broken in. I knocked on the door across the hall—the Fighting Frasiers—to ask if they'd seen anyone hanging around my door. I tracked down Salvatore, who was listening to his serial on the radio, which he said helped him perfect his English, and spoke—shouted—over the broadcast's narrator of *The Shadow*.

Who knows what evil lurks in the hearts of men? The Shadow *knows!*

Not so useful for polite conversation, I thought, but his English was improving, even if some of Salvatore's accented jargon (*front man* to describe his janitorial responsibilities, and *hunky-dory*—"the faucet no drip, is hunky-dory"), was straight out of the radio drama *Gang Busters—The only national program that brings you authentic police case histories.*

Anyway, nothing. No one noticed anyone at my door.

But, while gathering my mail from the box, James,

whose apartment was below mine, was coming in from the street. We spoke a few words. He asked after my father, a word about the weather, and then he congratulated me on my Bund rally reporting, having seen it in *The Morning Sun*.

I thanked him when he said, "It was very comprehensive." I felt a rush of gratitude. His good opinion meant a lot to me.

"This movement must be stopped, and people made aware of what is happening in this country!" He smiled and sent an inquiring raised eyebrow. "You must be very busy these days."

"Yes, a bit more than usual," I said. "But we have to get together next week for chess?" I said, "I'll bring the wine."

"I'll cook a goose. Say next Tuesday?"

"I think so. I just returned home from Papa's."

"I thought you returned yesterday."

"Just now."

"You know how sound travels—"

"You heard someone in my apartment?"

"My dear, at first I thought you were moving for good, not just for a couple of days to attend Archie."

"What time was this?"

"In the evening sometime. Furniture shifted about. I admit, I was a bit vexed."

"From all the racket?"

"No! The idea that you were moving! That you didn't tell me! And so, I came up to see."

"Someone was in my apartment, James."

"Yes, I know." He laughed shyly, embarrassed, and

surprising me. "I don't mean to be a busybody, I was just—But the fellow—"

"You met him?"

"Seemed like a nice young man. When I arrived, he was just outside the door. Said you weren't at home, but that he was the brother of a friend of yours from college, and you were putting him up for a couple of nights while in town from Philadelphia."

I see. . .yes, a friend. "What did he look like?"

"You don't know?"

"I never met him."

"Well. . . the hallway is rather dim—Salvatore needs to put in a higher wattage bulb—so I didn't—He said he was in a hurry. Perhaps thirty years old, tall—taller than I am. Scurried down the stairs before I could be hospitable and invite him over for a drink."

It might not be a good idea to tell James the truth. That my guest was a burglar with an intent more nefarious than stealing my jewelry. At the very least, he had been after my evidence; at worst, he meant me harm. Why drag my friend into a possibly dangerous situation? Since I'd been lying to everyone I cared about these past few days, how much blacker could my soul get by adding just one more, Dorian Gray?

"Well, he's gone now," I said.

At a little after eight o'clock, ensconced in the embrace of "Hugo," with Little Dick Trumble sitting on the edge of the chair across from me, slurping his Rheingold beer and chomping on peanuts I'd put out for him; shelled—I'd never serve peanuts in their shells to Little Dick, considering the cleanup—I let loose all I'd held back from him over the past few days.

The truth always wins out. But it didn't set me free.

I thought he'd be furious with me, but he wasn't, or didn't show it if he was. Little Dick wasn't one to hold a grudge. "It don't get you very far in life if you walk around with a chip on your shoulder or believe everybody's out to get you," I remembering him scolding Rudy, who'd spat out spiteful words at the news his colleague was going to marry his ex-wife. "What did Henry Hanover's wife have to say?"

"Not a thing. She left town—according to her next-door neighbor—for a holiday in Cuba."

"Glean anything from the neighbor?"

"Only that the couple—Henry and wife—were not such a happy couple. The old man who died right before his wife's funeral looked like he was in good health. Far as the neighbor knew, the old man didn't have a heart condition, like they told the reporter at *The Hour*, or their friends. The old man founded the company, Hanover Aeronautics. They had government military contracts, and the house they lived in is pretty grand."

"Well, that's something, anyway."

"No hard proof, though. No financials yet. Gossip. Speculation."

I told Dick about the break-in, that it was obviously a search for the evidence I'd gathered and had put in the shopping bag, returning with it just tonight. The burglar didn't know I was staying at Papa's and that I had kept the evidence stashed there until now. I did not, however, share my fears that the burglar meant me harm.

I picked up the Bergdorf Goodman's shopping bag and laid out its contents between us on the ottoman:

The little black address book.

The bill addressed to H. Werner sent from Dr. Armbruster.

Six eight-by-ten photos, taped together, of the Hanover Aeronautics blueprint.

Photo of the envelope addressed to Miss Mae Brown, Pittenweem, Scotland.

Photo of the enclosed letter.

Photo of a handkerchief, folded into a fan shape, in a flat celluloid-covered box.

Photo of the birthday card message.

The wristwatch and wallet pinched from a guy named Joe, who'd pinched them from the deceased Henry Hanover.

A broken briefcase buckle.

"All right," Dick started. "So, you think you've stumbled on a spy ring?" asked Little Dick, flipping through the address book.

While waiting for Little Dick's arrival, I once again perused the address book. I counted twenty-seven entries—names, addresses, and phone numbers of people in and around the city—and five telephone numbers attributed to people with only initials.

"I think the address book holds more information on Hedy Werner than is obvious on first glance. Nazis were meeting at her apartment, after all."

Little Dick, leaning in toward me with a confidential whisper, said, "We know now that this kind of espionage has been going on for years, right under Uncle Sam's nose. These spies have gotten away with stealing our industrial and military secrets, and getting them from our own citizens! Do you think like I do that Henry Hanover, an American citizen, was selling out his country? Was he a Nazi?"

"After seeing the twenty thousand Nazi sympathizers at the Bund rally the other night, it wouldn't surprise me. Unless he was a patriot, trying to get back the blueprints that someone else—Pudgy, perhaps—had stolen from the aircraft plant."

"Now, you are certain you heard correctly what Monty said about—"

"Yes. He told the man at the tailor shop," I said, grabbing my shorthand notebook from my tote and turning to the notes I made of the conversation.

"They said this:

Tailor: *I don't see how it can be ready any sooner.*

Monty: *Yes, but the ship sails at midnight tomorrow.*

Tailor: *I saw in the papers about—*

Monty: *It's been taken care of. All cleaned up. Hanover was—well, he's not a problem now.*

Tailor: *Is there any way—*

Monty: *I wouldn't worry about that. There's no connection to you. Our people are looking for him. The case is closed as far as the police are concerned.*"

Little Dick lit a cigarette and pondered the meaning of the conversation.

"Okay, I'd like to know who *'our people'* are, and *who* it might be that those unidentified people *'are looking for?'"*

"Yeah, Dick, if we knew *who* the lead players were, we'd be able to figure out who did what to whom. Maybe there are good guys and bad guys—or maybe all are bad guys."

"I'm getting confused with all the who's who owl speak."

"We don't have time to sort the villains from the victims right now. Something is going on that ship—a bomb?"

"Why would a Nazi put a bomb on the ship? Makes no sense! I figure it's that blueprint that's to be delivered to someone sailing to Germany."

He put the book down with the other evidence and picked up the dentist's bill, removing it from the envelope. "This is interesting," said Little Dick. "Nine bucks for a gold crown for a posterior molar. Think she had to sleep with Armbruster to get it at that price?"

He looked from the envelope held in one hand to the bill in his other.

"This is interesting."

"What? What did I miss?"

"Well, the date atop the bill says February twenty-first. That was yesterday. The postmark shows the bill was sent on February seventeenth. Now, isn't it standard practice to bill a person *after* the work gets done?"

The light went on. "That's not a bill; that's an assignation!" I exclaimed. "A message setting up a date, address—Armbruster's office—and the nine-dollar fee—nine o'clock!

The time of the meeting! *Posterior molar*—p.m.—post meri-diem! It was at nine when the big blonde arrived at Dr. Arm-bruster's office—yesterday, which was the twenty-first!"

"Oh my God!" I yelped, grabbing the photo of the message in the birthday card. "It's all code!

I scanned the handwritten message. It was almost too easy, I now realized.

"I don't know why I didn't see it before," I said. "It's sort of like an acrostic. A puzzle almost too simple, but then, who would think there's a message enclosed in a birthday card?"

I reread the card. There was something wrong, some-thing out of sync.

Well, I reasoned, "Peacock" is an endearment, per-haps, a nickname. . .

What's this remark about *chivalry*, I wondered?

And why phrase "This gift I sent," the object ahead of the verb, instead of simply saying, "I sent this gift . . .?"

The phrasing was odd. *Sent,* past tense, instead of *send.* I underlined it. It was the fourth word in the sentence. Deliberately done, I realized. I took my pen and underlined the fourth word in each sentence. A ridiculously simple key.

Happy birthday, My dear <u>Peacock</u>!
Chivalry is not <u>dead!</u>
This gift I <u>sent</u>. Was not the plan
I would have <u>delivered</u> it.
But I'm in <u>New York</u>!
Best regards from <u>Laura.</u>

I hope this <u>arrives.</u> Before you leave <u>Southampton.</u>
Auntie Belle.

"Peacock dead," I said. "Who is—was Peacock? A spy's code name? Henry Hanover, maybe?"

"Well," said Little Dick, "I suppose you might see that as a coded message of sorts, knowing what you know about a dead man, Hanover, the *plan* or blueprint, *New York* being the name of the ship that's sailing. Maybe an acrostic?"

He looked over the message, searching for possible combinations, calling out letters in vertical sequence, and when arriving at a dead end, counting over from the first letter, second letter and onward, stalling when words could not be formed. "Tibia? What the hell?"

"Maybe it's just that simple, what is written in the card. 'Peacock—Hanover—dead. Plan delivered (the blueprints) *New York*. Laura—the name on the passport—arrives Southampton.'"

"Okay, okay."

"Let me see the letter to the woman in Scotland."

"Miss Mae Brown, Pittenweem, Scotland. The sender's return address is a street in Cherbourg."

"Well, if the *S.S. New York* makes port in Cherbourg— let's find out if that's a port of call."

A telephone call to the city desk confirmed Cherbourg was the second port the *S.S. New York* would make, after Cobh; onward to Southampton before the ship's final destination, Hamburg. I told Little Dick to find out if we could get our hands on a passenger list.

"So, these letters are meant to be posted from France,"

I said, more certain than ever that the carrier was the woman, Laura Miller—if that in fact was her real name—and she would also be delivering the Hanover Aeronautics blueprints upon arrival in Southampton.

I looked at the photograph of the ticket. Cabin class all the way to Hamburg.

For the next half hour, I tried to decode the letter to Miss Mae Brown, Pittenweem, that had been enclosed in the package containing the birthday card and gift—the embroidered handkerchief. I handed the photo to Little Dick. He read the letter out loud:

"'Dear Mae,

The weather has been miserable here in Lisbon. Cold and rainy most days. I am planning to go fly-fishing in Spain next month with George. He knows the best rivers to go to. So don't expect me to return until the end of April.

Your brother, Ryan'"

"The end of April," I mused. What was planned for late that month?

But there was no obvious cipher to decode. I handed it to Dick to look over, and sat bewildered.

"Dick," I said at last, while he still strained for meaning in the three paragraphs. "That woman, this Laura, has to be stopped. We can't let her sail off with all this. We can't let her deliver the blueprint and then disappear in Germany!"

Dick put down the photo of the letter to Mae Brown with a disgusted sigh. "I can't see it. You'd think it was written with invisible ink, or something, 'cause I don't see—"

Together, we rose from our seats.

Of course! Invisible ink!

The horizontal lines of writing were spaced just wide enough apart to accommodate additional writing. Not so great a margin of white space to attract suspicion, but enough to insert the true message. Problem was we didn't have the original letter to test. Still, we had to intercept, not only these letters to Scotland, but the blueprint, as well. And there was no doubt in my mind that Monty had delivered the blueprint to the tailor, who would deliver it to Laura Miller before midnight, when the *S.S. New York* sailed. The thought popped into my mind when I thought about Monty's words to the tailor. Perhaps, when he stressed the time constraints for delivery, before midnight, it was about getting the plans photographed on microfilm! A much easier way to smuggle it out.

"We've got to go to the police, Dick."

"I wonder how these spies got the NYPD to drop the investigation into Henry Hanover's murder?" said Little Dick. "Unless they have people in the department who squashed the case?"

"So, we can't just turn this information over to the police. We have to stop her ourselves."

"Let's not get all excited, Filly. People are dead, you know?"

"What the hell are you saying? I can't just stand by. That blueprint obviously contains a device that's our government's secret. Something important to our national defense. Something important enough not to hesitate leaving a path of dead bodies. The Germans have been building their military, their air force, these past few years. They've been doing more than flexing their muscles, Dick. This is bigger than us."

"Yeah, yeah, I know that. They're on the march, and Hitler isn't shy about what they're doing, I know."

"So, we're just going to sit around—"

"We can't go to the cops. We can't do this alone. But what good will it do to add ourselves to the body count?"

"Why do you think we'll get killed? Not if we're smart, we won't! We don't have to confront the woman or her Nazi friends. She doesn't know who we are or what we're after. I'll get into her cabin right before the ship sails, and I'll get back the plans—now I'll know to look for: microfilm. She could stash it at the bottom of her cold cream jar, or in her jewelry box. I wonder if I could snatch a maid's uniform from the—"

"Hey, kiddo, do you remember Jack Mitchell? He used to write a political column."

"Yes, I remember when I was a kid, and he was writing about the last appeals in the Sacco and Vanzetti death sentences. What about him?"

"That's the man. He's the real deal. Kept at it week after week in his column about what they were doing to those poor Italians. The trial—the whole setup—looked fishy to him. He pretty much said that the judge was corrupt; the witnesses for the prosecution, paid; the men's alibis, substantiated by dozens of people in the community, discredited—well, let's say, the men were set up because of their anarchist beliefs and their fight for fair wages and improved conditions in the Boston factories. Anarchists don't organize; it's against their philosophy. They detest government, and anarchists hate the Commie propagandists, who were all about organizing—the unions, their main activity in the U.S."

"So, the labor unions were Soviet inspired?"

"Uniting workers for negotiating fair wages is a great thing."

"Well, yes, but—"

"Most Americans would agree," said Dick.

"What does this have to do—"

"Right! Well, Jack Mitchell took a job with the Federal Bureau back in '30, when he realized it wasn't the anarchists we needed to worry about but the Reds that needed tackling. He's at the New York office, at Foley Square, and I run into him once in a while. He doesn't talk much about his duties at the Bureau, but they're looking hard at the Nazis now."

"You forgot that *The Morning Sun*'s exposé made the Bureau a laughing stock last December, when they let that Nazi spy ring escape the country."

"Well, maybe they've learned their lesson."

"So, our paper makes the Bureau look like a bunch of morons and now they're gonna be glad to help us? They'll laugh at us, or discount us. What makes you think they won't see it as a trick to show them up as impotent?"

"I don't know. But look, kiddo, you've got the evidence here," said Dick, slapping the photos in his hand.

"Jack will at least listen."

"Should we call him?"

"I'll call him at home."

Something good or bad was going to happen tonight, depending on where you stood, and I was feeling the adrenaline rush. I took the photos of the evidence I found at Dr. Armbruster's from Little Dick, and looked them over once again, while Little Dick dialed and asked the operator to connect him with John R. Mitchell who lived on East Seventy-Eighth Street. I paced the floor, nervously popping peanuts in my mouth and mindlessly washing them down with beer. I spilled some from the glass, slopping the liquid on the pictures. I hurried to the bathroom and wiped them off with a bath towel. Little Dick called out to me.

When I returned to the living room, Dick said, "Jack's wife said he's upstate, and she doesn't know how to reach him. Seems his team is tracking a con broke out of Sing Sing."

"Oh crap. Maybe we have no choice but to call the cops. Who do you know at the Twentieth you can vouch for?"

"Plenty guys are on the level," said Little Dick, scratching his head. "But they won't take this seriously. Don't ask me why; it's the nature of the cop-reporter relationship. We're always fishing, and they're never biting, if ya know what I mean."

We didn't speak for a while, each of us privately trying to conjure up a plan for how to proceed. Finally, I broke the silence with resolve.

"We'll just have to stop it ourselves."

"You mean, you want to go down to the pier and—"

"Yeah, we go down to the dock and see who boards the ship."

"It's a passenger line. They'll be hundreds sailing, hundreds sending them off."

I said, "Well, you told me when you called the paper, they were sending a boy to run the passenger list down here."

There was a knock on the door.

"Speak of the devil," said Little Dick. He opened the door to receive the envelope from the messenger.

We looked over the list. Around six hundred passengers.

"Okay," I said, suddenly feeling the hours slipping by. "Let's just stay with cabin class people. That's where her ticket has her."

"That whittles it down to just ninety," said Dick with a sarcastic tone. "You'd think she'd have been booked tourist or third class."

"In plain sight, Dick. Cabin class people, above reproach. Ha! Who's gonna suspect she's smuggling when she goes through customs?"

I don't recognize anyone of any news interest at first glance, but the society columns publish the comings and goings of even minor celebrities and dignitaries. And if some swell is sailing, there's bound to be press there to see them off and snap their picture waving from the gangway.

"Here's our cover onto the ship. Look! Lord Meriwether, the sixth Earl of Pendrick is sailing with his wife, Lady Mildred. There was that scandal last year, and we're reporters."

"You think Monty's going to be there, lead you to the carrier pigeon?" said Little Dick.

"I doubt it. As much as I'd like to catch him in the act, that treasonous—he already delivered the package."

"But the blueprint?"

"If it's on microfilm, it might have been hidden—Oh God! Hidden under the folded handkerchief, do you think?"

"But he might be there. Have you thought what we're supposed to do when we catch him at it? Or if we're caught?"

"I haven't worked that out yet."

"It would be a good idea if you did. I mean, there's a possibility we'll become fish food. Henry Hanover didn't fare too well."

"I doubt Monty would go that far. Whatever he is, I do believe he loves my father, so he won't kill me."

"I'll bet he loves his own skin more."

"All right, I see your point. . ."

"There're cops at the docks—"

"Checking passports, looking for stowaways, yeah," I said.

"I don't like it."

"We can't *not* follow this through."

"All right. We only got an hour or so before boarding."

I dressed for a bon voyage party.

Wednesday, February 22, 1939
9:50 p.m.

Dressed in my black sleeveless Chanel cocktail dress (found in a resale shop three or four years ago when such finds could be had for a song, thanks to the ravages of the economy), Mama's pearl necklace and drop earrings, hair swept up in a swirl of curls and topped with a feathery confection of a hat (stolen from a store mannequin during a scavenger hunt last summer), dress pumps on my feet, and satin elbow gloves up my arms, a spritz of Chanel No. 5, and topped off with Mama's beautiful sable coat, Little Dick Trumble helped me out of the taxi at the West Side pier.

There were scores of vehicles unloading trunks and valises, porters pushing stockpiles of luggage, passengers and their send-off parties scurrying about, bottles of champagne tugged under the arms of swells in dinner suits, uniformed telegram boys scooting through the crowd on their determined missions, fruit and flower baskets toted in the arms of express delivery men charging the buzzing air with anticipation and festivity and warming the otherwise cold misty night. The ocean liner shone like a beckoning orb aglow in the night, I mused, as we walked toward the terminal; its stacks and edges softened by the fog.

How many times had I sent off my parents' friends, this friend or that colleague, sailing off to Europe, South America, distant parts? Oh, that I might one day board such a beauty to ride the high seas to a foreign destination! But there was work to be done; my desire for adventure had to be squelched for now.

We passed through the gates marked for visitors and joined the flood of people walking up the gangways onto the ship. Embarking passengers were directed to their decks—cabin, tourist, and third class accommodations. After giving Laura Miller's name, we were pointed in the right direction.

With Little Dick toting his camera case and walking a few feet behind me, I carried a bottle of champagne and a fruit basket I'd snatched off a table near the purser's desk in the Grand Foyer, an opulently appointed space alight with dripping crystal chandeliers, groupings of brocade-upholstered seating and twin staircases curving up to the cabin class deck, while an orchestra played an upbeat string version of "Make Believe" from *Show Boat*.

Little Dick chuckled at my larceny, but I paid him no mind as we briskly walked up toward the staterooms, passing a flurry of giggling girls, a boisterous wedding party spilling out of a cabin into the hallway, a middle-aged couple arguing over a mislaid hatbox, the joyful *"Hoowahh!"* followed by laughter at the popping of a cork, and the raucous, if gleeful, gales of a school song, shouted more than sung, by a gang of rowdy college boys in send-off of a fellow student. Yale no doubt: *Boola Boola!* Each cabin held its own little story. . .

Among the hoopla of the rowdy were the more sedate passengers admitting porters struggling into the cabins their loads of luggage, steamer trunks, and in one case, a bass fiddle.

Before we even arrived at the door we were in search of, I caught a glimpse of the blonde from Dr. Armbruster's office (and Montgomery Chase's nightclub companion) as she entered a cabin.

Laura Miller.

That I recognized her at all was a surprise to me, since she was not at all the glamorous woman I'd seen before, wrapped in furs and shimmering silk. It was the very distinctive color of her hair—a platinum silver blond—peeking out from under a simple brown felt hat, the upturned nose, the porcelain complexion, and her astonishing height, a head above many of the men who blocked the path between us, that gave her away. When suddenly the figure of Montgomery Chase posing as Otto Rust exited a cabin just a few feet from where we stood, I braced myself for a confrontation. But he never turned in our direction, never saw us, and instead he made his way farther down the corridor before entering the blonde's suite.

Without much thought given to what Little Dick and I should do next, and without consultation between us, I grabbed Dick's elbow, and entered the room from which

Otto Rust had just exited.

The cabin was not occupied, although several valises stood just inside the door. I looked at the labels hanging off their handles, and read that they belonged to Wolfgang Meyer, destination Hamburg.

And then, there stood Montgomery Chase, in the doorway, glowering at us with a look of both panic and incredulity.

"What are you doing here?" he hissed, closing the door behind him and turning the lock. He crossed to me with one giant step, grabbed my arm, and shook me. Little Dick moved in toward him from behind with a weak gesture of attack, his camera hanging from his neck and hampering his ability to affect a strike. Monty, still gripping me, flung his other arm in a backward motion, striking Little Dick across this head and causing the reporter to crumple to the floor.

I let out a cry of terror as I struggled, kicked him in the shin, and found myself encircled in a stronghold from behind, my flailing legs kicking nothing but air.

"You stupid, stupid girl!" he spat out in my ear.

"I know what you are!"

"If you don't stop struggling, I'm going to break your little neck!"

"A murderer! That's what you are!"

"Don't tempt me!"

I could not release myself from his hold, and the more I struggled the more pointless it became. The man was an athlete able to scale walls and swing from chandeliers while fighting off a score of swordsmen—at least on the screen. I felt like a twig waving about in a windstorm.

"All right," I said, conceding, biding time until I could figure out a plan of escape, if not retaliation. And Little Dick was of no use, sitting up now on the floor, rubbing his head, and reaching for his hat tossed off by the fall.

"Don't try anything stupid—although coming here is stupid enough! I'm warning you," he said, pushing me roughly into a chair. "Who's your brave, if ineffectual, friend?"

"Who's yours?" I demanded.

"What?" he said, grabbing Little Dick and shoving him onto the bed.

"The babe next door? The platinum floozy. Laura Miller!"

"What the—What do you know?"

"Enough to know that you're working for the Nazis. That you are a Nazi. A Nazi spy!"

This was met with a laugh. "You idiot girl!"

"What do you find so funny?" I replied, incensed. "Betraying our country? You're a traitor to your country!"

He turned to Little Dick. "Who are you?"

"Dick Trumble, reporter at *The Morning Sun*," he replied cautiously, with a hint of challenge, impotent, if brave, before the hulking figure.

"Are you with this madwoman?"

"You mean Filly?" he replied, glanced at me, and then cast his eyes to the floor. "Yeah."

Monty seemed to make a quick calculation as he

looked from one to the other of us. "You have no idea what you've just stepped into."

"Oh yes, we do!"

"Oh, just shut up!"

I didn't at all like his dismissal. I didn't like when he called me an "idiot girl." "Nutcase" infuriated me. So, I smashed my high heel down on his instep. Released from his grip, I kneed him "where he lived."

Bent over, a grunt blew out of his mouth.

I knew how to defend myself!

The last thing I remember was a fist coming at me.

Thursday, February 23, 1939
1:30 a.m.

R udely awakened, my face was being slapped, not so gently, either, and in my outrage I struck out, only for my hand to be wrestled down to my side. Drums were pounding in my head; I tried to open my eyes, but could barely achieve a squint, which I abandoned to escape the piercing pain of a bright and unrelenting light cast over me. Something thick and aching lay on the left side of my face—on my cheek, and when I raised a hand to remove it the brash contact smarted.

"She's coming around," said a voice from a distance. "There, there, you're all right. Some water?"

Shielding my eyes, I managed to open one eye, then the other, tried to focus, and when the fog cleared, saw Little Dick patting my hand.

"I think she's all right now," said Little Dick, hovering over me.

I was on the fainting couch in my apartment, Mama's

sable coat draped over me. And as I tried to sit up, something cold was slapped on the side of my face, pushing me down and obscuring the vision of one eye.

"You'll live. The steak will bring down the swelling," said Monty, standing there, looking quite pleased with himself. I broke through the pain to sit up again, the meat slipping from off my cheek.

"That prime cut cost me seventy cents from that restaurant down the street," he scolded, catching the beef, and slapping it back with force.

"Ouch!"

Emotionally, I was still on the ship; in reality, some time had passed since I had the daylights knocked out of me. I turned to Little Dick, and asked, "How'd I get—"

Dick broke in, "He carried you over his shoulder off the ship, into a cab, and up three flights. Turning to Monty he said, "You owe me the seventy cents, since I fetched the steak for you."

Monty delved into his trouser pocket and extracted a dollar bill from a sheaf of bills from a money clip and handed it to the reporter. There was a long moment before Monty said, "You owe me thirty cents." Little Dick searched through his pocket change.

"Oh, for God's sake!" I said, "Who the hell cares about petty change!"

"I should make *you* pay for the steak, after what you did," replied Monty. He had stripped off his Otto Rust persona—the push-broom moustache, the eyeglasses, and the fake nose. Still, the gray hair and eyebrows remained like ghostly vestiges.

"You!" said Monty, pointing to Little Dick and then sweeping his hand toward the door, "Out!"

"I don't know—" said Little Dick, hesitating, looking to me and then his eyes following Monty who opened the door.

"I'll see you tomorrow," he said to me, putting two aspirins in the palm of my hand and handing me a glass of water to wash them down. He slapped the meat back onto my left cheek. I winced at the impact. He winced back empathetically, before heading for the door.

"Dick! Don't leave me alone with this man!"

Little Dick hesitated, threw me a little smile, and shrugged his shoulders, while Monty opened the door for his exit.

"You're *leaving* me? Why—why, you little *Dick!*" I yelled at his back.

"You shouldn't call the fellow names."

"You shut up, you son of a bitch!"

"Don't call my mother names or I'll punch you again!"

"You—you woman beater!"

"Ball-breaker!" Monty shouted back, referring to my last act of violence.

"Lothario!"

He considered that for a moment with a raised brow, a nod, and a pout.

"Well, there is truth in *that.*" He shrugged and added, "And who can blame me?"

"Everything okay in there?" sounded a disembodied

baritone.

From out in the hall, a shadowy figure moved forward into the rectangle of light cast from the room: a brawny blond, square-jawed *Aryan*, undoubtedly the Superman model of the Super Race poster, in a trench coat, clutching a fedora. Monty took Dick's arm and handed him over to the Hun.

"Take him away, Günter."

"Günter? Really?"

"Careful, he's little, but he's wily," referring to Little Dick.

"I'll see you tomorrow, kiddo," croaked Little Dick, feebly, waving his free hand.

"Don't count on it," said my captor, slamming the door.

"Go suck an egg!" I yelled at Monty.

"I would, but your refrigerator is empty," he said. "Soon as you're done with that steak, you can fry it up. I've built up an appetite lugging your carcass up three flights of stairs. Got any potatoes?" He stopped short his wisecracking.

"Whoa! I see you've been busy," said Monty, holding up the envelope containing Dr. Armbruster's bill addressed to Hedy Werner. He slipped it into his suit jacket pocket. Rippling through the pages of the little black address book, he said, "Tampering with evidence from a crime scene. Very nice felony conviction awaits you."

"Are you kidding me?! A firing squad awaits you! Hey! Leave those things alone!"

I tossed off the blood-dripping Delmonico steak and bounded over—stumbled—into the living room, where Monty was riffling through my evidence against him I had left out on the ottoman.

Ignoring my objections, he scooped up all of my "evidence" against him and crammed everything into the Bergdorf Goodman's bag. Coat flung over his shoulder, he donned Otto Rust's homburg, and, shopping bag in hand, walked to the door.

"Wait! Those belong to me!"

"Not anymore."

"That won't stop me."

"I don't care."

I had all the negatives for all the pictures I'd taken of the evidence, but I wasn't about to tell him that—and, because I was careless and slopped beer on my photos from Dr. Armbruster's earlier, I had enough evidence to make my case stashed in my bedroom bureau drawer.

"What about your steak?" I said, as a last resort.

"I've lost my appetite."

"Wait!" I yelled, and my head throbbed in punishment, "You can't just leave! I'm going to the FBI tomorrow!"

If I thought that would stop him, threaten him in some way, my pronouncement elicited a surprising reply.

"They won't believe you," he said, before slamming the door.

I sat there, perplexed, to the thud of footfalls diminishing on the stairs.

If the pain from the strike to my face was not enough

to keep me awake, my thoughts did. When he'd left, I had a mind to follow him, but even the courage of my convictions could not overcome my disorientation. My head was too heavy a burden for my neck to hold up. I felt a little bit drunk, even though I'd not touched a drop. I found myself in a puddle of tears that I could only attribute to frustration at the whole debacle I'd contributed to over the past few days, and the humiliation after failing to stop Monty.

I'll fix him, I ranted, as I threw the Delmonico in the kitchen sink. I poured a couple of fingers of Jim Beam, circled the living room, collapsed on the sofa, then refilled my glass and stared into space, an idiot trying to decide what to do next. I poured a third drink, took to the fainting couch, and lay there for a time, waiting for the throbbing in my head to subside.

Thursday, February 23, 1939
7:10 a.m.

After a few hours of drug-like sleep, I gingerly lifted my head. The sun was rising; the dull light filtered in through the curtains. The pain had dulled. I looked at the mantle clock. I washed my face. The cold water soothed my hot bruised cheek.

There was no time to try to disguise the blackish swelling of my eye, so I put on my shoes, my sable coat, and after checking my face again in the mirror—not a pretty picture—donned a felt hat with a wide, low brim and added sunglasses. Just as I was about to leave my apartment, I heard the rumbling of multiple feet running up the stairs.

The door shook from a pounding fist. I froze.

"Filomena Devlin, open the door. FBI."

Holy shit! I thought. He's turned me in! Montgomery Chase had turned the tables on me, accusing me of crimes against my country—or, at best, tampering with evidence from a murder investigation!

There was no escape. No way that I could negotiate the fire escape in heels.

I held my breath, my heart racing from fear, and opened the door.

Three men came bounding in, pushed past me, guns drawn, scanning the room for anyone else in occupancy. Once the bedroom and bathroom had been deemed clear, the guns were holstered. One of the men turned to me and stated my name. I nodded, and he flashed his identification card.

"You've got this all wrong," I spoke quietly. "Whatever he told you is a lie. Montgomery Chase is a Nazi spy, and I found him out."

Why did I detect a flash of amusement in the fellow's face, the suddenly relaxed postures of the other two men?

"You'll have to come with us, miss."

~~~~

The Federal Bureau of Investigation's New York Field Office is located in Foley Square, in the federal courthouse, and that was where I was carted off to by the three agents in their black sedan, before being deposited into a windowless room, to sit alone and stare at the walls, without my satchel, in which was my shorthand pad. So instead of composing a scathing letter to J. Edgar Hoover about my mistreatment at the hands of his agents, I sat chipping away at my nail polish, silently reciting the poems put to memory during my high school days—Keats's "Ode to a Nightingale" (*My heart aches, and a drowsy numbness pains My sense, as though of hemlock I had drunk…*); "The Raven," (*Once upon a midnight dreary, while I pondered weak and weary. . .);* and keeping with the bird theme, "The Rime of the Ancient Mariner" *(Water, water, everywhere, And all the boards did shrink; Water, water, everywhere, Nor any drop to drink.)*—when, trying to remember what came next, after two hours and fifty-one minutes without a decent book to read, a man in a black suit entered, with a glass and pitcher of water.

Very funny.

He identified himself as Special Agent Jake Rufus.

"You know, you could leave a couple of magazines or a newspaper or two in here. And a cup of coffee would be nice. If this is how you treat your guests, it's a wonder you have any friends at all."

"I'm not interested in making you my friend, Miss Devlin."

"The feeling is mutual, though last night Little Dick thought you people could help."

"It's time to come clean."

"Why, 'I washed me face 'n 'ands before I come.'" I replied in perfect Eliza Doolittle Cockney. Shaw would be proud!

"Oh, a wiseacre, hmm?"

"You don't have to mince words with me."

"Fine. I'll tell you straight. You are going to be charged with espionage against the United States of America. Because you are an American citizen you will be charged with treason, a death penalty crime."

"Well, you don't have to be so—*what!* Did that-that *actor*, that *scoundrel* give you some song and dance about me?

"Who are you talking about?"

Was this guy dense? I decided to move on.

"I have people who can vouch for me."

"Do you, now?"

"There's Little Dick—I mean Dick Trumble, reporter at *The Morning Sun*."

"Is that so? Well, I hate to dash your hopes, but he's in the same hot water as you are, Miss Devlin. We picked him up last night."

"What do you have? The word of an overrated, over-sexed, aging movie star with heavy calves? You call that evidence? Don't make me laugh."

"Let's start from the beginning, shall we?"

"I invoke my Second Amendment rights."

"You want to form a militia?"

"Not that one—I mean, the—"

"Don't look at me; I'm not going to help you out here. This is just a friendly little conversation."

"Oh, so charging me with espionage is the icebreaker? You kidding me?"

"Well, if you're so innocent, why don't you tell me why you are innocent?"

This man was making me mad; these FBI jerks had just fumbled the Rumrich spy case. Maybe this was revenge against Papa for breaking the story, for exposing the G-men's negligence in his newspaper. Still, I was worried they'd smartened up after that recent fiasco, and believing me a spy and not letting me leave the building was absurd. Were they afraid I'd try to escape to Argentina?

"I want to talk to Jack Mitchell."

"Special Agent Mitchell is not available."

"He's the only one I'll talk with."

Thursday, February 23, 1939
3:00 p.m.

Special Agent Rufus dismissed me with a stern warning to keep my mouth shut, in the manner of an elementary school principal scolding a pupil sent down for raucous classroom behavior. The threat was wasted on me. It was not my first time in the principal's office. "Don't do anything stupid, Miss Devlin. We'll be watching you."

I was getting pretty tired of the word *stupid*, used first by Monty and now this Neanderthal. I wanted to smack his supercilious face, dunk his fat head in the toilet bowl, and twist his testicles—and that was just the beginning. But he was already out the door. I also wanted to get the hell out of there (the confines purposely claustrophobic and designed to intimidate), as well as out of the Chanel dress I'd been wearing since yesterday evening.

I hailed a taxi and when I settled in the cabbie looked at me funny. It was no wonder, I realized, when I caught a glimpse of myself in the driver's rearview mirror. I looked like I'd lost a bar fight; I quickly donned the sunglasses, even though the day was dark and dreary.

Once I arrived home, I managed to climb up to my apartment without crossing paths with any of the tenants. I was particularly leery of running into James. I knew he would demand to know what brute hit me—I was too tired to retell the events of the past few days, and I didn't I want to lie to him again.

I ran a hot bath, added salts, stepped out of my clothes, and soaked for a long time, exhausted, my thoughts drifting until I began to nod off. I was crashing down from an adrenaline high, barely able to lift myself up out of the water.

After drying off, I lay down under my bedcovers and dozed, until my mind began to replay dialogue from the past few days. Monty telling me to shut up, and that I was "a stupid girl" was just icing on the cake, the insult over injury that stung more than the fact that I might be in serious trouble—like facing execution. The very idea that Montgomery Chase should get away by casting the blame on me was enough to shake me awake, and his disturbing voice in my ear propelled a fierce indignation to rise in me.

Once out of bed, I realized I was starving, not having eaten anything since the cold meatball sandwich twenty-four hours ago.

I grabbed my chenille bathrobe, stepped into slippers, and went foraging in the kitchen. The Delmonico steak was stinking in the kitchen sink. "There goes your seventy cents, mister!" I said aloud as I tossed it in the trash, then scavenged through my cabinets. I stuck my hand into the box of cornflakes and stuffed a handful of cereal in my mouth.

Thank goodness there was coffee. And the pot was clean. I filled the pot with water, scooped the grounds into the percolator, and lit the stove.

That damn man!

I sat down on Hugo waiting for the coffee to brew.

Stop thinking about him!

Papa must have heard by now that I had not shown up at the paper today.

Thursday! I needed to approve the Sunday Women's Pages today!

I took up the telephone handset, dialed Skip's line, and told him I was ill. He needed to approve Sunday's copy. Then I asked after Dick Trumble. Not in the office, "probably chasing down a lead."

I was worried the federal agents still had him sitting in a dreary room, trying to pry out of him enough incriminating evidence to convict me. I dialed the paper's main number and asked the switchboard operator to leave a message for Trumble to call me.

One problem solved. But where was Little Dick?

And why had he left me alone last night with Montgomery Chase? Had Chase given Dick some song and dance excuse about me misinterpreting what I said I saw?

That fucking-two-timing-son-of-a-bitch-Nazi-bastard!

Sizzling sounds from the kitchenette told me the percolator was boiling over and hitting the flames. I stormed over, turned off the gas, grabbed a cup from a hook, poured the coffee, took a sip, and burned my tongue.

Of course, they'd all listen to him. The agents were all men, and Montgomery Chase was a "man's man." He was seen as above reproach, not just for reputedly making huge donations to children's hospitals and opening thousand-acre sanctuaries for rare and abused animals, not to mention the estate in Santa Barbara that he bought and converted into a retirement home for aged actors. No, it was the notoriety as well, the devil-may-care image he'd fostered that thrilled the boys who didn't get out much and carried lunch pails to work: getting headlines as the injured party when that starlet's husband comes after him with a machete while filming a jungle adventure on Catalina, by being more "in like Flynn," than Erroll himself! ("In like Chase" failed the alliteration test, but "Chaste with Chase" proved oxymoronic, though the phrase could also imply frigidity of the female partner or, more devastating for his career, impotence on his part. The slogan never stuck.) And when the studio decided to promote the term "swinger" to Chase, in a sexual context, rather than transportation via jungle vine, he was happy to exploit it.

Women adored him; the "bad boy" a girl shouldn't run with but couldn't resist.

I hadn't a chance of credibility against the wiles of Montgomery Chase. . .

So what, damn it, if he fences with Fairbanks and schmoozes with Selznick? *A Nazi is a Nazi is a Nazi!*

I jammed my hand down into the cereal box for another hit.

I'll telephone Juliet! She'll commiserate, if not offer

any good advice, though she rarely has any. Not advice; she's always had that. But good advice? Not so much. . .

Advice about what? How to proceed? How to take down Montgomery Chase? Or how to play the game he's forced me into? I needed to prove him a spy; I needed to find the way to discredit him.

While consulting the darker aspects of my personality for the means to that end, there was a sharp rap on my door.

"It's Jack Mitchell, FBI."

I cinched the belt of my robe tighter and opened the door.

I suppose I expected a friendly approach, because I'd known this man since childhood, but I received an officious, "You ready to talk?"

He looked the same as I remembered him ten years ago. A little grayer around the temples, perhaps, better dressed, and a little thinner. But the harried expression that emanated from his black hooded eyes—a little frightening when you're a teenage girl—remained; only now I understood that it was simple determination that drove him.

"Little Dick and I tried to get in touch with you last night—"

He just hovered over me, wearing that impatient look, and for a second, I felt like that teenager again, intimidated, until I shook off my trepidation.

I resent when big men throw their weight around.

"Montgomery Chase is a Nazi spy," I blurted out, and I could hear the whine in my voice like a silly schoolyard accusation.

This isn't going well.

"Have a seat, Jack." I motioned toward the sofa, but he took a chair.

Suck up, Filomena.

"Coffee?"

He shook his head. "Let's just talk."

"As I was saying, Montgomery Chase is a spy," I tried again, but now with a sharp edge of self-justification.

I could do better; this isn't a rehearsal.

"That's quite an accusation."

Modulate your tone down an octave, Filly.

"I have proof."

Better. . .

"Oh? What's this proof?"

Shit! I thought. Monty had left last night and took all my evidence.

"I have negatives! Photo negatives of the proof I had before Chase took everything out of here last night. And there's Little Dick—"

"Trumble?"

I nodded, "Yes, he can vouch for me."

"He's been picked up."

"That's what the other guy told me. Then, they didn't hurt him? The big guy?"

"What are you talking about?"

"The big guy? Oversize Hitler Youth in long pants? Günter? Pair of breast plates and braids and he's in Valkyries at the Met?"

The door opened and Montgomery Chase stepped

over the threshold; a short, wiry little man peeking around his bulk.

I was taken aback by the gall of him entering my apartment, but more so by the way he just stood there, appraising the scene, looking over the room as if he owned it and was surprised to see intruders had broken in. From his hand dangled the Bergdorf Goodman's shopping bag. My self-assured tone flew out the window.

The short man was to remain unidentified, for he tipped his hat at Jack in response to the agent's, "Thanks, you can go." And he was gone.

Jack Mitchell rose from the chair and walked over to Monty, offering his hand to shake.

"Mr. Chase, thank you for coming. It's a real pleasure to finally meet you."

Why should I be surprised at this gesture? I'd already determined that Chase was every man's ideal. That he was a traitor to America didn't seem to be important in the light of his fame. Not to say I wasn't pissed.

"Hey! What is this?" I said, rising from my seat.

"Any way I can help, Special Agent Mitchell. I've heard good things about you."

"Me too—about you—I mean, good things. Call me Jack."

"Call me Monty."

"And I'm Marie of Romania."

"Really, Miss Devlin!"

"Really what?"

"This man is a two-time Academy Award nominee."

"He's a real two-timer all right!"

"Third time's a charm, as they say, Jack!"

"You know, before you hotfooted out to Hollywood, I saw you onstage back in '26, with Katharine Cornell in—"

"Sorry to interrupt this meeting of the mutual admiration society—but what the hell are you doing here?"

I was getting testy: I was tired from lack of sleep, being threatened, and ordered around. My eye was swollen, my cheek aflame, and my passport needed renewing for my flight to Timbuktu.

"All right, all right, all right, Miss Devlin," whined Special Agent Mitchell, his voice a siren.

There was a knock on the door.

"It's probably a bible salesman," I said, "don't answer it."

Little Dick was led in from the darkened hall, his elbow locked in the grip of the big blond oaf, Günter. I wondered if he sported lederhosen around the house. I tried to visualize it, and it wasn't a pretty picture.

"Sit him down, Günter," said Jack.

"If I knew I was having a party, I'd've hired a band," I said with sardonic glee.

"Baked a cake," corrected Monty, shaking his head.

"What? No, it's 'hired a band.'"

"It's 'If I knew you were coming I'd've baked a cake'!"

"But I didn't say, 'knew you were coming,' I said, 'knew I was having a party.'"

"Stop mixing your similes."

"Metaphors."

"Same thing."

"Calling Cole Porter," bellowed Little Dick, in the manner of a bellhop paging the lobby, "We've a song title for you!"

"Oh, a wise guy. Sit down and shut up," said Jack, flashing me and Little Dick the evil eye.

Now comes the drill, I thought. *Tread carefully. . .*

"What did you expect me to do?" I said, after Mitchell asked me how I came to be at the rooming house crime scene.

"I was covering the Bund rally at the Garden. I saw Chase, dressed up in his pickle salesman disguise. Who wouldn't wonder why he was at a Nazi rally? I followed him and Pudgy from the Bund rally up to the rooming house on Ninety-Third Street—"

"What did you call him?" asked Monty.

"—and you followed him out after the gunshot. You pushed him in front of the car."

"I did not."

His outrage played along his face, his jaw locked hard, and he stood there stiffly, almost making me regret the accusation. I'd never really thought he had pushed the fellow to his death; witnesses saw nothing of the kind, but I felt a thrill accusing him. Getting my own back. He needn't have belted me so hard, even if I did try to relieve him of his family jewels.

"Oh, sit down, for God's sake, and stop hovering over me," I said to Monty. "I am not intimidated."

Mitchell scowled at Monty and indicated the sofa.

Monty took a seat, crossed his legs, and didn't look at me while I carried on.

"There were gunshots. Two shots. He chased Pudgy—I mean I saw them leave the house"—I turned to look Monty straight in the eyes—"and you stole his briefcase."

"I took it. He panicked and ran." He looked at me accusingly; he didn't need to say anything, the look said enough.

I said, "Aren't you ashamed of yourself? What would Papa say about what you're doing?"

He ignored me, and then his attention turned to my photo of the blueprint. "And where did you get this, as if I haven't figured it out?"

Caught. And then I didn't care if he knew I'd snooped in his room, pawed through his things, in drawers and closet.

"I know you stole it," I challenged him. "A man was murdered, shot—"

"Stabbed."

"Stabbed, shot, what's the difference? Henry Hanover is dead. All for this plan."

He said, taking out the watch I'd pickpocketed from the pickpocketer, "Where'd you find this?"

"Where'd you think?"

"From whose wrist did the watch come off?"

"Henry Hanover's."

"You robbed a corpse?"

"Is that worse than you shooting the man?"

"Stabbed. And I didn't."

"I didn't take it; it was the other guy took it. Then I took it off the other guy when he wasn't looking. What's this all about? Who do you think you are questioning me, an FBI agent?"

That's when Special Agent Jack Mitchell pulled the rug out from under me.

"He is."

"Is what?"

"Working for us."

"What, you turned him? You think you can trust him now?"

Mitchell looked inquiringly at Montgomery Chase, as if deferring to him. I didn't like it at all.

I sat there, listening to Jack Mitchell telling me that I'd been mistaken about what I thought was true but wasn't; what I believed to be true of Montgomery Chase but wasn't.

I turned to Little Dick in silent inquiry.

"This is news to me, kiddo. I thought we were just gonna tell the feds what we knew about Chase."

"All right, it's time we let her in, don't you agree, Jack, before she causes any more trouble?"

Jack Mitchell said, "Montgomery Chase has been working to gather intelligence for the Bureau.

"Since when?"

"For the past year."

Was it possible?

How could this be?

How could I have been wrong about Chase?

"You mean, he's a spy?"

"For America."

"Crap," said Little Dick.

I was rendered speechless. And ordinarily for me to be so dumbfounded I'd have had to be bound and gagged, and I wasn't, that's how stunned I was.

The revelations came quickly, like an avalanche, burying me.

"My father was the child of German immigrants, but my mother, as you may not know—or you would have known immediately that I could never be a Nazi sympathizer—was a Russian Jew, and only a child when she and my grandparents escaped the pogroms in 1881. And so you see, I am half-Jewish, Filomena. I would have thought you'd known, since our parents were close friends."

"That's a silly assumption. Why would anyone, Papa, or my mother discuss such things?"

"Well, I suppose not. Details of my background are not widely known. Hollywood may be run by Jews, but its stars are not encouraged to claim that heritage."

The Montgomery Chase I thought I knew was not the Montgomery Chase who sat opposite me, talking to me with candor and free of the pretense I had come to expect.

"Now," said Jack Mitchell, "what we need to know is exactly what you know. First, let's go back to your arrival at the rooming house."

I related how I had spotted Monty, disguised as Otto Rust at the Bund rally, and no, I had not followed him there that night. "I had wanted to cover the event on my own initiative, and when I saw Skip there with a photographer, he officially offered me the assignment. Your brief tête-a-tête with Pudgy made me curious. I followed you both uptown and waited as you entered the brownstone. While debating with myself what to do, I saw shadows moving violently along the lowered window shade, and then heard gunfire. I hid beneath the front stoop as Pudgy ran down, and then I watched you tail him down the street.

"I found the belt buckle on the ground—it came from the briefcase, and then I went up into the building to the second floor. The room's door was open. I heard a noise coming from the third floor and looked up, frightened of who might be lurking there. That's when I saw the couple, the young man coming down the stairs. He was buttoning his shirt, his girl was leaning over the third-floor railing, urging him to hurry, because her brother might be returning home any minute and Joe mustn't be caught there."

"Wait a minute," interrupted Jack. "What about the gunshots? What about this "Joe?" Who was the woman? Did they witness anything?"

"My impression was that the gunshots scared them, and, well, you see, the girl's brother didn't like this guy, Joe. That seemed to be more important to them than who might be dead."

"Did this woman have a name?"

"I didn't ask. I wanted to get inside the room where I saw the scuffle in the window."

"The man. . .this guy told you his name was Joe?"

"Well, later, when we were leaving."

"I don't get it. You went into the room."

"Yes."

"And this man, this Joe...?"

"He was watching from the hall when I discovered Henry Hanover. Only, I didn't know it was the same Hanover until the next day, when Little Dick told me."

"Wait a minute!" snapped Jack. "How could Dick know who it was, when you had the dead man's wallet? And what do you mean, 'the same Hanover?'"

"Okay," I said, trying to back up, but Dick interrupted.

"There was a story in the *Hour* a couple of days before, and Filly and I were going to investigate the sudden death of an old man, about whom we both suspected might, in fact, really have been murdered. The victim was Henry Hanover's father, Herbert. There was a photo of Henry and his parents—when the parents were alive, of course—and I recognized the face in the *Hour* with the face of the corpse in the rooming house."

"What were you doing there?"

"Covering the story. Came up with the rest of the reporters hanging around the precinct when the call came in of gunshots on Ninety-Third Street. The next day I told the detectives that I recognized the dead man, but they told me the case was closed."

Turning to me, Jack said, "Go on. Why'd you walk away with the crime scene evidence?"

"I just did. But I never intended to steal the dead man's watch and wallet."

An exasperated sigh from Jack, and a head shake from Monty prompted me to self-defense.

"Look, the door to the room was open, see? So, I went in. I saw the man lying on the floor, bleeding, and told Joe to close the door."

"You're telling us a man was in there with you? This fellow Joe?"

"Yeah, that's what I just said. And then the landlord came in, too."

"What about the rest of the residents?"

"Hiding behind their doors.

"I stanched the bleeding, and the man, Henry Hanover, tried to tell me something, but I just didn't understand. He lifted his hand, as if beckoning me, but even when I leaned in closer, his words were just a humming sound, made no sense to me. And then he died."

"And then?"

"The landlord came in and he started ranting about 'things like this don't happen in his house,' and who was I? I flashed my press badge and told him not to touch anything; the police should arrive soon. . .and I told Joe to cover the body. I grabbed my Rolleiflex from out my satchel and snapped pictures of the room and the dead man."

"I'll ask you again, why'd you steal the evidence?"

I had to think a minute. Was it because I thought there might be evidence there about Monty that would connect him to the murder? Was it because I had the crazy idea that I could solve the case and clear my father's godson? Or... incriminate him? I felt sure I had landed in a nest of Nazi activity. Whether Monty was involved wasn't the point. I was riled up after the hideous spectacle of the rally, I suppose, and then a man was lying dead, and someone had killed him.

"I don't know for certain why I took things. I just did."

"You said a while back that you lifted Hanover's watch and wallet from this fellow Joe?"

"Yeah. When I saw that the dead man's wrist was bare, where a moment before there was a wristwatch, I knew Joe had stolen it. And when he told me there was no I.D. on the body, I knew that men don't walk around town without their wallets, so when we were leaving, I picked Joe's pocket."

"And you think he didn't know you did?"

"I learned from the best—Freddy Four-Fingers. Remember him, Jack, from when you were at the paper?"

"Yeah, the stoolie."

"He was more than that. Earned a degree in mathematics from Northwestern. Just got in with the wrong crowd, Papa used to say. He's a Wall Street analyst now."

"From one bad crowd to another," chuckled Little Dick.

Monty cut in, "Didn't you say this Joe was in a hurry to quit the building because of his girlfriend's brother finding him there?"

"Yeah, but some people like living on the edge, you know, and he saw an opportunity to pilfer the goods."

"Like you did."

"I didn't feel right about it afterward, not until I saw the briefcase and found the blueprints. Then I thought—I thought—"

Little Dick kicked in, "She thought she was on to something bigger than a man getting whacked."

"That's true, Dick, but to be honest, what kept on playing through my mind was that we—Papa—was unknowingly harboring—"

"A Nazi spy?" finished Monty.

"Yes," I admitted.

Jack Mitchell picked up the pace. "So, tell me more about this man Joe?"

"Well, when we left the building, he just sort of got swallowed up in the crowd of reporters and neighbors who'd gathered out front when the police arrived."

"No, what I mean is, what's this Joe look like?"

"I didn't get a picture of his face, even though I took a dozen shots in the apartment."

I considered how best to describe Joe. I closed my eyes and put into play an exercise drilled into me by a professor at Columbia: the art of observation.

"Late twenties—maybe thirty; wavy auburn hair, light eyes—green or blue, five-ten—a little under six-feet tall, slim, reddish mole just under his. . .left eye. His breath smelled of spent tobacco. His hair tonic—lots of men wear the brand; I just can't tell you which one right now. His attire. . .well, he was buttoning his shirt when I arrived at the landing, and if he hadn't surprised me, I might not have noticed much. I had other things on my mind. But the fact that he was using the hallway as a dressing room. . .Well, the shirt looked odd on him—I can't say why—well, yes! It was too big, in the collar too big. . .and his girl helped him on with his coat. I'd say he was poor, because of the coat: old brown oversize tweedy overcoat, olive green lining— when the woman held it open at the shoulders for him to slip his arms in. There was a label—a red-and-gold lion in-signia, like a coat of arms. Not the sort of coat a young man would choose to wear. An old man's coat, you know? And worn at the cuffs, like he picked it up cheap at a secondhand shop. But wait. His trousers were well-fitting, not baggy. Suit trousers. Gray flannel. And the shoes. Good shoes, the leather shiny, their laces, new, clean."

"Well, that's pretty accurate," said Jack.

"A game we used to play," I said.

"Good."

"Oh, one more thing."

"Yes?"

"There was the trace of an accent in his speech. His *R*s were not rolled, but accentuated. 'ERRR'. When he said *brother*, referring to his girlfriend's brother, well most Amer-icans soften the *R* to a long *A—ahh*, maybe just the hint of the consonant. His was the kind of English learned in the classroom. Excellent, but not homegrown."

"German?"

I thought for a long minute. And then I remembered Dagmar, a German girl whose family immigrated to Canada from Bavaria when she was a child, before moving to New York, in time for us to become high school friends. Joe's ac-cent was familiar to me because I had heard in his speech traces of Dagmar's cadences, betraying her first language, German.

"Yes. Just like Dagmar. . ."

"Dagmar?"

"Never mind, I recognize the accent. Most definitely German."

"Well," said Jack Mitchell, "this is what's going to happen. You and Trumble, here, are going to pretend none of this happened. You will go about your business, back to doing what you usually do. Trumble, go back to chasing those police cars; Devlin, write your little stories for the ladies, if you know what's good for you."

"Why does that sound like a threat?"

"Because it is," he said, matter-of-factly. "Because if you interfere in a federal investigation, now that you know what you know, you will be putting lives at jeopardy, do you understand?"

"You've told us nothing, Jack!" I protested. "I've provided you with information and now you tell us to butt out?"

"It's over."

"*Over?*" I objected. "What do you mean it's *over?*"

Monty jumped in. "Look, Filomena, you stumbled into something dangerous. It's for your own protection that it ends here."

"For my protection?" I fired back. "You insinuate yourself into my father's house, you sock me in the face, you break in and search my apartment, and you talk about protecting me?"

"Listen—Archie knows what I'm doing. You and your friend, here, nearly blew my cover and that of another agent on that ship. And I didn't break into your apartment."

"You probably got one of your goons to paw through my things, looking for evidence."

Jack Mitchell interrupted. "What's this all about?"

"Just what I said. My apartment was broken into."

"When was this?"

"When? Couple of days ago. Don't tell me you don't know about it."

Jack looked inquiringly at Monty, who shook his head.

"Was anything disturbed? Anything taken?"

"What they were searching for obviously wasn't here. I'm sure your people were very careful, but they left their telltale marks of entry. Why, they didn't even bother to lock the front door when they left!"

"Are you sure it wasn't just an ordinary burglary?"

"What? Does a burglar rehang paintings, flip seat cushions, browse through bookshelves, and then leave behind gold jewelry and a sable coat?"

Grim faces avoided my eyes.

"So, you see it's not over for *me*."

Little Dick voiced what Jack and Monty would not. "Your Nazi friends are on to her."

"*They* broke in? Is that what you're saying?" I yelped.

"Well, we didn't."

"So maybe you think Dr. Armbruster—"

"What do you know about Armbruster?" cut in Monty.

"How do you think I knew you were going to be on the SS *New York* last night?"

"He. . .told you?"

"Certainly not."

Monty and Jack looked suspiciously at me.

"I've been following you for days. I saw you hand the envelope with the handkerchief box, the letter, the card, and the passport to the dentist. While in his apartment I opened the envelope—"

"In his apartment!" yelled Monty, incredulous.

"I sealed it back up again—don't get hysterical—and then I followed the big blonde from Armbruster's to the nightclub."

"For God's sake, Filomena!"

"I remember your discussion with the tailor about having something ready before midnight—"

"Wait a minute! You've been spying on me? You overheard what?"

"I just told you I've been tailing you for days. I put two and two together."

I got up, went to the bedroom to retrieve the evidence from the dentist's that I'd tossed in my bureau.

"Your G-men missed these. Smells like a beer hall, I know; they got spritzed."

"Holy!" said Jack, rifling through the photos.

Monty glanced over Jack's shoulder. "Those are photos of the doctored letters I passed to Peacock. They're with the range finder plans. . ."

"What was that?" I asked. "Doctored?"

"Peacock!"

"So Armbruster knows who you are. . ." said Monty.

"Certainly not! I wasn't stupid enough to tell him my real name."

"No," said Monty, "you were just stupid enough to enter a viper's nest!"

"He was very pleasant—not to say I wasn't a little frightened of the man—a Nazi *and* a dentist. I've always been scared to death of dentists since I was ten years old and Dr. Quinn pulled out a—"

"To hell with Dr. Quinn, or whatever his name was!" said Monty. "You're lucky you weren't caught."

Jack interrupted, his voice booming out over ours.

"You!" he said, pointing to me, "sit down!" Then pointing at my nemesis, he bellowed, "Chase! You sit over there while I try to sort this out."

"Good luck," said Monty under his breath.

Fancying himself the voice of reason now, Jack took a pad of legal paper and a pencil from his briefcase and handed them to me.

"Devlin, I want you to write down exactly what you did, when you did it, time and date—"

"Weather conditions?"

Jack rolled his eyes. "If it influenced your actions. I want to read every detail of your activity over the past few days, since you went to that damn Bund rally. You hear me?"

"Well, how could I not? You're shouting. I have a typewriter. Keep your pad," I said, walking to my desk, lifting the lid of the typewriter case, and fitting a sheet of paper through the roller. I sat down and began typing.

"Chase."

"What happened to 'call me Jack, call me Monty?'" I said.

"Monty. . .come on, now. Let's let Miss Devlin write up her story and we go down and get some dinner at the Italian place a couple of doors down?"

"Order the cannelloni," I said. "It's their specialty. Bring me back an eggplant parmesan. Dick? You hungry?"

"I could use—"

The agents were out the door before he could put in his order.

"Quick, Dick," I said popping up from my desk chair, "peek out the door and see if there're any Bureau goons hanging around."

"Kiddo, you're just gonna get into more—"

"Who are you? What did you do with the Dick Trumble I know and love?"

"I'm just saying. . ."

"Check the hall, for cryin' out loud!"

I hurried to the bedroom, tossed off the bathrobe, slipped into my underwear and socks, retrieved a turtleneck sweater from the dresser, pulled on wool slacks, and set my feet into a pair of low-heeled oxfords. Catching my reflection in the mirror I moaned. Where I'd never have been caught dead without makeup, I was glad that Monty got to see how badly he had hurt me. I remembered his expression that I'd interpreted as regret at his violence, whatever good that was; small justice since I was the one suffering.

There was little I could do except dab Max Factor Pan

Stik along the dark bruise that puffed up my cheekbone and eye. I swiped my lips with Coty's Tangerine lipstick, and was running the hairbrush through my hair when Dick called to me from the living room.

"Günter the Hun is guarding the hallway, sitting on the floor reading a comic book."

I pinned up my hair, angled the low-brimmed felt hat to cast a shadow over my swollen eye, secured it with a hatpin, and grabbed my camel coat with the big deep patch pockets below its wasp waist. I chose a pair of cashmere-lined deerskin gloves and walked out into the living room.

"Get your coat, Dick," I said, checking my Mark Cross satchel for the "necessaries"—wallet, press badge, notebook, pencils, handkerchiefs, makeup bag, keys, chewing gun, lemon drops, Cracker Jack box—to ward off sudden hunger pains—a pen knife, and my great big pearl-headed hatpin—protection from mashers and now Nazis. I retrieved a flashlight and put the small camera Juliet had lent me in one coat pocket and subway tokens and loose change in the other.

"What'd I forget?" I asked myself.

"Kitchen sink?"

"Too funny."

"Where'd'a think you're going with that big oaf out there?"

"He's staying there," I said, walking through my bedroom to the street-front windows, beckoning Dick to follow. I lifted the window sash, put my head out, and peered to the street, left, right, and down toward the entry door. No one appeared to be loitering, no one watching the house.

"Come on, Dick; don't forget your hat, now."

I climbed out onto the fire escape, urging Dick to follow.

Thursday, February 23, 1939
9:30 p.m.

Our escape to the street was easy, and once in a taxi heading uptown, we were free to speak our minds.

"We do have a right as reporters to continue our investigation into the death of Herbert Vincent Hanover, Dick, even if the old man's death could be related to the murder of his son, Henry."

"Freedom of the press, blah-blah-blah. I don't need a lesson, kiddo."

"So, do you agree we continue?"

"It doesn't matter if I agree or not. We've got the Bureau to contend with."

"More reason to exercise our right."

"Who are you trying to convince?"

"They have no right telling us what we can or cannot do, Dick!"

"Where are you taking me?"

"The rooming house."

"What do you expect to find there?"

"Answers to the questions Jack Mitchell and Monty won't give us."

"After the cops and the Bureau finished with the crime scene, what do you think is left to find?"

"Not much, you're right, Dick. No, there's something else I want to check out."

"Talk with the boarders, that kind of thing? From what you told me, nobody saw nothing."

"What do you suggest?"

"We go up to Bronxville. I got a hunch that's where the answers are."

We were moving right along up Eighth Avenue and approaching Columbus Circle. The traffic was light after we passed the Theater District—theatergoers deposited from cabs and into their seats as curtains rose over Broadway.

"You're probably right. . .but first I want to. . .explore something...some*one.*"

"Oh yeah?"

"Did you notice how Jack and Monty were very interested in this guy Joe, who was in the house when I arrived that night?"

"Yeah?"

"Why'd you think?"

Little Dick didn't respond right away, but when he did, it was as if he'd been pinched. "Holy crap! No, everything is fine, cabbie; just keep on driving." He turned to look at me and, in a whisper, said, "That guy Joe's story was bull crap."

"I'm sure of it now. He gave me the old Montague versus Capulet scenario. He wasn't there to romance his girl, he was there to shoot Henry."

"Henry was stabbed, Filly."

"Yes, yes, as I've been reminded. Shot, stabbed, he was there to do one or the other."

"Well, which? And why?"

"If we knew that—if Jack and Monty had leveled with us—we wouldn't be doing this."

My stomach was growling in protest. A couple of handfuls of cornflakes hadn't quieted it down. I told the cabbie to pull over for a quick stop at Zabar's.

"It's closed this time of night, kiddo," said Little Dick.

"Hot damn, I'm aching for a bagel and cream cheese!"

We got off at the corner Ninety-Third Street and Columbus Avenue and approached the rooming house, prepared to pretend a casual conversation near the brownstone's stoop. To get in, it was just a matter of waiting for one of the boarders to enter or leave the house.

"Let's hope this is quick, Dick. I'm freezing and I'm starving."

A cab pulled up to the curb and a woman got out. I followed her up the stoop, to the front door, fumbling through my bag for my key, ready with an excuse. But the ruse wasn't necessary.

Could this woman be the illusive Hedy Werner? I thought, as I lingered in the hall, shuffling through the post on the hall table, praying the landlord I met the night of the murder would not suddenly appear. Voices from a radio drama drifted through the house. The woman entered a room beyond the staircase.

I opened the front door for Little Dick. We walked up a flight and continued on past the crime scene—the splintery bullet hole in the room's door a bloodless, gaping wound. I rattled the doorknob. Locked.

Well, I hadn't wanted to look around that room; it was the third-floor rooms that interested me.

"Let's find Joe's girlfriend," I said.

Atop the stairs of the third floor, we faced three doors: a bathroom at center, its door slightly ajar, the slow drip of the sink faucet as steady as the ticking of a clock. Music was playing behind the door of the first room off the landing, in front of which Joe's girlfriend had leaned over the railing that night tossing down to Joe his hat and coat. I took a calming breath and knocked. The door creaked open and a woman, dressed in a floral pink wrapper from the past decade, her hair pin-curled and loosely covered with a red scarf, greeted us with a tentative, "Yes?"

This was not the young woman I had seen with Joe.

"I may have the wrong door," I said apologetically. "I'm looking for a young woman who lives here with her brother?"

She made a sound that sounded something like, "Phew," sniggered, and said, "Is that what she calls him?"

"Can you tell me which—"

"Downstairs, honey, second floor," she said, "but she's split. Went to nurse her sick mother."

I remembered the tenants coming out of their rooms—a screaming woman who emerged from a room on the first floor, a man in the old flannel bathrobe peeking out before retreating back into the room at the top of the second-floor landing, next to Hedy Werner's. There were only two rooms on the second floor, one Hedy's, the other, the bathrobed man's, the shared bathroom in between. She misunderstood me.

"The girl I'm looking for is blonde, in her early twenties—"

"Nobody looks like that lives here, honey."

I tried to put it all together. "You were talking about the woman downstairs, Hedy Werner? You saw her with a man who is her brother?"

"Hey!" she said. "I didn't mean that. I was joking around. I saw this fella go in her room one time, is all, and we're not supposed to entertain in our rooms, so I was just sayin'."

Light dawned as she scrutinized me. She slipped out the door to stand in the hall, her gaze running up and down Little Dick and then back at me. "You're the one found the dead guy."

"Yes. That's right. That's why I'm here. To talk with the girl who was here that night. She was standing right in front of your door."

"Oh yeah? That's funny. I wasn't home that night— well, not until after midnight, after all the excitement."

"How'd you know I found the guy?"

"Just a guess. The cops were looking for you. The landlord described you as dark-haired, green-eyed, with an attitude."

I ignored the critique, even though I wanted to heartily object.

"So, tell us about Hedy Werner, miss," said Dick, moving it along.

"Only saw her one time—passing on the stairs."

Something wasn't right.

"So, did you see Miss Werner *with* the man who entered her room?"

"Now that you put it that way. . .I saw the door open and the guy go in. Who else but her would—"

"Well, that one time you met her in the hall, did you speak? Introduce yourselves?"

"Ahh no. Just said 'hello,' and went on my way."

"What's she look like?" asked Dick, "Dark, fair, tall, pretty?"

"Yep."

"Whattaya mean?"

"Dark hair, fair skin, tall, and pretty. That's Hedy Werner."

"Good guess, Dick."

"If we add the 'attitude' we could be describing you, Filly!"

"I should say," said the woman, adjusting the red scarf to better cover the pin curls. Her hand fluttered as it brushed her breast. Did I get a sense that she was flirting with Little Dick?

"Well, I'm still wondering about this blonde girl I saw here, in front of your door."

"Maybe old Ronnie knows." She thumbed the door at

the end of the hall. "You think she did it?" she said.

"What?"

"Killed the guy."

"The young blonde girl or Hedy Werner?

"Either one."

"Ah no. I don't think so," I said, "I wanted to ask her about the man named Joe she was with."

She crooked a finger to follow her along the hall and knocked on the door of the next roomer. A man peeked out.

"Ronnie, these folks are looking for someone."

The man, around forty, bald, and sporting a five o'clock shadow and a tee-shirt that had seen cleaner days cast suspicious raccoon eyes over us.

"Yeah? What do I know about it?"

"We're looking for a young woman with blond hair who was here—"

"Only in my dreams, honey."

"—the night of the murder downstairs."

In his hand was a newspaper, which he rolled up tightly; he began smacking it in his other palm for emphasis.

"Has nothing to do with me."

Smack!

"Of course not, but—"

"So, why you asking?"

Smack!

"She was with a young man, calls himself Joe—"

Smack!

"For God's sake, Ron, nobody's saying nothin' about you having a lady in your room or anything."

"Then why you knocking on my door, Francie?"

"Just thought you might've seen her night of the murder."

"I seen nothing; I wasn't even here. Go out for a pack of smokes get back and the place is crawling with cops. I don't want no trouble."

Smack!

"Sorry to bother you, mister," I said, backing away from his door.

Francie, whispered, "He's starting over, you know?"

"No, I don't know."

"Spent a year in the pen."

"Oh, he's bitter."

Ronnie must have heard us, because he suddenly opened the door wider, stepped out into the hall, and said, "I don't want no trouble, see."

"The cops hounding you?" asked Little Dick.

"I done my time."

"Oh yeah?" said Dick. "Then why they fingering you?"

"Trying to pin it on me, why else? Can't leave a fellow be, oh no!"

"They question you?"

"I didn't stick around for that. I was in for a burglary rap, nonviolent offender. When I got back to the house, I saw something big had happened, so I made for a bar on the avenue. Stayed at my sister's place. This morning I saw they trashed my room."

I asked, "The cops?"

He nodded.

"Took anything?"

"What do you know about it?"

Paranoid, to boot!

This hothead scared me a little. I wondered if he wouldn't sock me in the face if I pressed him. I didn't need another black eye to match the one I already had; he appeared to be left-handed, by the way he clutched the rolled-up newspaper, both hands squeezing and twisting it now at its center. A visual metaphor for my neck.

Dick said, "Just asking."

He looked at me with wide eyes. Tortured eyes; sleepless eyes. We'd make quite a pair: raccoon couple. I'd've felt a little sorry for him, if that T-shirt wasn't so grimy. I chanced he would control his anger.

"Yeah. Overcoat and shirt." This was said with an air of wonder, like I was a fortune-teller revealing secrets from his past. Suddenly, the chip fell off his shoulder.

"Why would they do that?"

I suspected to see if there was any blood of the victim on his clothes, but I didn't say it.

I was putting it together, now, recalling in my mind's eye not only what I saw, but my *impressions* as I watched Joe and his girl hurriedly attempting his escape. I had unwittingly relayed those impressions to Jack, when he asked me to describe Joe. I had learned the skill of observation in school, but I had not applied the ability until then, had not searched though my memory of that encounter to really *see* what had been presented before me. I was mad at myself for being duped.

"What makes you think the cops took those clothes?"

"Who else? I heard there was a lot of blood. Listen, lady—"

"Cool down, will you? I'm not accusing you of killing the guy. Was it an old tweedy coat with a green lining that got taken?"

The look of amazement lifted his eyebrows.

"It wasn't the cops broke in your room," I said.

"How you know that?"

"The guy who 'gave it' to the man downstairs broke into your room."

"Why'd he do that?"

"Beats me," I lied. "Thanks, mister," I said.

"It weren't the cops?"

"It weren't," I said.

He seemed to appreciate the reassurance; he lightened his grip on the newspaper.

"Thing is, there was a blonde babe with the guy," said Dick.

Francie said, "I still don't know about any blonde hanging around here."

"So, Hedy Werner she wasn't."

"I only saw that Werner woman one time. On-the-road saleswoman I heard. Saw the guy I told you about one time."

"This guy. . .what he look like? This?" said Little Dick, showing her the press clipping from the elder Hanover's funeral story in *The Hour* and pointing to Henry Hanover's photo.

"Yep, that's the guy," said Francie.

Little Dick didn't give her much chance to read the headline, much less the story of the double funeral service; he folded the sheet quickly and popped it back into his breast pocket.

"I missed all the excitement for a movie date with a masher."

I thanked Francie for her help, and then handed her my card, asking that she call me if she remembered anything more about Hedy Werner.

"Well," said Little Dick as we walked to Ninety-Sixth Street, "we now know that Henry Hanover visited Hedy Werner's room sometime before the night of his murder."

"Yeah, according to Francie. More important, we now know that Joe was the killer."

"How you figure?"

"Simple: so-called "Joe" stabs Henry, and Joe's probably covered with blood. He retreats to the floor above the crime scene when Monty and Pudgy arrive, wants to get away by the roof or the back apartment's fire escape—out of Ronnie's apartment. Can't hit the street in bloody clothes, so he ransacks Ronnie's sad wardrobe, finds a shirt that's too big for him—but beggars can't be choosers, as they say— grabs a coat off the hook, and then I come along before it's a done deal."

"Who's the babe with him?"

"Hedy Werner?"

"But Werner's not a blondie."

"But, just a few minutes ago, Francie said something that made me think that Hedy and the blonde I saw with Joe might be one and the same woman. There are wigs, makeup—you know. I figure Monty and his friend Pudgy interrupted Joe—or whatever his true name is—from getting the blueprints from Henry. Monty must have thought the murderer escaped, but the fact was, the murderer never left the building. The killer was the guy named Joe I met in the hall."

"Yeah, kiddo, but why was it necessary for this guy 'Joe' to kill Henry? Whose side was Joe on? Were Joe and Henry both Nazis? Can't figure this one out."

"All we have is speculation. We haven't any facts. Yet."

"So, let's go get some, kiddo."

~~~~

We took a cab up to Bronxville. As we walked along the residential streets, shadows of the bare tree limbs cast haphazard geometrics along the sidewalks from the yellow glow of streetlamps. The snow of the other day had not melted here, where in Manhattan it had been shifted and stomped and driven over into gray slush. Here, snow draped the expansive lawns along the neighborhood, and the figure of a snowman stood like an eerie sentinel within an iron-fenced front yard. I'd have had a hard time finding the house on my own in the darkness, but for Little Dick, who'd been there yesterday to investigate.

As we approached the big brick and timber Tudor

mansion, befitting the recently deceased elder manufac-
turer and his wife, and where also had lived his son and
daughter-in-law, Dick hesitated.

"What's wrong? Is this or is it not the house, Dick?"

"Yeah, it is. But the house is dark; no one's there," he
said, throwing a hand in its direction. "What are we supposed to do? I mean, it's late, even the neighbors are asleep."

We stood at the entrance to a wide semicircular driveway. I appraised the situation, looking at the height of the
lower floor's leaded glass windows, trying to assess how to
get in. That's when I saw a dim light tracing the windows of
the ground-floor right wing.

"Someone's inside," I said to Dick, who hadn't seen
the light. "Well, then, we don't have to break in."

"What are you talking about *break in*?" he said, in a
hoarse whisper. "We didn't talk about anything like breaking in, Filly!"

"Well, we won't have to now."

His relief was palpable when he sighed.

"Why else did we come here?" I said. "A neighbor
told you Henry's wife left the country. Her husband and in-
laws are dead. No one else lives here."

"I figured maybe a maid or somebody would be here."

"The housekeeper answered the phone. What are you
doing?" hissed Dick, as I strode up the driveway to the porte
cochere at the right side of the house. "Filly, stop!"

"I'm just going to ring the doorbell, silly, not break in
or anything."

"But it doesn't make sense that someone is in the

house walking around with a flashlight."

"Burglar?"

"Oh right . . ."

"Wait. When Henry's wife beat it out of town, maybe she had the electric company shut off service."

"That still doesn't tell us who's in the house. Up to no good, I'll bet."

"Let's find out," I said, continuing to the porte cochere. Dick hurried after me. I turned and stopped him in his tracks. "Wait. You go over to the front door," I said, pointing to the public entrance to the house. "Ring the doorbell. If whoever is in the house has a legitimate reason to be there, they'll answer the bell. If whoever is in the house shouldn't be there, they'll leave through the side, where I'll be stationed."

"I don't know. . . There must be more than just the two ways out."

"Yeah, sure, but I'll see 'em leave. I'll be where there's a view of the rear of the house, as well as the garages. Now keep ringing the bell, and don't be polite about it."

"You mean, lean on it? I don't know why I let you— oh, what the hell?" he said, tugging the brim of his fedora down low over his brow and stuffing his hands into the pockets of his overcoat. He turned and I watched as he sashayed toward the front door like a teetering coatrack come to life. After he reached his destination, he was lost to me in the shadows.

I dashed along the driveway to the porte cochere and continued past to an arbor, which in the summer must be covered with roses, but in winter was a mass of prickly frozen sticks. Here I had a view of the back of the house and the sprawling lawn.

But the sky was dark, no moon had risen, and the shadows of the house, thrown wide by the streetlamps, hung over me. The rear of the building was pitch black. I nestled within the arbor to wait, listening.

It wasn't long before I heard the *swoosh* of a door opening and the crunch of footfalls on the crusty snow-cover. Looking through the lattice slats, my eyes, now adjusted to the dark, caught movement—shadow overlapping shadow—moving from the back of the building and heading in my direction.

What the hell do I do now? I asked myself. What was I going to accomplish standing here, hidden? I was frightened by what might happen if discovered.

But wasn't that why I was here? To affect a confrontation? To catch a thief?

People had been murdered, I realized during those seconds as I heard the approach, and there I stood, unarmed.

I had been cold a moment before, and now sweat was trickling down my back, and my heart raced. There was nowhere to hide.

What the hell was I doing?!

I hadn't time to think it out—I should have done that before I was in this predicament—so I was flying by the seat of my well-tailored trousers when I dug deep into my bag and my hand gripped cold metal.

I switch on my flashlight and the light caught the figure of a man. Was I seeing things? Isn't that "Joe" from the rooming house?

After a second of disorientation, a hand thrown up against the glare, he barreled toward me, like a runaway truck on a downhill trajectory, toting a small boxy suitcase. My midsection suffered a fierce wallop. Knocked down on the crusted snow, my shoulder bag strangling my neck, I felt the hard kick of his foot as he stomped over me before disappearing into the dark.

What did he have in that case? A bowling ball?

Winded and in mind-numbing pain, I staggered to my feet, and then fell to my knees, where I surrendered to the ground. Doubled over, I tried to find my voice to yell for Dick, but all I could emit was a hoarse gasp.

I was impervious to the cold, to the snow, to my environs, to sight and sound; I was trapped inside the pain. I was calling out, but I didn't hear my voice, even though my mouth was forming silent pleas.

And then, as the sharp biting pain eased into a throbbing ache, I heard from a distance the bark of a dog, its frantic, frenzied keening breaking through the night's silence. Returning to the world, I became aware that the whole neighborhood of dogs joined in the chorus of outrage. I heard a light thumping, like horse hooves on turf, before I realized I was about to be beset upon by a canine posse. What to do?

I rolled over onto my chest, my ribs burning, and stayed motionless, submissive, despite my terror. The black monster pounced on me, pinning me down. The creature growled; hot, steamy breath blasted the back of my neck; slobber whipped at my hair, my hat now a chew toy.

I was nudged repeatedly as the dog began to whine when I didn't respond to his bullying.

"Daisy!" yelled out a voice. "Daisy! Get over here, for cryin' out loud!"

"My God! What have you done, you bad dog?"

With a click of a metal, the hundred pounds lying on my back was lifted. I rolled over. A dark gloved hand helped me rise to my feet, and steadied me as I tried to regain my balance. Apologies were profusely offered, as well as offers of assistance to the warmth of the house next door.

"Are you sure you're all right?"

"Yes," I managed to say. "I just fell."

"Yes, I see that. Daisy thought you were a fox," said the man. "I am so sorry she knocked you down. What were you doing out here in the middle of the—?"

I had to think quickly. I used the few seconds of brushing off my coat and retrieving my battered hat and satchel to compose a story.

"I just stopped by the Hanovers' to offer my condolences to Henry and Margaret on the death of his parents," I said, lying through chattering teeth, "but it appears no one's at home."

Wow! I thought, *the lies are just pouring out of me tonight. I should run for Congress.*

I tried to breathe, but the very act of filling my lungs hurt. Broken ribs?

"Be still, Daisy!" The man chided the dog, a black Labrador retriever. Her owner was a husky man of middle age and out of breath from the exertion of the chase. He turned back to face me, assessing any possible injuries caused by his runaway pet, who was now smacking the backs of my knees with an exuberant wagging of her tail.

"Then you haven't heard the news?" said the man, his tone weighty with regret. I waited, dumb, for him to continue.

"Henry is dead, I'm afraid."

I made the appropriate sounds of shock—*What? Oh no! Say it isn't so! Poor Margaret! I must go to her*—but no one *is answering the door!*—which sent Daisy into an empathetic round of nuzzling at my hand. The man elaborated as I knew he would.

"First the old Mrs. Hanover, Lillian, dies from a fall down the stairs, and then her husband, Herbert, dies of a heart attack the day of the funeral! But who'd have thought that within only a couple of days, their son, Henry, would be attacked and killed on the street by a knife-wielding robber!"

So that's the story they gave—whoever *they* were— people: mugged on the street.

"Oh my God! Say it isn't so! How could this be?" Blah, blah, blah. . .

"Yes, it is true."

"And Margaret?" I said, "I must go to her!"

"Margaret? All alone in that big house with only servants to see to her needs, well, she just picked up and flew away."

I thought, I could be alone in my house with only servants to see to my needs and I'd be happy as a clam.

"Well, that explains why the house is dark and nobody's home. But I must go to her!"

"Cuba."

"Cuba?"

"Yes. She flew off to Cuba. For a rest, I presume."

"When does she return?"

"I don't know."

"You said she went to Cuba for a rest. How do you know for sure?"

"Well, yes, that's what Roger told our gardener. We share the same man, you see. Lawns and borders in the summer, snow removal and pruning in the winter. . . ."

"Roger?"

"Margaret's brother."

"Oh yes, of course, her brother. Where can I find Roger?"

"I can't say—I mean, I don't really know. I suppose he left when they closed down the house."

"He was living with them?"

"Well, yes! He was living with the family. My wife mentioned that she saw Margaret and Roger together at some restaurant, she didn't know he was her brother, and for a minute she thought the worst, but it turned out that Margaret wasn't stepping out on Henry, which was her first impression, but had stopped for a bite to eat after she'd picked Roger up from the train station when he first arrived here. You know how gossip gets started, these women."

I wanted to say that men are of equal fault when it came to gossip and rumor—after all, no one can easily measure the vitriol of Walter Winchell—or Alexander Woollcott. Take a seat at any bar, men's club or locker room and you'll get an earful. But I didn't want to dam the flow of information this man was giving me, so I kept mum.

"I haven't seen Margaret for a long time. Has Roger been here long?"

"Since autumn—yes, around then."

"How nice that the family took him in."

"Roger? I don't know him, really. Never met him. Just waved at him when I saw him a couple of times."

Something flashed over the man's face; the sudden shift in his attention, as if he was shutting down the discussion. I took a giant leap.

"Well, if I remember Margaret telling me, Roger was a handful when they were growing up."

The fellow immediately perked up and was back in my game.

"I'd say it's never easy when an in-law moves in—I've got a sister-in-law I could do without. Came for a week and stayed three months!"

"I pity you!"

He laughed, and then, finding me sympathetic, said, "No love lost between Henry and Roger."

"They didn't get on?"

"I should think not."

"They argued?"

"Well, yes. But it was the elder Mrs. Hanover; her

complaints were quite audible," he chuckled. "Warm October night, windows open—sound travels, you know."

He leaned in conspiratorially, and continued, "I think the old gal wasn't crazy about her daughter-in-law in the first place, and she didn't like the brother."

"Oh?"

He nodded, as the retriever pulled hard on the leash. The dog was bored with the conversation and anxious to nose out some enticing scent along the hedge border.

"Well, servants talk, you know. Our maid and the Hanovers' maid, well, servants talk."

"What tragedy! *Tsk, tsk, tsk. . .*"

So, I wondered, did the daughter-in-law push her mother-in-law down the stairs? I wanted to talk with these maids, but it would raise suspicions if I asked to talk to this man's servant now, at this late hour. Tomorrow, when he left for the office I could come by his house. . .

If all the Hanovers are dead, I wondered, what's to become of Hanover Aeronautics? Who inherits? Does the young Mrs. Hanover, Margaret, get it all? Or were there other heirs to the kingdom? I had to find out. In the morning would *not* be soon enough.

After we said good-night, I pretended to walk down the drive and toward the street, until I was out of sight of Daisy and her master, then doubled back around. I figured a door or window at the back of the house would have been left open when Joe made his escape.

As suspected, a French door off the stone-terraced patio was ajar.

I felt suddenly nauseous. After throwing up into bushes lining the patio, my churning stomach settled. I walked through heavy drapery, closed the door, and pulled the curtains.

The light of my flashlight swept the wood-paneled room, its beam illuminating photographs hanging on the wall, images of the elder Hanover, Herbert, shaking hands with Woodrow Wilson, sharing a laugh with Al Smith at a political rally. There was Herbert side by side and in conversation with Franklin Roosevelt, the men posed before an aeroplane hangar identified as Hanover Aeronautics, its legend emblazoned over the bay. Was that General Pershing dining out with Herbert and Lillian?

A desk dominated the room. I turned on the lamp.

From the disarray of piled paper and the drawer of a wooden file cabinet gaping open, I knew the room had been searched. Probably before Little Dick had surprised him ringing the doorbell. Which brought me to the realization that my friend might still be outside, around the front of the house, unaware of the commotion on the side lawn and my mauling by an overcurious canine.

As I started to leave the room, my eyes alighted on photographs placed in a niche between the bookcases. A tintype of Herbert and his wife, Lillian, exiting cathedral doors, a crowd of top-hatted gents and bustle-skirted women lining their path.

Next to the silver-framed elders stood the wedding photograph of Henry and Margaret, taken during the midtwenties, by the look of her tightly fitted, brow-skimming cap and veil. This photo was posed in a studio, the couple at center standing before a scenic backdrop, a dozen members of the wedding party trailing to the edges. All the women held huge bouquets; the morning-suited ushers posed at three-quarter profile, three flower girls and a ring bearer on the floor at their feet. I was about to abandon my scrutiny of the photo, remembering Little Dick standing out in the cold, when my eyes were drawn back to the photo. I leaned in for a closer look. The bride wore sleek silk charmeuse. . .

Now it was coming together.

I walked to the door, entered a short hall, off of which were several rooms. I continued straight, in the direction of the center and front of the house. Turning the corner into a large pillared space, my light fell on statuary and potted ferns; under my feet was the checkerboard pattern of terrazzo tiles. When the fan window crowning the front door caught and reflected light back into my eyes, I cupped the bowl of the flashlight and switched it off. I sensed movement at my side, and upon turning, startled, my flashlight now a weapon, my arm swept out in defense of imminent assault but instead made contact with the great vase filled with a silk floral arrangement on a table positioned at the center of the room. The resulting crash of fine porcelain rang through the house as I felt my flailing arm caught in a tight grip.

Oh crap! I thought. Joe had followed me back into the house!

After a moment's panic, my instincts took over. My

bag slipped off my shoulder as I backed up close to my captor. In one swift movement I grabbed the offending hand that restricted me, bent my right leg at the knee, kicked my foot back to make heel-to-shin contact, and moved into position to flip the attacker over my shoulder.

As I attempted the maneuver, pain wracked my rib cage. I aborted the move and instead threw him over my thigh. My attacker was a lightweight—weighed less than me. The cry of helplessness, as coattails in flight grazed my hat, rang familiar.

Poor man, I thought as I recognized the bag of bones at my feet, thinking he could certainly use a little fat on those bones.

The moaning stopped when he regained his senses and the air in his lungs. But he looked up at me with a perplexed stare, as if awaiting my answer to his question.

"The back door was open, Dick," I said, offering a hand around his back to support his rise. The gesture caused a stab to my torso. I winced and croaked out, "How did you get in?"

"Cellar door."

I told him about the various tussles I'd endured with both man and beast while he was rummaging around the house.

"Sorry if I hurt you, Dick."

"No sorrier than me," he said, rubbing the back of his head.

"Find anything of interest while I was in the wrestling ring?"

"Sure did; found this," he said, removing from his coat pocket a small cylindrical metal object, pronged on one end.

"What is it?"

"A spent tube. For a radio. Specific to a radio, see? It's a 6SC7."

"I see. What's it mean other than the Hanover's owned a radio?"

"One of the Hanover's was a shortwave radio ham. The radio itself is nowhere to be found. There's a workshop room in the basement. I found this because one workbench surface was completely clear of clutter, while the rest of the room was a mess with stuff. It was this pad," he said, offering up the notepad to me, "that drew my attention, see? The only thing on the otherwise clear workbench."

"It's blank."

"So it is. That's when I caught sight of the radio tube on the floor."

I took a pencil from my bag and positioning the lead tip of it at an angle rubbed it along the paper's surface. There, revealed in the depressions, was a series of letters. It was hard to discern any meaning from the symbols, but I knew that what I was looking at was a coded message, the ghostly remains from the original writing paper torn off the pad.

"You found this in the cellar? So, where is this radio hidden?" I asked Dick.

"Can't find the radio."

I nodded and thought, small suitcase. I remember thinking the wallop registered against my stomach made me think of a bowling ball—and I was the pin.

So, this was the Nazi spy nest. And the Hanover family were the Nazis.

"These people had a shortwave radio station here, out of their basement. There's wiring. I followed it to a disabled antenna out back of the house."

Everything had changed over the past twenty-four hours. The evidence I'd gathered and witnessed firsthand had brought me to the false conclusion that Montgomery Chase was a Nazi spy.

Assumptions—my cynical, unsubstantiated machinations arisen from that little weekly Bronx newspaper, *The Hour*, suggested to my mind a black comedy—by the sheer cheerfulness of the reporting of the double deaths—that the double funeral was a convenient way for a son to gain monetarily. A multimillion-dollar aeronautics company had dropped into Henry Hanover's lap, along with whatever fortune his old man had personally accrued.

Evidence pointed to Hedy Werner operating as a Nazi operative; that Joe, who was at first just a guy named "Joe" and an opportunist, stealing a watch and wallet from a dead man.

It was all wrong!

I had been prejudiced against Monty and had lost all objectivity. Something nagged at me. Something that I saw or heard that didn't make sense. But what was it?

The evidence we'd accrued led me down dead ends because the motives of the main players were far from certain. Then I recalled the lesson one of my professors had stressed: *when investigating a story, one should not ignore ev-idence that might be contrary to the journalist's preconceptions. Don't interpret evidence to fit one hypothesis. The best journalist is also a good detective. Both are bound to seek the truth, and rather than try to fit the evidence into establishing a fixed hypothesis, allow all the gathered evidence to determine the hypothesis.*

I could see that I had been steering toward conclusions that would prove my preconceived notions. I knew now, by remembering details of that murderous night in the rooming house, that Joe had played a more sinister role.

I could make a lot of excuses—that Jack and Monty didn't tell me what-was-what and who-was-who in the scheme of things. National security.

But the truth was I had wanted to believe Montgomery Chase was a Nazi. To fault him. And my ego (as well as my eye) was bruised when I learned Monty was not a spy. I had been even more frazzled to learn he was an important figure in our country's fight against Fascism. That he was not the vacuous movie idol I'd perceived him to be, but a patriot employing his skills as an acclaimed actor. My uneasiness around the man had prejudiced me because of my feelings about him, those teenage crush feelings that I'd been embarrassed about.

And the special place he had in my father's heart.

I'd heard Papa once say to Mama that Monty was like the son he'd always wanted. So, no matter how many Giants games I went to with Papa, no matter how hard I tried to be the newspaperman that would make him proud, I was not enough by the very chance of gender. So, truth be told, I hadn't wanted to look beyond casting blame on Monty.

At the moment, I didn't know for sure what roles any of these characters played in the drama. I told Little Dick of my discovery of the wedding photograph.

"Where could Joe have gone?" asked Dick.

"He could be anywhere. I doubt he'll keep the identity of Roger, Margaret's brother."

"Beating it out of the country, I'll bet."

"He won't be easy to find. If he's a spy, he might have multiple passports."

"We better telephone Jack so they can stop him at the docks. Maybe he's heading for a train out of the city, or even at the bus station," said Dick.

"Or he's got a car."

"That poses a problem. Who knows what he's driving!"

"No time to call Jack," I said.

Big house. . .rich people lived here.

"Let's go to the garage."

"Around back, end of the driveway past the porte cochere."

I hadn't seen or heard a car pass down the drive, even though I was no more than fifty feet from the driveway, under the arbor when my attacker dashed by. But then, I was doubled over in pain before being terrorized by a slobbering canine.

"Maybe he parked it on the street, or around the block for all we know. Let's check out the garage."

We hurried out through the French doors, the way I'd

come in, stopping for a moment at the office desk to take another look at the paper pad under the student lamp. I tore off the top sheet and held it in front of the light. Now, the paper translucent, I was able to see what I'd failed to see with just the light of my flashlight. It confirmed my hunch.

"Let's steal a car, Dick!"

"All right."

"You sound agreeable."

"Just resigned. What's grand theft auto after breaking and entering?"

"Right," I replied. "But we need to get there before he does."

"Before he gets where?"

"Wherever *there* is."

"We gotta call Jack at the Bureau, Filly!"

"We will. Just as soon as we know for sure."

"Know what, for cryin' out loud?"

"If he winds up where I think he's going."

"Well, that tells me exactly *nothing!*"

"Well, well, well," I said, as we entered the huge garage bay through a side door, "looks like we've got to decide on the Silver Ghost, the Daimler or the Caddy sedan. The Dusie is too ostentatious. Oh," I sighed, "but what a lovely ride."

The little room to the side of the bay held the keys to three automobiles on the wall rack. The fourth key was missing, under the label *'36 Auburn*. I figured that was Joe's getaway car.

Dick opened the garage doors and I scooted into the

Daimler's driver's seat and started the motor. I hadn't driven a car in ages, maybe years, and I forced the stick in reverse, popping the clutch a couple of times before I got the feel for it.

"Hey! Try to keep this thing from hopping down the street."

"Driving's like riding a bicycle. You never forget."

"Well, your memory is failing, if you ask me," he said, over the grinding of gears, as I attempted to put the clutch in first. Soon, we were hopping down the long drive and approaching the street when headlights glared and a siren blared in our path, nearly blinding me and stopping my heart. I stamped on the brake pedal, forgetting to engage the clutch pedal at the same time and the automobile shuddered to a stop, the engine stalled.

"Get out of the car!" came a disembodied voice. There were shadowy figures breaking through the bright glare. I could make out the column of automobiles, some with flashing lights, blocking the gate and lining the driveway.

"Holy shit!" said Little Dick. "Stop, Filly! What the hell are you doing?" screeched Dick, as I swerved the car sharply to the left off the drive and gunned the engine. We crossed the front lawn, clipping the boxwood hedges and narrowly avoiding the vehicular homicide of the Greek goddess. The expression, "pedal to the metal" popped to mind, and that's exactly what I did, once we hit the pavement with a mighty lurch off the icy snow bank that bordered the road.

"This thing is a yacht," I said. The front end extended the length of a football field. It took a while for me to get the hang of turning corners without leaping over the curbs.

The urgent whine of sirens got louder; we had the advantage of distance; the cops had to hop back into their vehicles, had to back out of the driveway, scramble around and into position for the pursuit.

There was no sign of the Auburn. Few cars were on the street at this hour. This wasn't Manhattan where the city never sleeps. But we had to shake the cops; the car stood out like a diamond broach on a thrift shop rag.

Ahead was a commercial strip of buildings. I turned a corner in an attempt to get off the main road, and as we approached, I saw the sign of an A&P grocery store up ahead. I slowed. A driveway off the street was shielded by a canvas-covered truck parked on the street and vegetable stalls lined the other side obstructing the view from the street. I pulled into the drive, no bigger than an alley, and drove back to the store's loading dock.

I dashed the headlights.

"Why don't we just let the boys catch us?" said Little Dick. "Saves us the nickel for the phone call."

"Oh yeah? You want to spend the next three or four hours trying to explain what we were doing in the house? They probably think we're burglars. Why else were they at the house? Somebody saw us prowling around and—"

"You're right; we'd have a lot of explaining to do."

"So, we've got to shake them."

"Then what are we waiting for? Let's ditch this luxury cruiser!"

"Hold your horses, Dick! We need transportation."

"But they're looking for this car, Filly!"

"Listen, will you?" I said as the sirens got closer, and then, after a few moments of breath-holding, receded into the distance.

"Good, we're all right now."

"For the time being," I said, slowly backing out of the alley before turning on the headlights. "Now where the hell are we, Dick?"

"Beats me."

"Well, we got to find somebody by the name of Breslau. Ever hear of him?"

"How would I know? Wait a minute; let me ask the great and powerful oracle."

"Dick, don't be obtuse." I handed him the notepaper that had yielded a ghostly impression under the graphite. He shone my flashlight over it.

"There're numbers after the name. Looks like a phone number."

I said, "What're we supposed to do, dial it and ask for Breslau?"

"No. We need to call the telephone company and ask for them to check it in the reverse directory for the address of that line."

"Why didn't I think of that?"

I'd seen a neighborhood bar on the block before I'd turned into the alley. It was difficult, but I managed to turn the car around after a couple of bumps on the back fender and maneuvered the "tank" to return the way we'd entered. I parked just at the alley entrance, and I got out of the car.

I sidestepped where an overindulger had wretched on the sidewalk and walked into the bar. It was a dark and depressing place, the atmosphere rife of spent whiskey and stale pretzels. The barkeep pointed to the rear of the room when I asked for the phone booth.

Passing a lineup of mostly elderly men on the barstools, the downtrodden refuge of our Great Depression and failed Prohibition, I spotted the phone booth beside an unsavory restroom. I was stopped in my tracks when I saw who entered the booth, illuminated in a flash of light as he closed its door.

He cracked open the bifold just enough, so the booth's light went off, dropped a coin in the slot, and dialed. I slunk back along the wall near the foul toilet room to eavesdrop Joe's side of the conversation.

Had I been fluent in German, I would have gotten more than the gist from Joe's tone that he was harried and hurried.

Until. . .

"Lindenhurst. . ." said Joe with a question in his voice. "Ya, Shorty's, Merrick Road, danke."

The receiver was replaced, and the door swung open. I held my breath, praying that he would not need the restroom. As I watched him walking down the aisle toward the front door, I went into the booth, pulled a nickel out of my pocket, and dialed the telephone number imprinted on the notepaper. The operator came on the line and demanded ten cents more for the long-distance call.

A familiar voice greeted me after the first ring. Shook

to my core, I hung up.

I picked up the receiver, dropped the nickel in the slot, and dialed.

Eva picked up.

"Is Monty there?"

"He's out."

"What about Rocco?"

"You mean Rory; he told us to call him Rory."

"All right, Rory! Is he home?"

"He's in his room, I think."

"Eva, can you get him to the phone? It's important."

"But he may be asleep."

"He'll want you to wake him."

"Well, let me call up to him."

It seemed to take forever, but finally, Rocco picked up on the second-floor extension.

"Let's get crackin'!" I said when I returned to the car.

"Filly, while you were belting back cheap gin, I saw a guy drive past in an Auburn, late model. How many of those do you see around?"

"That was Joe, Dick," I said, pulling out of the alley. "Which way is Lindenhurst?"

"What? You want to go to Long Island this time of night? Oh right! Long Island! That's where Lindenhurst is!"

"You're going in the wrong direction."

"You know how to get there?"

"Merrick Road, sure."

"How do you know that? I didn't tell you yet."

"I don't know. I was hoping you could tell me."

We could go on like this forever. So, I briefed Little Dick of the overheard conversation.

"Aside from a detail here or there, I believe I've figured it out!"

"Want to share this revelation with me?"

"Where to begin? All right, from the beginning. Although the story in *The Hour* put us on this trail of a couple murdering the family patriarch for monetary gain, we had it all wrong!"

"Let me jump ahead for a moment: it was Joe—or as he posed in the Hanover household, Roger. It was he who stabbed Henry in the rooming house."

"How did you work that out?"

"I think Joe was in cahoots with Henry's wife, Margaret. I doubt they are brother and sister, even though they identified as siblings.

"I think what happened was the old woman, Lillian, Henry's mother, discovered their conspiracy—found out they were Nazis. So, Joe or Henry's wife, Margaret, pushed the elder Mrs. Hanover down the flight of stairs to her death. According to the neighbor I encountered tonight, there was strife in the household between the daughter-in-law, Roger, and the elder Hanovers."

"Hanover Aeronautics designs parts and develops new applications for the Air Force and Navy, as well as commercial airliners. They have government contracts."

"Yes, Dick, that's exactly what I suspect. Many of the company's inventions would be valuable to an enemy nation planning on waging war against us. I'll bet the old gal found Joe and Margaret out and would have exposed them for the Nazi spies they were, so she had to be silenced. And when she died, and the old man suspected something unsavory was going on, Joe and Margaret done him in. I don't believe Henry had anything to do with the deaths of his parents."

"Okay, but that's a great leap."

"First, only a madman kills his own parents, even when there is a lot of money to be gained from their murder. And second, if you took a tour of Henry's office, there on the walls is the evidence of the man's American patriotism. Both he and his father, Herbert, and the company they built, have only *contributed* to the benefit of America's military defense. *And* Henry fought in the Great War. He flew fifty-eight missions against the Huns."

"You discovered all that after a glimpse at a wall?"

"I could read what kind of people the Hanovers were. Yes, it was documented on the walls. Henry was not a traitor to his country."

"So, Henry wasn't part of the spy ring?"

"The questions are: Had Henry been lured to the rooming house for nefarious purposes? Was Henry's intent to stop Joe from delivering the blueprints to his Nazi cohorts?"

"Remember Monty said the plans he delivered to the *SS New York* were doctored? I'll put my money on the scenario that Henry called the FBI and was working with the G-men to snare Joe. But something went wrong. Monty didn't get to the rooming house in time to stop Joe from killing Henry. Either way, Henry was a hero!"

"We could have known for certain if Monty and Jack had leveled with us about what went down," said Dick. "How did you arrive at this. . .*twist*?"

"Well, it was Joe. His shirt was too big—the one he was tucking into his trousers when I first saw him at the rooming house."

"That's a stretch."

"And the shabby overcoat. It just didn't square with his high-end shoes."

"Okay. . ." said Dick, fitting the pieces together. When it finally hit him he shouted out, "*Okay!*"

I shivered as I remembered Henry Hanover's terrified expression as he raised a shaking hand to point a finger toward a place beyond me. I thought the gesture was the dying man's focus into *the Beyond*. Now I understood that he was pointing to his murderer, standing near the door.

Hmm, he'd moaned, blood choking his hard-pressed words.

Him!

At the time, had I understood that Henry was pointing in accusation against the man standing inches away, I might not have made it out of the rooming house alive. I shivered. Yes, Joe played his part as frustrated lover very well.

"So, it was the shoes gave him away?"

"To be truthful, Dick, I didn't fully grasp the clues that were right in front of me until Monty and Jack pressed me for a description of Joe. But the shoes spoke volumes. The clothes he arrived in must have been bloodied after he stabbed Henry. Why else don oversize clothing? It was all he could get his hands on in his attempt to escape down the fire escape off Ronnie's back apartment."

"What about the gunshots? That's what brought the police to the scene."

"I think Monty shot at Joe when he discovered him fleeing, after I saw a scuffle in the window before the shot rang out. Monty obviously missed his mark; the evidence was the bullet hole in the door. Monty didn't know Joe ran up the stairs to the third floor, not down and out of the building. When I discovered the briefcase in Monty's closet the next morning and saw the gun, I knew it had been fired recently. I could smell the gunpowder.

"I figure Joe didn't have time to retrieve the briefcase without getting shot. Monty thought he'd run out the front door of the house, but he was just upstairs, in that fellow Ronnie's room with Margaret, intending to return to Hedy Werner's room to fetch the briefcase. He couldn't escape the rooming house in blood-covered clothing."

"Wait a minute!" said Dick, causing me to slam on my brakes. "You think the blonde Joe was with was Margaret Hanover? How'd you arrive at *that*?"

"Why, the photo of Margaret and Henry's wedding I discovered tonight. I recognized her. Margaret and Hedy Werner are one and the same person."

"Holy canary!" Dick said, as I restarted the engine. "Why, then, didn't Monty and Jack tell us that Henry Hanover wasn't a Nazi spy?"

In my mind, I flipped through the various possibilities, the reasons why the agents had not just told us the truth.

"I suppose they didn't want two gung ho reporters trampling through their investigation. And we were doing just that, weren't we? When it comes to national security, they weren't obliged to tell us anything. They figured we would just do as we were told, toe the line."

"That's never been my style, and after tonight, I see it's not yours. Well, this is a new angle," said Dick. "I suppose Margaret got out down the fire escape."

"And Pudgy saw the opportunity to grab the briefcase that held the plans," I said. "If he hadn't been killed those blueprints would have been lost to Germany."

"Turn left at the next corner. We're heading for the Tri-Borough Bridge."

"So, tell me, what's in Lindenhurst?"

"Nothing much. It's a town off the Great South Bay that was settled last century by German immigrants. And—you were just a kid—bootleggers ran businesses out on the Island. Irish rumrunners shipped their cargo from Europe via the Great South Bay. Merrick Road was a fuel line to the city. Turn left here," Dick said.

The new Tri-Borough Bridge loomed ahead through the rising fog; its lights eerily glowing orbs.

Friday, February 24, 1939
2:45 a.m.

After a nearly two-hour drive through the Bronx and Queens, a stop for gasoline, and a dark, increasingly foggy drive along the Sunrise Highway, we picked up Merrick Road.

Soon visibility was reduced to only a dozen feet beyond the Daimler's headlamps as the fog thickened. I rolled down my window. A warm front was coming in. I could smell the salty tang of the sea. Condensation dripped off the foggy interior of the windshield. Dick kept it wiped off with his scarf.

"How in hell are we supposed to find the place in this pea soup?"

"We're looking for a garage," said Dick. "How many garages could there be on this strip?"

Through the thickened atmosphere, the lonesome call of a distant foghorn sounded its lament.

Past boarded-up clam stands and variety stores, seafood restaurants and bait shops, many closed for the winter, we rolled eastward along Merrick Road.

And then, just as I was about to groan a complaint at Dick, I spotted the garage. The place appeared totally dark and I couldn't see a legend above the shack, and if it had not been for the Texaco signs on the pumps we might have passed right by it. But we knew it was Shorty's Garage because there was an Auburn parked at the side of the building. I pulled to the other side of the two-lane highway and parked at the rear of a tackle shop, out of view of the garage.

"Dick, you stay in the car."

"What do you mean?! You're not going anywhere. We have to wait for Monty and the feds to arrive."

"I'm going to sneak over there and see if Joe is inside."

"Well, we know he's there, because the Auburn is there."

"He might have met this guy Shorty and left by now. Ditched the car."

"All right, but hurry up. You never know. . ."

"Never know what?"

"I don't know. You just don't."

I threw my satchel over my shoulder and crossed the road. I was afraid of being seen from the little window in the shack, so I made a wide curve and crept around the bay toward the rear of the little building.

A faint light glowed from the shack's rear window, affording me enough light not to knock over the trash can I was about to stumble upon. I gingerly crept closer and ducked down, and in a daring moment popped up to peek inside.

A hurricane lamp illuminated the faces of Joe and another man, one I didn't recognize. The telephone number he had called earlier was at the home of Dr. Armbruster, but it was not he who arrived at this rendezvous. Was this Shorty? He was taller than Joe. . .

I could hear their muffled conversation, but they refused to speak in English! I was getting nowhere fast spying on these Germans. I decided I would return to the Daimler and we'd wait it out, keep an eye on the place, and see what they did next, while we waited for Monty and his G-men to arrive.

But before I knew it, I heard movement, then the creak of the back door opening. I scrambled away and ducked down in the shadows. I held my breath—I'd been doing a lot of that this night. Amazing I was still alive.

"Ist es weit von hier?"

"Nein."

"Gut."

A negative answer to a question. And *goot*. . .good!

What could I make of this?

But judging from their body language, Shorty was bringing Joe somewhere and it was walking distance, since they abandoned the Auburn and began walking through the sandy yard behind the shack and to where the property met a road just off Merrick.

I had to make a decision: go back to Little Dick and follow in the Daimler—the headlights alerting the men that they were being followed—or wait for the posse to arrive?

I ran back across the street to the car, scared Dick half to death when I opened the driver's side door, jumped in, and started the motor. The headlights off, and at a very slow speed, I pulled into the side road. The entrance was lit by a streetlamp and the fog had dissipated enough so that I could see the men walking ahead. That's when Dick said he knew where we were.

"Glad you do, 'cause I don't."

There was dark water to our right as we entered the road. Boats were moored, most covered with tarps for the winter.

We passed a tall venetian column with a winged lion atop it. "This is the entrance to American Venice."

"Okay, where are the gondolas?"

"You laugh, but there were gondolas. Look, a little bridge, fashioned after those in Venice. This was a vacation development started in the early twenties, modeled after the Italian city for New York City folk to buy summer homes, bungalows built along the canal systems which open into the Great South Bay. It never took off because of the Crash."

And walking over the bridge was our quarry. I pulled the car as far off the road as I could to wait for the men to clear the bridge. I didn't want to follow too closely for fear they would hear the engine. When they were out of view, I decided we should continue.

But I had not anticipated that the side of the road would be a sandy shoulder. All sand, and we were stuck in it. I revved the engine, turned the wheel first left and then right, put it in reverse and then in first, but it was futile. And getting out and pushing the car wasn't going to work. The car was a monster built of steel. We needed a tow.

We were going to lose them!

"We're going nowhere fast," said Dick.

We bolted out of the car.

"I'm following them," I announced. "You need to get back to the garage and wait for the troops to arrive, and if they haven't, break in, and use the phone to call the police. I'll see where these guys go and come right back to you."

"If you ask me, I don't like it."

"I'm not asking you. One of us has to find out where they end up. I'll join you as soon as I know."

I didn't wait for a reply, and walked toward the bridge.

The low tide reeked of the decay beneath the calm waters of the canal and rose with the thickening fog. It hit me: I was walking into danger. Danger I was ill-prepared to deal with. But it struck me, too, as a metaphor for the wave of putridity rolling across Europe, smothering and annihilating, and now extending its foul reach to our shores.

I was scared.

What was I going to achieve, alone, unarmed, following these criminals into an unknown place other than to probably get myself killed? For surely, if caught, these men would not hesitate to kill me. They'd already left a trail of dead bodies, so what was one more murder? But I'd come this far to give up now; I had to go on. I was compelled to go on. Too much was at stake.

I stiffened my spine, and with false courage, forced myself to walk quietly over the little Venetian-style bridge.

But as I passed over it in my pursuit of the men, the fog dissipated. I was vulnerable now, no trees, no vegetation--nothing to shield me if they turned their heads. I stopped, paralyzed, as they turned left onto a side street.

Off the bridge now, I cut diagonally across a plot of sandy soil that bordered the canal and ran parallel to the road, scrub oak my only cover. I lost sight of the two men, but I scrambled along, spirals of ghostly mist rising from off the black water, a visual fence from plunging in to guide me.

The foghorn sounded repeatedly like the forlorn moans of a wounded animal, boat rigging creaked along the canal, a buoy bell clanged somewhere at the mouth of the Great South Bay. The night was closing in on me, its cold swirling breath filling my lungs, chilling my resolve.

Suddenly, light punctured the darkness, and I could see it came from within a structure across the road. I braced myself and headed toward it, stumbling over knotted grasses, and catching my coat sleeve on thorny bushes in my progress. A small creature skirted past and the image in my mind, if not in reality, was of something rat-like scurrying by, its gurgling squeak of surprise in response to my muted gasp.

"Pull yourself together, Filomena!"

The man from Shorty's Garage broke the small rectangle of light from a small bungalow. I scooted across the road, and flattened myself against the wall of the building, invisible from view of the window. Gingerly, I crouched down and moved toward the window ledge, took a breath for courage, and peeked in. Three men were in the room, one, seated at a table before a boxy black appliance with knobs—a radio transmitter!—the man from Shorty's Garage tapping a lever sitting on a small desk. I knew enough to identify code being transmitted. Where was Joe?

I sensed him before I ever saw him. The hair at the back of my neck rose, electrified, and I turned to see the dark shadowy hulk coming from around the rear of the house. It was too late to hide, even had there was a place to hide. The house sat on sand, nothing but low brush across the road near the dark water.

I turned the corner toward the front of the house, in a dash away from his line of vision—or so I thought. The sharp retort of gunfire gripped my heart, took my breath, before adrenaline kicked in and I beelined toward the canal where the fog was thicker. There, a lone leaning weeping willow, dipped its bare fingers over the water, its trunk provided a moment's cover. But he was following my path. I willed the fog to shield me from view, but it did not obey.

This is the test of the Coward verses the Brave Warrior, I thought. I could bluster and posture with feigned heroism, but the truth was I was scared shitless, a pathetic, whimpering coward in the field of battle.

My latent Catholicism kicked in and I prayed to Mary, full of Grace and Our Father Who Art in Heaven when another gunshot sounded, and then another. Frantically searching for a place to hide, I prepared myself for a leap in the canal, shrugging off the Mark Cross satchel to crawl in the darkness toward the timbers at the canal.

Barreling toward it, and ready to leap, a structure appeared—a boat, a fishing trawler, I surmised, by the rigging, was hitched to the dock a short sprint away. I might be trapping myself but the alternative at the moment was grim. The next bullet would hit me; my coat would drag me down in the water, or I might freeze from hypothermia if I had to remain in the canal for very long. I chose the boat.

He fired another shot, the bullet that whizzed past me hit metal with a crisp ping. I leaped onto the platform.

The fog thickened again, and I acted on instinct. Let him think he hit me or that I jumped into the canal. I needed to make the sound of a big splash. I searched for anything that was not bolted down and finally found a tackle box. I tossed it into the canal, feigning my leap into the dark waters. Now to find a place to hide, not somewhere he would think to look. Not below, not the cabin. . .

There was a hatch in the floor, and I twisted the handle open, but there were convoluted mechanics and little space. I was getting frantic now. There had to be some space that would hold me.

I turned, and there it was. A deep metal box. I pried the latch up, looked inside, and in the darkness found my hidey-hole. The sour reek of fish made me gag. I braced myself and stepped inside. With both hands, I brought the heavy cover securely over me.

More gunfire—two, then three shots—sounded outside my cocoon. Joe was firing at a phantom figure, I thought with relief, shooting at some "thing" he thought was me clinging to the wall of the canal.

Minutes passed—or were they hours? —and then I heard the thumps of footfalls and felt the boat rock. I was filled with renewed terror of discovery, shivering, and trying not to cry out in the pitch-black trap. And then I pulled out of my paralyzing fear. All was silent. I breathed deeply the air of the foul fishhold, a hoarse sigh rising in my throat. Although still vulnerable, I had been granted another minute of life. And for the first time in my life, I viscerally understood the precious and vulnerable nature of my existence.

I remained motionless but for the sound of my breath and the gentle, muffled lapping of the water against the hull of the boat. How long could I survive in the fishhold before the air ran out? The lulling of the boat rocked me almost to a state of semiconsciousness.

I waited, waited for the moment when I could escape the coffin of the hold. Time passed, and still I waited. I was not afraid of being immersed in the darkness rather, it was comforting, somehow.

But for the lack of air. . .

Slowly, I began to emerge from that safe place within myself as it became harder to breathe. Regaining my wits, I knew I couldn't remain where I was much longer. I hoped the men had gone by now, had made their dash from the bungalow, from the town, or were captured by Monty and the G-men along their way.

But what if Joe was patiently waiting on the deck, aware I was in hiding, a gun ready to shoot me when I lifted the lid?

I had to chance it, as I was struggling for air, and

raised a hand to push up the hatch. But from the way I was positioned, I couldn't get leverage against the heavy metal cover.

The latch must have fallen over the bar and secured itself when I brought the cover down. I was trapped! I wanted to bang on the cover, to scream my terror aloud but did neither. I had to think. . .

My satchel. I could find something in my satchel to help pry myself out. The memory of throwing it off near the willow tree dashed that hope.

I tried to sit upright, to push the hatch open. My bruised ribs burned with my efforts. If I got out of here alive, I thought, I would enroll in weightlifting classes.

Footfalls pounded overhead, the boat rocked, metal scraped, fresh air flooded in, and I braced for a bullet.

I love you, Papa...

I could barely see him in the dark, but I knew it wasn't Joe or the other man. He brought with him a faint scent of Guerlain's Mouchoir de Monsieur cologne to momentarily override the stench of dead fish. I breathed like I had never breathed before.

But he didn't help me out, no! He pushed me roughly aside and forced his way into the hold, before the lid came down on both of us!

He lay on top of me. We were face-to-face, his mouth at my neck, the brush of his cheek against mine, rough; he needed a shave, I thought, ridiculously. And although I felt an initial shock at his sudden closeness—his weight on mine was not unpleasant—my alarm soon melted into a feeling of calm, of security when he whispered in my ear that soon he would get me to safety, that I should just remain quiet and still.

In the pitch-blackness, I reached a hand to his head and my fingers brushed through his hair. I realized what I had done and drew away, but he grabbed my hand, turning my palm to meet his lips. I heard what sounded like a laugh, a sigh, really, and I wished there had been light, light enough that I might see his eyes, the expression on his face. Had I misunderstood or was I deranged, I wondered, but was he nuzzling my neck, was he kissing my throat and now my cheek, and now my lips? I wanted to protest, but I could not protest. And then I realized that I didn't want to protest. I didn't want him to stop, I wanted more. . .

He gasped and shifted his weight, pressing harder against me. I felt a hardness at my hip.

"Please," he whispered urgently.

This was sheer madness! But madness though it might be, I pulled his head down to my breast.

"Please," he pleaded again.

"Oh yes," I whispered, my hands wrapped around his neck now, urging him on.

"Please, Filomena, you're pressing against my Luger."

Is that what he called it? Men often had funny names for their —

"*What?*" I screeched, pushing him away, his head smacking hard against the lid above us. "*Argggggghhh!*"

"Are you trying to kill me or just maim me?"

I wanted to crawl up and hide in disgrace, but I was

already crawled up and hiding. I was glad he couldn't see my embarrassment—I tossed off the shame I felt with an attack. "I'd. . .I'd like. . . You bet I'd like to kill you, but you've got the Luger! Get off me."

"I can't. There's no place for me to go. Maybe if we shift our weight, we can lay side by side."

I moved to my left side, he to his right side, and we wound up side by side and face-to-face.

"This isn't good," he said. "Turn the opposite way."

I twisted over so that my back was to him. This position proved no better. We were spooning and his arm draped daringly around my waist. I couldn't reach to slap it.

Footsteps thumped overhead, the boat rocked, and a few moments later, the motor roared deafeningly, shaking us in our little sardine can.

"What's going on?" I said.

"Isn't it obvious? We're going on a little ride."

"But—"

"Don't worry."

"What are you going to do?"

"I'll think of something, I suppose."

"That doesn't inspire much confidence."

"I guess not, but the plot thickened, thanks to you. My next move will fly on a wing and a prayer."

"What are you inferring? And why are you speaking in clichés?"

"Clichés are all that come to mind, but the truth is, if you'd left it to me and my colleagues, we wouldn't be here. Now because of your interference, plans have changed. Not to worry."

I wanted to yell, *What do you mean not to worry!* but suddenly the boat lurched forward, and then we were cruising along the canal. Were we going toward the ocean?

A minute later, the engine whined in a higher key and the shift in speed threw me closer in his embrace.

"We've entered high water."

"You mean—"

"We're out of the canal and in the Great South Bay."

"Shit—damn it!"

"Don't curse yet; wait until we're in real trouble."

"I don't see how it can get any worse. We've no way out of this box! We'll die first of suffocation!"

"Ye of little faith."

"There you go again, another chestnut!"

I felt him shift his weight, and then suddenly a great gush of air washed over my face. A thin stream of weak light poured into the space.

There were no voices to be heard over the noise of the motor.

"Wait!" I said, grabbing him by the coat collar. "Be careful."

And with that said he hoisted himself out of the hold and before the latch fell in place, I raised a hand to stop it, allowing a thin stream of the dawn's light and fresh air to pour in.

I pushed the opening wider to listen. When no sound other than the roar of the motor could be discerned, I peeked through and took a chance to escape my prison. I was halfway out when I looked up to the wheelhouse. Two men were in the shelter, and Monty was sneaking up behind them, gun pointed. I gasped, fearing that one or the other might overtake him. This was not a movie. No director would yell cut. He was in mortal danger, and I could not just remain in my little hole hoping all would work out, that he would not be shot or worse, killed.

I needed to help, to be ready to help, anyway, if I had to. I searched the deck for something, anything I could use as a weapon—something to throw, to wield.

A harpoon was secured against the inside of the hull. It took a minute, but I released its holdings. I looked to the bridge and was shocked to see Monty in combat with Joe; the other man was still at the wheel. The boat was speeding up now, accelerating and bobbing and bouncing wildly against the waves. Nearly toppling on the deck, I steadied myself to proceed toward them, the harpoon in tow.

A shot rang out above the din. Monty's weapon flew through the air and landed on the deck a few feet from where I stood.

I had to help Monty, and there was no time for hesitation. I grabbed the gun, tossed away the harpoon, and ran to the wheelhouse.

Pausing below the landing, I watched as Monty landed a punch at Joe's head, then another to his stomach. But the man at the wheel turned and was about to fire his weapon at Monty.

I pulled up a step, and he caught my eye. Then he turned the gun on me.

I ducked as he fired, and I heard the bullet ping on the deck below.

There was no doubt in my mind that he was coming for me now, and I wouldn't find cover in time. And when he stood over me, his eyes hard, his lip curled in a cold-blooded sneer, I felt a weakening and a tingling run through me.

So this is how it ends. . .

The boat listed on its side; I felt the drag, and while I held on to the rail, I wondered if falling to the deck might land the shot to my leg or arm, instead of between the eyes as I knew he intended.

But before I could make that leap, the expression on the man's face changed from hateful determination to surprise. Monty, on his feet, knocked a club across the back of the man's knees. When they buckled, agony crossed his features: his mouth agape, his eyes narrowed and wet. His balance precarious, all Monty had to do was push him over with a kick of his foot. He landed on the deck.

But Monty's victory was fleeting, as Joe, bloodied and bent, picked up the man's discarded weapon and rushed in behind Monty.

It was all of a split second; I'd never fired a gun before, and my grip on the weapon was shaky. The boat was running in circles now, as no one was manning the wheel. I might hit the wrong man, but Monty was dead one way or the other if I didn't fire.

Monty saw my speechless terror when he looked down at me pointing the weapon. He bolted headfirst to the deck as I pulled the trigger.

The recoil knocked the gun from my hand. The smell of gunpowder and the heat of it against my freezing fingers shook me to the core. Had I just killed a man?

I stumbled. The nameless man lay groaning in his world of suffering. Still, the gun I'd dropped was within his easy reach, and I was taking no chances. I retrieved it and held it over him, all the while trembling, emotions heightened, on edge, believing that I had taken a life. A man named Joe. A man known as Roger. A Nazi spy. A murderer!

Too shocked to cry aloud, hot tears rolled down my face as I gripped that gun stiffly, unyieldingly. When the engine stopped, the boat rocked wildly, but I kept my balance. As the ringing in my ears quieted, the *lap-lap-lap* of the waves hitting against the boat was all I could hear. And then, the hum of another motor, waves rocking the vessel, wildly.

The blast of a horn shook me out from my reverie. When I looked up from guarding my prisoner, there appeared a Coast Guard cutter. Someone in uniform was talking though a loudspeaker, but I couldn't make out what was said at first.

Oh, they wanted me to drop the gun.

I tried to let go of it, but my fingers were frozen in place, no matter how I tried, I could not will my hands to release it.

"It's all right, Filomena," spoke a voice. It was a good voice, of rich baritone timbre, and I felt arms envelope me like a warm blanket drawn over my shoulders. My fingers yielded to his touch, and I relinquished the weapon. He gently turned me around to face him. I buried my face in his chest.

"Is he dead? Oh God! Did I kill him?"

Words poured out of me in a rush, with my tears. "But I had to! He was about to shoot you, and I couldn't let that happen. No! I couldn't let that happen!"

"Hush, Filomena, hush, my darling. He's *not* dead. You put a bullet in his shoulder, that's all. He'll live, but he won't be joining the prison bowling league for some time."

"Is Little Dick all right?"

"He's just fine."

"Papa must never know of this!" I said, looking up into his dark eyes. "I can't have him worried about me."

"He won't, my dear, I promise," he said with a smile. "But this won't happen again. This was a one-time thing, something you chanced into. I made you curious, and I wasn't in a position to explain. But you'll have to keep the knowledge of what I do a secret, you understand? My work is important, Filomena."

"Yes, I see that it is," I said, my head resting on his shoulder. "And that's why I'm going to help you."

"What?"

"Be a part of the fight."

"But—"

"No "buts". I just saved your life."

"Yes

"And I have questions."

"I'm sure. . ."

"Yes, so you might as well answer them."

"I suppose I can."

"Where were these guys going?"

"To be picked up by a German U-boat a couple of miles offshore."

"German subs? In our waters?"

"Yes."

"I suppose Henry caught his wife and Joe scheming, right? And after his parents were murdered he called the Bureau, right?"

"Why, yes."

"As I thought. He was a good man, a patriot. I could tell."

"He was, but how did you—"

"A shame, really."

"Yes."

"And who was the pudgy man you met at the rally?"

"Max Lucas. An engineer. Worked with the Bureau. He was going to redo the plans, make small but crucial changes so they'd be useless in the hands of the Germans."

"Why did he run from the rooming house?"

"He must have thought I'd been killed by Joe when Joe lunged at me with the knife he used to kill Henry. Max couldn't risk the plans being taken."

"A shame, really," I said, referring to his accidental demise.

"Yes."

"I'm very sorry I thought him a Nazi."

"Yes. . ."

"Who is Hedy Werner? Was she the blonde woman I

followed from Dr. Armbruster's, posing as Laura Miller?"

"Laura Miller is the alias of a German girl, whose father and mother were beaten and left for dead by Brownshirts. She carries falsified documents to Germany. She's one of us."

"So, is Margaret Hedy Werner?"

"No. You could say I'm Hedy Werner," he said.

"What?"

"There is no Hedy Werner, just a room in the rooming house I acquired in her name."

"But people have seen her."

"They may think they have, but she doesn't exist."

"Explain about the handkerchief—the birthday gift?"

"It wasn't an ordinary hankie. It has tiny holes cut into it. When placed atop a particular map, it reveals locations for resistance activities."

"What's a range finder?"

He laughed, and I felt my own laugh bubble up inside me.

"It's a device that can register altitude changes. It measures the distance from bomber aircraft to ground targets."

"You'll have to explain this all to me more thoroughly."

"They'll explain it."

"Who're they?"

"The people at the spy training school."

"There is such a place?"

"Oh yes."

"Will you enroll me?"

"Do I have a choice?"

"I'm ready for the fight."

"Who am I to get in the way of Filomena Devlin."

"It's a beautiful morning, isn't it?" I said, recovered now. "It's good to be alive," I said, looking out over the expanse of ocean, the sunrise sparkling on its surface, gulls screaming while diving for their breakfast.

"Yes, my dear one. Beautiful."

"Ouch! Your Luger is pressing on my hip."

"That's not my Luger."

Afterword

In high school, my history teacher, Dr. Schwartz, pre-sented the theory of a cycle of governing posited by Poly-bius, the Greek historian of 2000 years ago, who first sug-gested the separation of powers in a governing democracy.

Polybius's cycle included democracy, aristocracy, and monarchy, which would eventually devolve into degener-ate forms such as ochlocracy (mob rule), oligarchy, and tyr-anny. I remember asking, stating actually, to Dr. Schwartz, "That can't happen here, though." He smiled, and said, "It almost did happen here with the rise of Fascism in Europe." I had yet to read Sinclair Lewis's novel, *It Can't Happen Here*, which addressed the demise of democracy.

It was later that I learned about how and why Fascism swept through Europe leading to America's involvement in World War II, and that it was only a confluence of events that ended Fascism's imminent threat in the United States.

Dr. Schwartz's lesson stuck with me, and throughout

my lifetime, I have watched governments around the world prove this theory sound: Democracies rise and fall, tyrants rule, and then people revolt. Still, I never believed American Democracy was vulnerable to shifting toward authoritarianism in my lifetime. Now, I'm not so certain, because today, we are experiencing the almost identical political and societal conditions which led to the rise of strongmen like Hitler and Mussolini a hundred years ago, proving if we don't learn from history, we are bound to repeat it. It's something to think about, learn from, and work toward shoring-up the foundation of our democracy if we hope to keep our constitutional freedoms.

On a lighter note, a decade ago, I chanced upon a news article in the *Tampa Bay Times* about a two-for-one funeral of an elderly couple who had passed away within days of each other, "Frugal Father's Two-for-One Funeral Fits His Style." It was funny, if a bit macabre. As a writer, I stored this little gem in my memory bank, not thinking it would be the germ of a subplot to one of my mystery novels.

About the Author

Agata Stanford, author of the popular and acclaimed Dorothy Parker Mystery Series, brings her storytelling talents to this World War II mystery. In addition to being a prolific novelist, she has written seven plays and two musicals.

Her brilliant and witty dialogue in her novels was honed by her background as a trained actress, singer, and dancer beginning with her attendance at the prestigious High School of Performing Arts in New York City. She has acted in/or directed fourteen Equity productions, performed on tour, on and Off-Broadway, as a nightclub performer in New York and resort clubs and appeared in more than fifty films and thirty stage plays.

As a native New Yorker, she loves the history of the city, especially from the last century, and her books are filled with rich descriptions of earlier times with historical accuracy.